THE DEAD AND THE BURIED

DETECTIVE INSPECTOR MARC FAGAN

JASON CHAPMAN

Author's notes

This novel is a work of complete fiction. The names, characters and incidents portrayed in it are the work of the author's imagination. Any resemblance to actual persons, living or dead, events or localities is entirely coincidental.

For mum and dad

Thank you for teaching me patience, perseverance and the value of hard work

P R O L O G U E

DAY 1
Skenfrith Castle – Monmouthshire – 12:36am

Professor Robert Turner pushed his exhausted body forward. With every agonising moment, the horror of his imminent death became more apparent. Turner could sense his lungs filling with bodily fluids. Regret, anger, and terror raged through his mind.

His assassin held back, stalking a few dozen yards behind the stricken victim. As if they were enjoying a midnight stroll.

Turner glanced up into the crystal-clear night sky. A full moon shone down on the ruined castle. Casting shadows off the surrounding trees, like hooded spectres, clawing out into the darkness.

An owl shrieked into the gloom, seeking a mate. A few moments later, a reply came back.

Turner struggled to regulate his faltering breath as he staggered towards the castle entrance. The moonlight provided helpful visibility for the aging lecturer. He struggled to reach a gangplank that crossed the castle's dried up moat. A handrail provided a welcome balance for his failing body. The pain was unbearable. With every weakening step he could feel the dagger his attacker had driven into his back. The first instinct was to remove it. But Turner knew this was the end. His car had been driven away, and he was too weak to call out for help. The row of cottages that were a few hundred yards away were shrouded in darkness. Turner stared at the cylindrical castle keep in the distance. He managed a glimpse behind.

'Consider this your dying confession, old man.' A voice

loomed out of the blackness. 'Tell me where the journal is.'

Turner summoned his remaining energy, stumbling towards the opening of the keep. Eventually, he reached his target. His strength failed. He dropped to his knees, peering up through the circular opening into the star filled sky.

The cloaked figure entered the keep, planting a firm hand on Turner's shoulder to stop him keeling over.

'This won't change a thing.' Turner gasped.

'You have desecrated an ancient site.' The stranger explained. 'Your sins will be cleansed on this night.'

'You think killing me is going to discourage others? It's simply a matter of time before the markers are found. With, or without, the journal.'

'Time, Professor Turner, is the one thing you are out of.'

Turner felt excruciating agony as his executioner wrenched the dagger from his back.

The killer took their steadying hand off Turner's shoulder.

The frail man fell forward onto his face. His breathing became shallower with every gasp. Turner sensed his heart pumping away fiercely.

The stranger rolled their victim's frail body onto his back with ease.

Turner gazed at the heavens.

A shooting star streaked through the atmosphere, bursting into a magnificent but brief light show.

The attacker straddled the victim. Clutching the bloodied dagger with both hands. 'For her!' The murderer declared before plunging the dagger downwards deep into Turner's chest.

Turner let out a final, agonising gasp. Moments later, death claimed him.

CHAPTER 1

Skenfrith Castle - 07:43am

'The call was made by the landlord of the pub across the road. He always walks his dogs on the grounds of the castle. To make sure no overnight visitors have been dropping litter.' Detective Sergeant Sean Watkins explained. 'They've been having problems with fly tippers recently. As well as the odd gang of teenagers looking to smoke weed. The local police do their best, but this is a relatively large area to cover.'

Detective Inspector Marc Fagan walked across a wooden gangplank that led to the interior of the ruined castle.

CSI officers were patrolling the grounds. Two officers stood guard outside the entrance to the keep. The usual inner and outer cordons had been established.

A CSI ducked under the police tape and approached. 'You're going to love this one, Fagan.'

'What have we got?'

'One male in his mid-seventies. A stab wound to the upper chest. It also looks as if someone had plunged the dagger into his back. Before flipping him over and shoving it through his chest.'

'You mean knife.' Fagan corrected him.

The CSI shook his head. 'It's definitely a dagger. And from the looks of it, I'd say it's old. At least a few hundred years.'

Fagan stared towards the opening of the castle keep.

'Let's have a look, shall we.'

A tent had been erected to protect the body. Another CSI was scouring the walls of the keep, putting rubbish into an evidence bag.

Fagan entered the tent first. 'Jesus.' He gasped, gawping at the sight that confronted him.

The man was naked, lying on his back. His arms and legs spread out. At the centre of each palm appeared to be a metal spike, which had been driven through each hand. His feet also had similar treatment, with a metal spike forced through the bridge of each foot, exiting the sole.

The CSI pointed at the hand. 'Whoever did this must have used a sledgehammer or something heavy. This is pretty solid ground.'

Fagan looked the body up and down. 'Some sort of ritualistic killing?'

The CSI nodded. 'It looks that way, doesn't it. The way the body has been positioned and everything. Also, whoever did this must have had an accomplice.'

'So there could be two murderers.' Watkins speculated.

'it's possible, yeah.'

Fagan spotted what appeared to be a parchment next to the body with a message scrawled.

All sinners will perish

'This murder has it all.' The CSI remarked. 'And before you are wondering, the ink is blood. Really gruesome stuff.'

'The victim's blood?' Watkins guessed.

'We won't know until we've done a lab analysis.'

Fagan looked towards the entrance to the keep. 'A long way to carry a body.'

'I don't think he was dead before he reached this point. He was murdered here and laid out in this spot.'

'So the murderers, whoever they are, lured him to this location.'

'It's very probable. I don't think he would have just been naked when he turned up here. There's also discolouration around his mouth. I'm not sure, but I'll have to run a full analysis of his blood. There's more than a simple stabbing going on here.'

Fagan spotted a mark on his forehead.

'It was made by a hot branding iron.'

'I can't be sure, but it looks like a letter A.' Watkins said, squinting at the marking.

'Time of death?' Fagan stated.

The CSI puffed out his cheeks, scratching his head. 'He's been here a good few hours. I'd say about midnight, maybe.'

Fagan looked around the keep.

'Pretty remote area.' Watkins pointed out. 'The suspects would have been able to take their time.'

'How long would it have taken our murderer to present his body like this?' Fagan asked.

'Everything has been done carefully. Which means they took their time. But not too much time as to risk being caught. It wouldn't have taken long to remove his clothing. And there being two of them would have speeded things up.'

'What about CCTV?'

'Around here, are you joking? Look at this place, it's like Midsomer. Everyone knows each other, everyone trusts each other. There's no need for CCTV. Besides, many of the people out here are retired. Some of them probably haven't got the internet.'

'Surely the local pub has cameras.'

The CSI shook his head. 'The local farms probably have surveillance to protect their equipment, but nothing of use.'

'We'll have to knock on doors in the row of cottages that have a view of this castle. There must be someone who saw something.' Fagan looked at the body. 'So, they lure our victim out here, kill him, then leave.' He looked back towards the gangplank. 'You couldn't get a vehicle up here, could you?'

'No, just to the entrance to where the walkway starts. But there are no fresh tire marks on the grass outside. And the car park will be jammed with sightseer vehicles. This place is very popular with people from all over. People come here to walk their dogs. Others come for picnics. Obviously, you get your history buffs around here looking at the place.'

Watkins stared down at the body, mulling things around in his mind.

Fagan noticed his expression. 'Is there something you want to share, DS Watkins?'

'I was thinking, boss, about Dan Brown?'

'Isn't he a novelist?'

Watkins nodded. 'He's written a series of books about a Harvard academic called Robert Langdon.'

'Are those the Tom Hanks films?' The CSI asked.

'Yeah. Not a fan of the films, but I love the novels.'

'What's your point?' Fagan shrugged.

'This is like something out of one of his books. *The Da Vinci Code*.' Watkins pointed at the body. 'The way the body has been positioned. It's in the form of the Vitruvian Man, a drawing by Leonardo da Vinci.'

'I am familiar with Leonardo da Vinci.' Fagan had bought a few puzzles in the past of Da Vinci's famous artwork.

'This murder has all the cliches of a Dan Brown novel.' Watkins continued. 'The murder weapon that looks old. The message scrawled in blood. And the symbol branded into his forehead. Whoever carried out this murder knew what they were doing.'

'So you're saying this author, Dan Brown, murdered him?' Fagan pointed at the body.

Watkins frowned at his superior, who was smiling back at him.

'Ha ha, hilarious boss. What I'm saying is that the clue here is the symbol branded into his forehead. It obviously has a significant meaning. And the way the body has been laid out. Nails through his hands and feet. This man has been crucified. Which means whoever murdered him was sending a powerful message. And then there's the note, scrawled in blood. '

'When are we likely to get an ID?'

'Couldn't tell you.' The CSI answered. 'It will be a few hours before we can remove the body. It's not like he's just been dumped. This was a carefully constructed scene.'

Fagan looked at Watkins. 'You said the suspects may be trying to send a message. Who to?'

'All depends who he is. All sinners must perish.' He read the message scrawled on the parchment aloud.

'I take it the landlord is available to chat?'

'Yes boss, I told him not to move until you've had a word with him.'

Fagan pulled his smartphone out of his pocket and took a picture of the dead man. 'Better have a chat with the landlord.'

CHAPTER 2

8:11am

After doing a patrol of the castle, Fagan and Watkins called at a pub called the Bell at Skenfrith.

'Do you walk your dogs every day on the castle grounds?' Fagan asked, looking at two black Labradors sat by a large fireplace.

The landlord looked visibly shocked after discovering the body. He nodded. 'It isn't something you expect to find daily.'

'What do you usually find?'

The landlord shrugged. 'Bits and bobs, you know. The summer months are busy. I usually go around the castle to make sure no one has dropped anything. I have found the odd needle. At the height of summer I find quite a few used condoms. Disgusting things, I wish people would do that kind of thing in their own home. We've also been getting problems with fly tippers.'

'I'm sorry to have to do this to you, but I need to show you a photo of the man you found this morning.'

The landlord shuddered. 'Something I won't forget in a hurry. I didn't get close enough to the body to see his face. I'm not a morbid sightseer or anything like that. The dogs were the first to find him. They lay down near his body and howled like wolves. When I went to the opening and saw the poor bloke lying there.'

'That's ok. You say your dogs lay down near the body. They didn't approach and sniff around it.'

'No.'

Fagan called up the picture on his phone. 'Do you recognise this man? Has he called in the pub recently?'

The landlord looked visibly distraught as he stared at the picture. 'Sorry, I don't recognise him at all. I'm familiar with most of the residents on the cottages across the way opposite the castle. We get people from all over, coming for food. People from Abergavenny, Monmouth, a few from Usk and Raglan. Get a couple of regulars from Ross on Wye every Sunday for lunch.'

'But you have never seen this man?' Fagan asked.

'No, but then again, we get strangers all the time through here. Mostly enjoying the castle and the countryside.'

'Do you ever get any trouble in here?'

'Good lord no, this is a country pub. There's no one to cause trouble out here. Most of the people who come here are older folk. Wanting a bit of peace and quiet. None of the younger ones come out here because there's nothing else to do but enjoy the country. You hear the odd roar of an engine occasionally in the night. There was a bad smash last year. You know what it's like on these country roads. Every boy racer wants to drive like Jeremy Clarkson. It's a wonder nobody was killed. The car left the road and ended upside down in the river. Three boys were in the car. One of them had to be airlifted. The emergency services arrived quickly.'

'Have you seen anyone acting in a strange manner?' Watkins asked. 'Walking around looking like they were scoping the place out.'

'What, besides the people who come to scope out the castle? Everyone who comes through here wants to be nosy. Especially when it comes to the castle. This time of the year, the Druids like to come here and do whatever

Druids do. You know, like the ones who go to Stonehenge.'

'Have you seen any of these druids around lately?'

'There were loads of them here last week. Hang on a minute.' The landlord remembered something. 'I was walking the dogs last Thursday evening. There were a couple of druids arguing with a man and a woman who had state-of-the-art camera equipment. One druid claimed they were stealing the spirit of the land or something like that.'

'You actually overheard them saying that?' Fagan asked.

The landlord nodded. 'Other than that, nothing really happens around here. Certainly not a murder. I have been running this pub for thirty years. This is by far the worst thing that's ever happened.'

Fagan held up his phone again. 'Do you think it could have been this man these druids were arguing with?'

The landlord looked doubtful. 'I was too far away to see faces, sorry.'

Fagan packed away his notebook and thanked the landlord for his time. He left a card on the bar should the landlord remember anything else.

Both detectives emerged onto the road and started walking back towards the row of cottages opposite the castle.

A taxi pulled up outside one of the cottages.

Fagan recognised the logo.

Jamie Evans climbed out of the car and walked around to the passenger side to let an elderly woman out. 'Here you go, Mrs Jones, back home safe and sound. I'll get your bags.'

'Oh dear, what is going on here?' The woman asked, spotting the array of police vehicles.

'What indeed.' Evans followed through, laden down

with bags. He spotted Fagan approaching. 'Morning DI Fagan.' He looked over at the crime scene. 'What's going on here then?'

Fagan smiled back at him. 'I'm afraid I'm not allowed to discuss it with members of the public.'

'I do hope there hasn't been any more trouble.' Mrs Jones commented.

Fagan zeroed in on the old woman. 'Trouble, madam?'

'A really nice man was arguing with some of those do-gooders.'

'Do-gooders?' Watkins enquired.

'Yes, they come out here every summer and dance around in robes and all that nonsense.'

'Do you mean druids?' Fagan recalled what the landlord of the pub had mentioned a few minutes earlier.

'Yes, that's them. Bunch of silly old twaddle if you ask me.'

'And what trouble have you seen lately?'

'Just this really nice man I was talking to last week. He was here every day. So I gave him some tea and biscuits. Very intelligent man. Seemed to know a lot about the castle. He told me he was a teacher.'

'So what did you see?'

'He was arguing with these druids yesterday morning, I think. If I recall. They were shouting at him. Said he didn't belong here.'

'Can you remember what time this was?'

'Just before lunchtime, I think.'

Fagan scribbled away in his notepad. 'You say you gave him a cup of tea and some biscuits?'

'Yes, he came around here every day last week. He was with a much younger lady. But then on Friday he was on his own. That's when I offered him a cup of tea.'

'Mrs Jones, isn't it?'

'Yes dear, but folks around here call me Annie, except for this young man.' She looked at Evans.

'How many times have I said Mrs Jones. It's called respect your elders.'

'Annie, I have a photograph here. I would like to show you. Only it could be a little frightening to look at.'

Annie held out her hand, stroking Fagan's cheek. 'Bless you dear, but I was a wren during the war. I was stationed in Dover, taking care of the American GIs as they came back from Omaha beach. I've seen it all.'

Fagan called up the picture on his phone and held it up.

'That poor man.' Annie said, staring at the picture.

'So, this is the man you were talking to?'

She nodded.

'Did he say anything to you that might help us find out who did this to him?'

'He mentioned he taught at Cambridge and he was here looking for Alice.'

'Alice?' Evans said, smiling.

Fagan glared at him. 'Haven't you got any fares to pick up?'

Evans nodded. 'I'll see you next week, Mrs Jones. You can tell me all about it.' He walked back to his car and headed back to Abergavenny.

'This gentleman you were talking to, didn't tell you his name, did he, Annie?' Watkins asked.

Annie recalled the conversation she had a week earlier. 'Yes, Robert, Robert Turner.'

'Brilliant.' Fagan jotted down the name.

'So who is Alice?' Watkins questioned. 'Is she someone who lives locally?'

Annie chuckled. 'No, Alice is someone who lived around here a long time ago. She's known locally as Alice of Abergavenny. I remember Robert telling me he was interested in the history of this area. He said that he and some students came up from Cambridge and were staying over at the Agincourt Hotel just outside Monmouth. It's a very posh place.'

'Annie, you have been fantastic.' Fagan smiled at the old woman.

'I really hope you catch the horrid people who did this to such a nice man.'

'Don't worry Annie, we will.' Watkins assured her.

CHAPTER 3

Agincourt Hotel – Monmouth – 08:36am

The Agincourt Hotel was situated on the outskirts of Monmouth on the old Abergavenny road. Just under a mile from Vine Road Music Studios. The hotel was surrounded by tall ancient oak trees, making it invisible from the road. Two gargoyles were mounted on decorative plinths attached to a very old iron gate. Fagan smiled as he drove past the gargoyles, singing a poor rendition of the Adams Family theme tune. He parked his car as near to the main entrance as possible. Although there were no CCTV cameras visible, there were plenty of warning signs threatening clamping if anyone parked illegally. Fagan paid no attention to the signs. He knew as soon as he flashed his warrant card, no one would challenge him.

'Annie wasn't joking. This place is posh.' Watkins commented, looking around at the expensive furniture and décor. Ancient looking wooden beams crisscrossed the ceiling. A suit of armour guarded a doorway leading to the bar. There were no signs of modern technology.

Fagan had rung the bell twice before a tall, thin man appeared out of the manager's office.

'Yes gentlemen, how can I help?'

Fagan held up his ID. 'Detective inspector Fagan, this is Detective Sergeant Watkins. We need to see the manager immediately.'

The man looked down at his waistcoat. 'I'm sorry, I should have my badge around here somewhere.'

'Then I take it you're the manager.' Fagan guessed.

'Yes, how can I help you Inspector Fagan?'

'I need to know if you have a man called Robert Turner staying here?'

The manager scrutinised Fagan for a moment before reluctantly opening the guest register. He nodded. 'Yes, I recall now. Professor Robert Turner. He's left strict instructions not to be disturbed this morning.'

Watkins and Fagan exchanged a quick glance.

'We want immediate access to his room.' Fagan requested in an authoritative tone.

The manager disapproved of the two detectives showing up and demanding to see one of the guest's rooms. But judging by their expressions, he wasn't going to be able to stop them. He turned and walked a few paces to the key safe, which was guarded with a combination lock. He plucked a key from the safe and closed the door.

Fagan watched him carefully. 'I would have thought an establishment like this would have key cards.'

'We did, but our guests complained. A hotel as old as this needs to be more traditional.'

'What about CCTV?'

'We have a camera near the main gate, but that's about all.'

'You're not worried about crime then?'

'We are in the middle of nowhere, Inspector Fagan. Crime out here is non-existent. Again, as with the keys, our clients don't want to feel their every move is being scrutinised. We have had the odd intruder wanting to see if anyone from the music world is staying here. Vine Road Music studios are very well known.'

'How old is this hotel?'

'It was established in 1416 by a serving knight that fought at Agincourt with Henry V, hence the name

Agincourt. Many of the soldiers that fought alongside Henry were local.' He put the key on the desk.

'Thanks for the history lesson.' Fagan grabbed the key off the desk and headed for a staircase.

'Not a fan of history then boss?' Watkins commented as they climbed the stairs.

'Definitely not. I hated the subject at school.'

'Depends what it is.'

They both approached the door to the room they were looking for.

Fagan looked at the key number. 'Room twenty-six.'

'Hold up, Boss.' Watkins pointed at the door.

Fagan noticed the door was already partly open.

Both men slipped on latex gloves.

Fagan pushed the door. It swung open with ease.

The room beyond had been ransacked.

Watkins was already on his phone requesting a CSI team.

Fagan stepped into the room.

Drawers had been pulled out and emptied. An overturned suitcase was on the bed, which had its covers stripped off. Someone had also lifted the mattress. A wardrobe had been emptied. Coat hangers strewn across the floor. A few shirts were still attached to their hangers. A pair of trousers lay on the floor with their pockets turned out.

'Someone wanted something pretty bad.' Watkins said.

'Yeah, question is what?'

'From what little we know about this Turner, he was a teacher. The manager addressed him as Professor Turner.'

'Professor in what I wonder?' Fagan mused, surveying the carnage that engulfed the room.

'A simple break-in, boss, or something else?'

Fagan shrugged. 'It's hard to tell at this point. What do

we know so far? He's been identified by Annie, but we need a formal identification. He's been visiting Skenfrith castle lately and had an argument with some druids. Not really an open and shut case. And now someone was determined enough to turn this room upside down.'

'Oh my god.' A voice called out from the entrance to the room.

Fagan put his hand up. 'This is a crime scene.' He produced his ID badge. 'DI Fagan with Merseyside.' Fagan stopped before correcting himself. 'Gwent police.'

'What's happened? Where is Robert?' The young woman asked.

'I'm sorry, you are?' Watkins asked.

'I'm Doctor Sarah York, Robert's assistant.' York took in the chaos in front of her. 'What has happened here? Where is Robert?' She asked again.

'Are you referring to Robert Turner?'

'Yes, we were supposed to be having breakfast this morning. The Manager just told me police were here wanting to speak with him. Now, could you please tell me where he is?'

'We need to seal this room.' Fagan suggested, looking at York. 'Where is your room located?'

'I'm in room sixteen.'

'We need to talk in there.'

Watkins remained outside the room waiting for forensics to arrive while Fagan and York returned to her room.

York sat on the bed.

Fagan left the hotel room door wide open.

'Please tell me where Robert is.' York began to sound agitated with Fagan's lack of information.

'This may come as a shock to you, Doctor York. But we believe Robert Turner was found dead this morning at

Skenfrith castle.'

A tsunami of shock and grief engulfed York as she processed what the detective had just revealed to her.

Fagan knelt down in front of her, producing his smartphone. 'Can I call you Sarah?'

York shrugged. 'If you want.'

'I know this may be difficult for you Sarah. But I'm about to show you a picture of who we believe is Professor Turner. I need you to make a formal identification. You will also be asked to go to Nevil Hall hospital this afternoon to make another identification of his body.'

York nodded. 'Ok.'

Fagan called up the picture on his phone and held it up in front of her.

York clasped her hand over her mouth and sobbed.

'Sarah, is this Professor Robert Turner?'

She was too distraught to answer.

'Take your time.' Fagan encouraged calmly. He had lost count of how many pictures of the dead he had shown to people over the years. Every time he was tasked with this procedure, it always felt like the first time.

Watkins appeared at the hotel room door. 'Boss, uniform has just turned up. CSI is half an hour out.'

York seemed inconsolable as she continued to sob.

'Sarah, please, this is vital to our investigation. Can you confirm that this is Professor Turner?'

York took a deep breath, managing to nod. 'Yes.'

'I'm afraid I am going to have to ask you some questions regarding Professor Turner. Let's get you out of here and go downstairs to the restaurant. I don't know about you, but I get a little shaky when I haven't had coffee first thing in the morning.'

Ten minutes later they were sitting in the hotel's main restaurant.

The waitress set down a tray with coffee and fresh croissants.

York had calmed herself down, but was still visibly distraught at the picture Fagan had shown her.

'When was the last time you spoke with Professor Turner?' Fagan asked, biting into a croissant.

York picked up her coffee cup with a shaking hand, taking a sip. 'Last night, we had dinner here.'

'What time was this?'

'About seven o'clock.'

'How long did you spend with him?'

'Around three hours. We finished our meal quickly but ordered a bottle of wine.'

'A long time to drink a bottle of wine.' Watkins remarked.

'Robert was a bit of a wine connoisseur. He ordered quite an expensive bottle of red wine, from the local vineyard. They have an exclusive wine cellar in this hotel.'

'How was your dinner with Robert? Did he seem nervous about anything?'

'He was on edge. Yesterday afternoon he got a text from someone.' York recalled the time. 'It was about three o'clock. I remember Robert walking to the other end of the field. Even from that distance, I could tell he was having an argument with someone.'

'You didn't catch any of what he was arguing about?' Fagan asked, scribbling furiously.

'No, sorry.'

'During your meal last night. What were you talking about?'

'We were discussing the dig. We're currently working just outside Abergavenny.'

'Dig?' Fagan questioned.

'We've been here about two weeks now. Part of a team

from Cambridge working on an archaeological dig. Our group has been excavating a site near Bont.'

'Where is Bont?'

'It's a mile off the Abergavenny road. In the middle of nowhere.'

'What are you looking for in such a remote location?'

'Professor Turner was working on a theory. He believed there may have been an old manor house out there. We didn't think we would find anything at first at such an out of the way spot. But we found a medieval sword buried. So we carried on digging and discovered the foundations of a large structure.'

'And there's a team working out there at this moment?' Watkins said.

'Yes, it's one of three teams we have around the area.'

Fagan recalled the name that Annie had mentioned earlier. 'Who's Alice of Abergavenny?'

'She was a local noble woman. She apparently had great wealth and lived around here.'

'At Bont?' Watkins asked.

'No, we're still looking for her main dwelling. The place we're currently looking at is thought to be one of her deputies, a knight sworn to protect Alice.'

'Find anything valuable at this dig?' Fagan asked.

York nodded, taking another sip of coffee. 'The sword itself is worth a small fortune. It had a large diamond in its hilt and the handle was encrusted with gold leaf. We also recovered a chest with jewellery. Necklaces, pendants, broaches, rings and bracelets.'

'Worth quite a lot of money then?' Fagan said.

'Yes.'

'Where are these items now?'

'Professor Turner had them shipped straight to his college at Cambridge.'

'Must have attracted a lot of attention, finding all that treasure.'

York shook her head. 'Professor Turner wanted everything kept under wraps. He didn't want a hoard of treasure hunters disturbing the site. There was a metal detector enthusiast out there last week kicking up a fuss.'

'What happened?'

'He said he was from a local club and that the farmer had always given him permission to detect on the surrounding fields he owned.'

'Do you think this metal detecting enthusiast could have known about what you found?'

'I don't know. Wherever we go, we always encounter people who don't like archaeologists. Mostly amateur treasure hunters wanting to strike it big.'

'So what happened to this metal detecting enthusiast?'

'Robert told him that he had paid the farmer a significant amount of money to excavate the site.'

'Do you know how much?'

'Twenty thousand pounds.'

'That's a lot of money.' Watkins remarked. 'Just to dig around in a field.'

'The sword is probably worth ten times that much. As for the chest we found, probably in the millions. Professor Turner believed that there are more artefacts to be found at the site.'

'So what is this site got to do with this Alice?'

'Robert believed the site may have a marker. One of three that will reveal where Alice had her main manor house. It is believed to hold a vast treasure that she had acquired throughout her lifetime.'

'Although you say he kept things under wraps, there must have been other people who knew what he was looking for?'

'Just other academics and our benefactor? I was the only member of the dig team who was fully briefed on the project.'

'Benefactor?'

'Damien Thackery. He's a London based businessman who's funding this dig.'

'I would have thought something as significant as this, Cambridge would have been funding the dig?' Fagan considered.

'Unfortunately no. Robert was a bit of a maverick when it came to archaeology. He always went after the most obscure legends. Alice of Abergavenny happens to be something of a lifelong passion of his.'

'We have a witness who saw Professor Turner arguing with someone last week. A druid.'

Sarah let out a snort of derision. 'Bloody tree huggers. They accused us of desecrating their beloved land.'

'Have you ever had any other trouble with them?'

'Yes, they turned up when we first started to excavate the site. We usually ignore them. I did film them hurling abuse at us. I've encountered many people throughout my career who have always had a problem with archaeologists. It doesn't matter what we find, there are always those who will oppose what we do. Especially when it comes to religious artefacts.'

'Religious artefacts?'

'That's what Professor Turner was most interested in regarding Alice.'

'So he was out here looking for a religious artefact that belonged to this Alice?'

'Yes, she was supposed to have owned a relic called the Splinter of Christ. It's a solid gold cross with a piece of the true cross embedded into it.'

'True cross?' Watkins said.

'The cross that Jesus was allegedly crucified on.'

'Allegedly.' Fagan remarked. 'I take it you're not the religious type?'

'Not really.' York answered. 'The splinter of Christ is just a legend. But Robert believed Alice could have come into possession of it. Along with other important artefacts.'

'The person who ransacked Professor Turner's room. Do you know what they could have been looking for?'

York shook her head. 'No, everything of value was taken back to Cambridge.'

'Following the argument he had with someone on the phone yesterday afternoon. How did he seem?'

'Robert seemed agitated during dinner last night. Kept checking his phone.'

Fagan jotted down more notes before snapping his notebook shut. 'Well, I think that's about all for now. We'll let you get on with your day.'

'I need to tell the team what has happened.'

Fagan nodded. 'You say there are three sites being excavated. Where are the other two?'

'There's one out at Brynderi and another one in Llangattock Lingoed.'

'Thank you.' Fagan handed her a card. 'Here's my number. If you can think of anything else that will help us with our enquiry, then please call.'

'At least we have some idea as to what this is about now.' Watkins remarked as they headed back to Newport.

'We need to visit all the sites that York mentioned.'

'I've a feeling because of what's involved here people are not just interested in ancient artefacts. There's obviously a lot of money at stake here.'

C H A P T E R 4

Newport Police HQ – 09:45am

Fagan stood in front of a whiteboard. He scrawled Turner's name at the top.

PC Andrew Brooks had been assigned to help with the investigation. Chief Constable Paul Griffiths had e-mailed Fagan earlier that morning to say that he could only spare one officer at that present time. The scene of crime officers at Skenfrith castle were ordered to sweep and clean the crime scene and return to the constituencies they had been on loan from.

Fagan had the feeling that since Rebecca was murdered plus his investigation into Benny Nelson, the Chief Constable was trying to make his life awkward. He turned to face Watkins and Brooks. 'So, we have the deceased found at Skenfrith castle. He's been crucified and stabbed with a dagger. He picked up a printed picture of Turner's body and stuck it on the whiteboard. 'What do we know about the victim?'

Brooks looked at a tablet he was holding. 'Professor Robert Turner, renowned archaeologist. Also described as a modern-day Indiana Jones, according to his webpage at Cambridge university. His speciality has been tracking down religious artefacts stolen from the Holy Land during the crusades. He's been credited with a number of finds across Europe, including part of the crown of thorns worn by Christ during the crucifixion, and also part of the robe he wore when he carried the cross. He's an expert on many events throughout history, most notably the crusades. Apparently he has written eleven books on the crusades and royal history in the UK.'

'He's an expert then.' Fagan cut Brooks off before he could monologue any more.

Brooks nodded. 'That about sums him up, yeah.'

'So, he's here looking for the Splinter of Christ, or whatever it's called.'

Watkins looked at his smartphone. 'It's basically what Sarah York described this morning. It's supposed to be a golden cross which is encrusted with diamonds and has a piece of the one true cross embedded into it. It was stolen in 1172AD from the Church of Solomon in Jerusalem. Apparently a bunch of marauding knights stormed the temple, killed most of the monks before making away with the valuables, including this Splinter of Christ. A bunch of Knights Templar were dispatched to hunt them down.'

'Sorry to be a bit of a buzzkill here.' Fagan interrupted. 'But is everything going to be a tedious history lesson during this murder investigation?'

'You have to admit boss, this isn't your average murder. The way the victim was killed for a start. Spread eagled in a castle keep. Crucified, with a dagger sticking out of his chest. Plus, he's got that insignia branded onto his forehead. And let's not forget the note written on parchment scrawled in blood. It's like I said this morning. It mimics a plot out of a Dan Brown novel.'

'What about the blood on the scroll?'

'We won't know if the blood belongs to the victim until the lab contacts us.' Watkins' phone pinged. 'Talk of the devil.' He said, reading the message. 'They have just removed Turner's body. It's been taken to Nevil Hall mortuary.'

Fagan took a deep breath.

'Which means boss, for now, we're stuck with the history lesson.'

Fagan rolled his eyes and sighed. 'Fine, what about suspects?'

'We're a little thin on the ground with that sir.' Brooks explained. 'Sarah York left Turner last night at ten o'clock. I spoke with her earlier to see if she was able to remember anything more. She told us that Turner was one of these go to bed on time types. He went to bed at ten thirty every night and would wake at six thirty every morning. Apparently, Professor Turner liked to get eight hours of sleep every night.'

'Wouldn't we all.' Watkins yawned. 'I was up at three feeding the baby this morning. Couldn't get back to sleep.'

'But last night Turner wasn't the go to bed early type.' Fagan pointed out. 'At some point he left the hotel. York mentioned he was constantly checking his phone during their meal last night. The question is, what lured him away from the hotel? I take it all the vehicles parked in the vicinity of the castle have been run through the DVLA?'

'Yes boss.' Watkins nodded. 'All have checked out belonging to residence within the area. There was one vehicle that didn't have tax on it.'

'We need to find out if this Professor Turner arrived in his own car. According to Annie this morning, Turner had some sort of altercation with local druids. They must have some kind of club. They've probably got a social media presence. Anyone who wants to make their mark in the world usually has a social media page of some sort. Doctor Sarah York also mentioned the head of the local metal detecting club hanging around the dig site at Bont.' Fagan made eye contact with Brooks. 'I want you to go to all three sites where they have been digging and start taking witness statements from everyone at each dig site.'

'That could be quite an undertaking boss. Sarah York said there are dozens working at the sites.'

'I don't care if there are ten thousand people. We need to know everyone who is involved in this dig. As soon as we get more uniforms, I want them taking names.' Fagan looked back at the whiteboard. 'So he was a noted archaeologist, author. Been all over Europe digging for religious artefacts. What is the motive for his murder?'

'I think this speaks for itself.' Watkins said. 'Obviously buried treasure is at stake here. Not only that, but Turner was looking for what he's claiming to be the Splinter of Christ. That in itself is enough to send most religious groups into a frenzy. Sooner or later news of his death will spread. Then we'll have every tom, dick and harry treasure hunter descending on the area.'

'The murderer must have known he was here looking for this splinter.' Fagan speculated.

Watkins nodded. 'Which gives us a wide scope of people. Everyone on the archaeological group is a potential suspect. They've all got stakes in this dig. If this splinter is found, then it will be one for the history books. Every member of that dig team will want to pin their name to this.'

'Sarah York said that Cambridge university wasn't funding their dig. It was someone called Damien Thackery. We need to know why Cambridge university wasn't funding the dig. You would have thought someone with Turner's reputation could get funding for anything.'

'Unless someone didn't want him looking for this artefact.' Brooks suggested.

'What do you mean?'

'There are those who believe that the past is the past and should stay there. But again, this is like the *Da Vinci Code*, the Vatican bending over backwards to stop the possibility of information about Jesus having a bloodline leaking out.'

'So this Turner could have been murdered because our murderer didn't want him finding this splinter of Christ.' Fagan speculated. 'The question is9barmy who?'

Watkins shrugged. 'This is a long haul investigation boss, no suspects yet, but plenty of motive for murder.'

Fagan looked despairingly at the whiteboard. 'We'll have to start kicking over stones. Find out if this Turner has any enemies. We need to get in contact with Cambridge university. Perhaps we'll turn up something there. I suggest you both get going with your assignments.'

'What are you doing boss?' Watkins asked.

'I'm going to learn some history about this so-called Alice of Abergavenny. You've said it yourself. Looks like this is going to be more of a history lesson than a murder enquiry.'

CHAPTER 5

Lower Monk Street – Abergavenny – 10:56am

Fagan stepped through the door of George Walker's house. 'Here you go George. The shopping you ordered from Iceland.'

'Thanks Marc. I don't know what's up with Iceland's delivery service lately. That's twice I have ordered something and had to send someone after it. I don't want to take up your time if you're on the Job.'

'I'm on an extended lunch break.' Fagan smiled.

George chuckled. 'In that case, I'll put the kettle on. I always used to find time to pop home to Mary when I was on duty.'

Fagan sipped the coffee George had just made, along with a plateful of biscuits.

'I hear you found a body out at Skenfrith castle.'

Fagan smiled. 'I see the Evans news service has been in full swing today.'

'He's excited that you're back in town. I suppose everyone is. I understand if you can't talk about it. Back in the day, if anything happened in this town it was all over the place. The police back then weren't exactly discreet.'

'Today you have to keep a lot of secrets. I revealed too much about Rebecca's murder. I'm surprised it didn't land me in the shit.'

'People would have eventually found out the grisly details. You have to still deal with the trial when it happens. That will dig up a few ghosts again.'

Fagan nodded slowly. 'It will. I have to see a councillor at some point. My superior seems to think that Rebecca's death affected me.'

'Has it?'

Fagan considered the possibility. 'I suppose.'

'So what happened at Skenfrith this morning?' George asked changing the subject.

'We found the body of this university Professor. I have seen a lot of dead people in my time, but I don't think I was even prepared for this one. The victim in question was found in the castle keep. He'd been stripped naked and crucified to the floor. There was an old dagger impaled into his chest. A very nasty killing. Anyway, I have to look into this man's background which involves a lot of historical research.' Fagan recalled his school days. 'History was never my thing when I was in school.' He looked over at George who had a strange look on his face. 'You ok George?'

'Did you say the fellow was crucified?'

Fagan nodded as he bit into a chocolate bourbon.

George stroked his chin, recalling a memory. 'June 1975, I was called to a similar case at Tintern Abbey.'

'Really.' Fagan expressed surprise.

'He was a University Professor as well, Cambridge I think.'

'You mean it was a similar murder George?'

'Apart from the dagger and the bloke being naked.' George mused. 'The man we found had a broadsword sticking through his belly. Caused quite the stir in Tintern. The locals thought that Jack the Ripper had come to town. I remember the fellow had a mark carved into his forehead. The letter A, if I recall.'

Fagan pulled his phone from his pocket and located the picture of Turner. He zoomed into the brand that had been burnt onto his forehead.

George put his reading glasses on and stared at the picture. 'Yeah, that's definitely similar.'

Fagan was amazed how detailed George remembered the scene. 'Did they catch the person responsible?'

'Good lord no. This wasn't an open and shut murder. This was something entirely different. No one had any idea how he wound up in the abbey. There were no forensics that you have today.'

'Not even any suspects?'

'No, it was a total mystery. I found out he'd been staying at the Angel hotel at the time. If I recall, he was one of those people who likes to dig around in the dirt.'

'How did you know he had a room at the Angel?'

'He had a box of matches with their name stamped on it. Most places used to do that back then. Unlike your victim he was fully clothed.' George drank from his coffee mug. 'I remember speaking to the hotel manager after they found the chap. He gave me the keys to his room to have a look around, but someone had been in his room before me.'

'Someone turned over his room.' Fagan stated, thinking about what happened earlier at the Agincourt hotel.

'I have the case file in the back shed if you want to have a look.'

'How have you got case files George? I would have thought even back then that would have been a big no no.'

'When I was recruited into Operation Countryman, I was asked to copy case files. I'll be honest with you Marc. I was keeping stuff way before Countrymen. The men running the operation were afraid that any bent copper in the force would be able to make stuff disappear. Bob Benson certainly had a knack for doing that.' He stood up. 'Come on, I'll show you what I have.'

A few minutes later, they were in the shed where George stored his case files. 'I've kept this place dry all these years. Otherwise everything would have gone mouldy. I come out here a couple of times a week to read through stuff. It's better than watching those god-awful quiz shows on the telly in the afternoon. They'll rot your brain more than anything. They're all repeated after a few months.' George seemed to know exactly what he was looking for and went straight to the filing cabinet. 'I keep everything in date and order so it will be easy to find.' He opened a drawer and thumbed through the files. 'Here we go, here it is.'

Fagan opened the file that contained a photograph of the victim who was spread out in a similar position to Professor Turner. Except this man was fully clothed. A sword was at an angle impaled into the victim's chest. Fagan looked at the other documents, which consisted of just four pages with names and brief statements. 'This is incomplete George. Where's the rest of the file?'

'That's all there is I'm afraid.'

'How come?'

'The evidence disappeared a few days after they found the body.'

'Stolen?'

'That was my theory at the time. There wasn't a lot of evidence. We kept the sword and his clothing. But everything vanished, so there wasn't really anything worth investigating.' George pointed at the file. 'There's a few names of people who I interviewed.'

Fagan looked through the brief list. 'It says here the victim's name is Norman Cuthbert of Cambridge university.' Fagan then spotted Robert Turner's name at the bottom. 'Well I'll be dammed.' He pointed at the name. 'I don't suppose you remember talking to this man here?'

George looked at the name before nodding. 'Yes, a young man. I think he was a student. I remember him being very upset about his death. Blaming himself. I also remember he was clutching an old journal he claimed belonged to Cuthbert and that he had given it to him the night before he died. Said it contained Cuthbert's life's work.'

'Did he tell you what they were digging for at Tintern?'

'Something to do with buried treasure or something like that.' George pointed at the files. 'I scribbled down some notes.'

Fagan studied the file. 'Alice of Abergavenny.' He read aloud.

'That's her. They were also looking for the holy grail.'

'Or The Splinter of Christ.' Fagan pointed at more notes scribbled on a page. 'George, do you mind if I hang on to this?'

'You are more than welcome to help yourself to anything in this shed Marc. I miss the old days. It shattered me when Bob told me to go.'

Fagan remembered the conversation they had a few months previously. 'I'll make sure I get this back to you.'

C H A P T E R 6

Llanover – 11:26am

'Thanks for seeing me at short notice Nigel.' Fagan said.

'I was just packing to go to New York for a week.' Nigel Thomas revealed. 'I'm jumping on a plane at ten o'clock tonight. Got an interview with an American news network about a documentary I narrated on the War of Independence. I doubt if they're going to be happy. You know what the Americans are like. If it doesn't fit in with their narrow-minded view of the world, they bitch like mad.'

'I was hoping you'd be around for the next few days.'

'Why what's up?'

'I've had a dead body turn up at Skenfrith castle and I am looking for information about what this bloke was interested in. He was an archaeologist.'

'Not my particular area of expertise. I've watched a few episodes of Time Team whenever they're in the area. What have you got?'

'The victim in question was found naked and crucified to the floor of the castle keep.'

'Ouch.'

'Ouch indeed.' Fagan called up the picture on his phone and passed it to Thomas.

'Jesus Fagan.' Thomas recoiled from the phone. 'I didn't think you were going to show me the body.'

'What can you tell me about this?'

'Apart from the fact the poor bastard has been crucified

to the floor, not a lot.'

'The CSI said the dagger is ancient. Could be a few hundred years. It's been sharpened recently.'

Thomas composed himself and zoomed in on the dagger. 'It looks ceremonial, but I can't be sure.'

'The man also had a mark branded on his forehead.'

Thomas studied the image. 'Interesting.'

'What?'

'It's a seal, you know, like the ones they used to seal envelopes with wax in the old days. And if I'm not mistaken, this particular stamp belongs to Alice of Abergavenny.'

'So you know who this Alice is?'

Thomas picked up a tablet from his desk. 'Just bits and bobs I'm afraid. She was a local girl. Lived in the 12th century. Supposedly just a servant girl. She took a lover who was a local knight. Looks like she wanted to be more than just a serving wench at the local tavern.' Thomas scrolled down the screen. 'Her lover's name has been lost to history. In 1170AD Alice travelled to Ireland with her knight and witnessed a battle in which he died. It is said that she was both heartbroken and filled with rage. During the battle prisoners were captured from the opposing side. The commanding officer was going to release the prisoners in exchange for a ransom. However, Alice had different plans. She got a blacksmith to forge her seal with her initial. Then she went to the commanding officer and told him that any prisoners should be executed. He was somewhat dismayed at her request and said that she'd have to do it herself. So, in one afternoon, Alice beheaded seventy prisoners.'

'Seventy, Jesus.'

'She marked each head with the seal the blacksmith had made for her and returned them to the opposing side.'

'Not someone you'd want to piss off on a first date then.' Fagan joked.

Thomas laughed. 'No, not really.'

'What happened to her after that?'

'No one knows. That's where Alice's story ends.'

'I find it hard to believe this woman chopped off the heads of seventy men in one afternoon and did not develop a taste for killing.' A dark memory stabbed at Fagan's mind. 'One of my first major murder investigations involved a serial killer. A number of prostitutes had been found dead around Liverpool. The killer was sending notes in all the time. Fancied himself as the Yorkshire ripper. One note said, once you've killed once, you'll never go back.'

'Chilling.' Thomas remarked.

'We never caught him, even with all the technology at our disposal.' Fagan glanced at the tablet Thomas had. 'So, you see, once you've chopped off seventy heads, there's no way you're going to stop at that. The archaeologist we found this morning was supposedly out here looking for something called the splinter of Christ.'

Thomas rolled his eyes. 'Jesus, that old chestnut.'

'You've heard of it then?'

Thomas leant back in his chair, folding his arms. 'I have lost count of how many nutjobs e-mail me, or have knocked at my door expecting me to know the location of this Splinter of Christ. It's like the search for the holy grail if you believe in all that nonsense. How much do you know about the Skirrid mountain?'

'My mam once told me it's supposed to be haunted. Something to do with a farmer's daughter, ill-fated love and all that. She was supposed to have committed suicide on the mountain when her father stopped her from marrying a local boy. Her ghost haunts the mountain on a misty day. She's dressed all in white.'

'That's very good Inspector Fagan, a popular story as well. What about how the mountain became the shape it is today?'

Fagan shrugged. 'Not a clue.'

'If you're a geologist, you know that a landslide occurred during the last ice age. But if you're religious, you will say the mountain split in two, the moment Christ was crucified, so the story goes. It's another local grail legend. Along with the splinter of Christ.' Thomas closed his eyes and recited some verse. 'The heavens opened and God cast down his wrath upon the mountain side. As our lord Jesus sacrificed himself for man, Satan dined in the mountain's gaping wound.'

Fagan smiled. 'The devil's table. That pile of rocks that looks like a toadstool. We used to dare each other to climb on the top. I think Tyler was the only one who did it. What is that line you just quoted?'

'It's an old poem that was written by a man called Gerald of Wales, who was the Archdeacon of Brecon. He was massive in his day, educated in France and visited Rome several times meeting the Pope. He wrote a tonne of religious texts. As for Satan's table, that's another local legend which has no merit.'

'So where does this Splinter of Christ legend come from?'

'It's one of many grail legends that have been touted for generations. Lord Malcolm Barry, who incidentally lives out by Skenfrith castle has been peddling the Splinter of Christ legend for years.'

'Why is it associated with the holy grail?'

'There are loads of grail legends that have passed through this way. Several years ago, an artefact was stolen from a church in Herefordshire. It was known as the Nanteos cup. Another medieval grail fake that has turned up over the years. The cup was found eventually by west Mercia police as part of an operation to track down stolen religious artefacts. Apparently there is a growing trend in it.' Thomas suddenly stopped talking. 'Hang on a moment.'

'What?'

He held out his hand. 'Give me your phone. I want to see a picture of that dagger.'

Fagan handed over his phone.

Thomas scrutinised the dagger impaled in Turner's chest. 'Of course. Why didn't I see that?' He handed Fagan his phone back. 'Don't turn off that picture.' He searched for a webpage on his tablet. 'Here it is.' He handed Fagan his tablet.

Fagan studied the picture of four daggers in a display case. He then looked at the dagger on his phone. 'They're the same, or at least one of them is.'

Thomas nodded.

'Where did you find that picture?'

'The Abergavenny Chronicle.' Thomas answered. 'I had an interview with them about a major theft.' He checked the date on the news article. 'In January 2020, Abergavenny Museum got broken into. The thieves were able to deactivate the alarm system. I remember the museum curator Tony James calling me on the morning of the robbery. Poor bugger was in pieces. He'd spent two years planning a medieval artefacts exhibition at the museum. He was interviewed by BBC Wales news at the time. Tony had been collecting stuff for years. Mostly things local metal detectors would find. But the pride of his collection were these four daggers that were supposed to be a centrepiece for the exhibition.'

'Where did he get the daggers from?'

Thomas stalled on an answer.

'Were they stolen?'

'Not exactly, well at least not that I know of.' Thomas replied. 'They were loaned to him sometime back in the seventies.'

'But he never gave them back.'

'No, and I'll tell you why. Tony was an archaeologist back in his day. He told me that he was at a dig at Tintern Abbey when they came across a significant find, including the daggers. There was some bigwig archaeologist at the site. A Cambridge man there, overseeing the dig. He was Tony's former teacher, when he studied at Cambridge.'

Fagan picked up the file he had brought with him, opening it. 'This big wig archaeologist, was it someone by the name of Norman Cuthbert?'

'Yeah, he was the Indiana Jones of the time. Before anyone had ever heard of Spielberg's fictional archaeologist. I remember Tony saying that Cuthbert was interested in the legend of Alice of Abergavenny. When they found the daggers Cuthbert was all excited.'

'Why?'

Thomas held up the picture on his tablet. 'Take a look at the picture you took this morning.'

Fagan stared at the image for a few moments before spotting what Thomas wanted him to see. On the hilt of the Dagger was Alice's seal. 'Shit.'

'One of these daggers is the one you took a photo of this morning. Tony told me that Cuthbert had given him the daggers for safekeeping. But a few days later, they found Cuthbert's body in the grounds of the abbey. Tony said he was so terrified he hung on to the daggers and never told a soul until he told me decades later. He also told his daughters how he came across the daggers.'

Fagan showed Thomas the photo of Cuthbert's body at the abbey. 'Here's Norman Cuthbert as he appeared in 1975.'

Thomas glared at the image. 'Where did you get this?'

'George Walker gave me this just an hour ago.'

'The picture is too old to make out any detail on the sword.'

'Can you give me Tony's contact details? I'll need to speak with him.'

'Sorry Fagan, Tony died in May 2020, during lockdown. Poor sod had been lying in the centre of his living room for a few days before his daughter found him. I had a visit from the police about his death. I received a text from him. Tony text me to say he knew who stole the daggers.'

'Who?'

Thomas exhibited a look of sadness. 'That's the thing, he never answered me. His phone record revealed he'd tried to ring me about five days before they found him. I remember seeing the calls and tried to phone him back. All I got was his voicemail. I was in London at the time giving a lecture at the British museum.'

'Cause of death?'

'A heart attack apparently, but then again, it was during the lockdown. So many people died during that time. It was chaos to tell who was dying of what. I even went to the police with the text. But they didn't want to know. Too busy making sure that no one was breaking lockdown rules. Shortly after his death, his daughter came to see me. She claimed her father had died in mysterious circumstances.'

'What kind of mysterious circumstances?'

'The murderous kind.'

'Did she tell the police?'

'I think so, but it was lockdown. They insisted he died of a heart attack. I even showed her the text Tony sent me. She told me she had collected evidence she found. But again, the police didn't want to know.' Thomas stared at the black and white image of Cuthbert. 'That exhibition was everything to him. I remember Tony telling me he had a massive argument with Lord Barry about the daggers. It was just after he had an article published in the Chronicle about the exhibition.'

'Did he tell you what the argument was about?'

'Lord Barry was furious that the daggers were part of the exhibition.'

'Why?'

'Said they belonged to Alice's descendants.'

'But you just said Alice disappeared after she killed all those prisoners.'

'And that's the mystery isn't it, Inspector Fagan? We are talking nine hundred years ago.' Thomas handed back the photo. 'Listen, I'll be away for over a week and I know you want to get to the bottom of this quickly. So, against my better judgement, I'll give you the name of the woman who runs Abergavenny Museum.'

'Against your better judgement?.

'After Tony died, I contacted Monmouthshire council and said I wanted to take over the running of the place. Tony had already told me he wanted me to do it after he had gone. I just wasn't expecting it to be so soon.'

'What happened?'

'They told me they'd already found a suitable curator for the job. Since the museum was shut for over a year, I couldn't get access to anything. When it finally opened back up, this Amanda Rhys had rearranged the place. Tony's hard work wiped away. He knew her. She moved to Abergavenny in 2018. Tony took a shine to her.' Thomas frowned. 'He ran that museum for over forty years. There was so much she just threw away. The woman has no respect for local history. She claims that she's a local girl at heart. Despite her being from Cambridgeshire. She's into genealogy and all that stuff. Apparently, Amanda is from noble stock that lived in Wales over a thousand years ago.' Thomas let out a snort of derision. 'The woman is full of it, makes out she knows everything about history. Every month she gives talks at the Angel. There's a lecture being held tonight.'

Fagan smiled at Thomas. 'I seem to remember a young boy at school knowing everything.'

Thomas chuckled. 'The good old days. Speaking of which, I have been going through pictures from the London Hotel. Quite a few interesting people used to go there back in the day. When I get back from New York, we'll meet up at some point.'

'Sure.' Fagan's phone buzzed.

'Boss, where are you?' Watkins asked.

'I'm doing research on this Alice woman.'

'You need to get out to the dig site in Bont. All hell is kicking off here.'

'I'm on my way.'

CHAPTER 7

Bont – Monmouthshire – 12:09pm

Even from a distance of several hundred yards, Fagan could hear shouting as he climbed out of his jet-black Jeep SUV. He looked out across the field, taking in the enormity of the archaeological site. At the side of the dig a group of people were huddled together. Fagan spotted the florescent jacket of constable Brooks, who was in the middle of the affray.

Watkins pushed through the group of people, spotting Fagan approaching. 'This is bloody ridiculous. We can't get a word of sense out of these dicks. Bunch of bickering school kids if you ask me.'

Two men were squaring off against one another as Fagan approached. He could hear Sarah York trying to diffuse the conflict.

'The both of you, just calm down. We can't be fighting like this.'

One of the feuding men glared at her. 'Look who's decided to be the boss of us all, Miss fucking special herself.'

'What's going on here?' Fagan shouted, louder than anyone else. He waded into the centre of the group, standing between the two arguing men.

'Who the fuck are you?' One man snarled.

'Detective inspector Marc Fagan.' He shoved his ID in the man's face. 'Now, do you mind telling me who you are?'

The man took a step back from Fagan, acknowledging his ID. 'David Spooner.'

Fagan glanced at the other man, who was scowling at Spooner. 'Jay Dayton.'

'Ok, now can you two promise me you won't start arguing again?'

Both men nodded in unison, maintaining a menacing stare at each other.

Fagan stepped back. 'Right, would someone tell me why it's all kicking off?'

'They were arguing about the way forward regarding the dig.' York spoke for them.

Both Spooner and Dayton glared at her before looking back at each other.

'A way forward?'

'We were deciding if we should concentrate our efforts at another dig site. These two think there is nothing else to be found here.'

Fagan looked at her. 'But you do?'

'Yes.'

'What exactly are you hoping to find out here?'

York remained silent.

Fagan looked at the men. 'Are any of you going to answer my questions?'

More silence. Other members of the archaeology team turned away and started walking back towards the dig.

'Like that is it.' Fagan stated, looking at Watkins. 'Sean, phone this in. I want more bodies here on the double.' He looked at York, Spooner and Dayton. 'The three of you will come back to Newport central HQ for questioning.'

'What.' Spooner protested. 'But we haven't done anything. You can't just arrest us.'

'I'm not arresting you. Unless I need to. We want to ask you a couple of routine questions.'

'You can ask them here.' Spooner folded his arms and stood firm.

Fagan stepped up to him. 'Either you come in for a routine questioning, or I will arrest you in connection with Professor Turner's murder.'

Spooner glared back at Fagan. 'Don't think you can threaten me, plod.'

Fagan stood toe to toe with him. 'I wouldn't get clever if I were you. A man has been brutally murdered up the road at Skenfrith castle. I appreciate you wanting to carry on. Sarah York has already revealed the significance of this find. However, the facts stand, all of you are part of an active murder investigation. Now either I'll arrest you for being linked to Professor Turner's murder. Or you can come voluntarily. What's it going to be?'

CHAPTER 8

Newport Central police HQ – 1:05pm

'Interview with Sarah York and myself, Detective Inspector Marc Fagan. So let's start at the beginning shall we. How long have you worked with Professor Turner?'

'About fifteen years.'

'I take it you studied archaeology at university?'

'No, my major was knitting.'

Fagan wasn't impressed by her sass. 'I don't need this shit Sarah. And for your information, I've met many people who attended university but ended up doing different things.'

'Yes, if you want specific answers. Archaeology was my major at Cambridge. I graduated top of my class.'

'Did you study under Turner?'

'Yes.'

'I take it archaeology is a hard line of business to break into.'

'I suppose. When I left university, I was fortunate. Professor Turner offered me a position as his personal assistant. He said I had potential.'

'Potential in what, exactly?'

'If your real question is, was I screwing Robert? Then the answer is no. Jesus, he's old enough to be my grandfather.'

'I wasn't suggesting that.'

'Yes, we were close. Robert reminded me of my father, who died when I was sixteen.'

'I'm sorry to hear that. So what were they arguing about

at the site in Bont?' Fagan checked his notes. 'Spooner and Dayton.'

'Those two are always arguing. Whenever Robert started a new dig, he'd hire a new team. I was the only one he would keep. Spooner and Dayton had a problem working with us from the start.'

'When I spoke to you this morning at the Agincourt hotel regarding Robert's room, you said you had no idea why his room was ransacked. Have you had anymore thoughts on that?'

'No. I told you, everything of value was taken back to Cambridge. Robert didn't want items of value at the dig site.'

'Well, there must have been something worth stealing in that room.' Fagan recalled what George had said to him earlier that day. 'Did Robert ever keep a journal?'

York hesitated before answering. 'Like a diary, you mean?'

'Yes, like a diary.'

'He kept plenty of notes on his work. But I can't remember a journal or a diary.'

'How obsessed was Robert about finding this Splinter of Christ?'

York considered the question for a moment. 'This was to be Robert's last significant find before he retired. So yes, I'd say he was quite passionate about finding it. He always used to say, he owed it to his former mentor.'

'That wouldn't be Professor Norman Cuthbert, would it?'

York stared back at Fagan. 'How do you know that?'

Fagan opened the file George had loaned him, pointing at the photograph of Cuthbert. 'This photograph was taken in 1975. Cuthbert was murdered in similar fashion to Robert. But with a sword, not a dagger. Did Robert ever mention anything about this?'

'He used to talk about Norman all the time. Professor Cuthbert was an expert on the Knights Templar. He travelled to the Holy Land in search of their origins. His passion was Grail myth and other religious artefacts stolen during the crusades.'

'The dagger we found this morning used to murder Robert was one of four daggers that were stolen from Abergavenny museum in January 2020. Would you know anything about that?'

'Why would I know anything? I have no connection to this town.'

'They were originally found by Norman Cuthbert in the ruins of Tintern Abbey.'

'Come to think about it, Robert did mention them, because they were supposed to be the first marker.'

'Marker?'

'To mark the path to the Splinter of Christ. But he said the daggers were stolen just before Cuthbert was murdered.'

'They were more borrowed than stolen. My source told me that the daggers were lent to the former curator of the local museum, who hung onto them for over four decades.'

'This is all new information to me.' York claimed. 'Robert had often spoken of the missing daggers. I always thought he was talking about another mythical artefact. We have had many red herrings over the years regarding Alice of Abergavenny. It used to annoy the hell out of Robert whenever someone would try to lead him up the garden path.' York remembered something.

'What is it?' Fagan asked, noting York's expression.

'Robert contacted the museum curator. He had just been turned down by Cambridge for funding for the dig. So he contacted Abergavenny museum and asked if the local authority would be interested in funding the dig.'

'I take it they turned him down?'

York nodded. 'Despite the fact he offered thirty percent of anything recovered. Which would have been priceless if we found what Robert was searching for.'

'Had found?'

York inhaled. 'For a while I was caught up in the legend of things like the Holy grail, King Arthur, Viking gods marauding through the landscape. Then, after a while, you learn that legend and myth are just that. I sometimes wonder why so many people still read the bible. Robert always encouraged me to read it. To look beyond the spiritual aspect and read it like a story. You know what I've discovered after fifteen years of studying it?'

Fagan shrugged.

'It's simply what Robert said it was. A story, and that's it. Yes, you can read through it and discover who you are.'

'And have you discovered who you are Sarah?'

York stared at the wall. 'I'm just another lost soul in search of answers she will never find.'

'Surely Robert's work can't be forgotten. I was reading up on him earlier. He accomplished a lot during his lifetime.'

'And gained nothing.' York remarked. 'I was the only family he had. He never married or anything like that. After Cuthbert was murdered, he said he wouldn't let the petty things in life distract him until he caught up with whoever killed Norman.'

Fagan thought about his own views on marriage. The job always came first. Marriage was something for people who wanted to throw their lives away. 'Do you think the same person killed Robert and his mentor?'

'God, no. We're talking almost fifty years ago. If it is the same person, then they'd have to be ancient.'

'You just mentioned that Robert always hired a fresh team whenever he started a new dig. And that you were always kept on.'

'Of course, I was his personal assistant. As much as a brilliant man he was, there were times when Robert couldn't even tie his own shoe laces.'

'So the fact he hired a new team with every new dig didn't raise cause for concern.'

'What do you mean?'

'What I mean is that he was one of the top archaeologists in the country. His reputation would have followed him around. So everyone would have wanted to be on his team, including whoever murdered him.'

'I suppose, but Robert never hired anyone from outside the archaeology department at Cambridge. He would to say to me he wanted to give as many of the students the benefit of his experience as he could. Robert loved to share knowledge.'

'What about the two who were arguing earlier?'

'Spooner is a complete dick. I lost count of how many times Robert had to tell him to toe the line. To respect what he was doing. Come to think of it, only yesterday, Robert threatened to throw Spooner off the team.'

'Why?'

'He was never there for a start. And when he was there, he wasn't interested in getting his hands dirty. Spooner comes from a money family. He was just going through the motions doing the degree. What did he say to me a few weeks back? I'm taking the least path of resistance through university, which is why I chose archaeology. He's an arrogant prick who will have a successful career because his path is already laid out before him. Unlike the rest. As for Dayton, I know little about him. He's usually the quietest of the team.'

'And you've no idea what they were arguing about?'

'I arrived not long after your first officer arrived.'

A few moments of silence followed.

'So you've no clue who could have murdered Robert?' York stated.

'At this moment in time, no. All avenues of enquiry have hit a dead end. There's no CCTV at the hotel.'

'That's why Robert chose the Agincourt. He phoned the manager of the hotel a week before he arrived and asked about cameras.'

Fagan scribbled a line in his notebook. 'Interesting to know. Did he have any rivals in Cambridge?'

'Chester Jameson was his biggest rival. Professor Jameson is also big on myth and legend and all that stuff. But he was more of an Arthurian more than anything. Jameson would tell Robert he was wasting his time. And vice versa. I always thought it was silly, given their age. It was like two grown-up children bickering.'

'What about the man financing the dig?'

'Damien Thackery, biggest prick on the face of the planet.'

'Why is that?'

'Ten years ago, he funded a dig in France. It was to excavate a Templar site. Only these weren't mainstream Templars, they were a breakaway faction. Robert believed they had connections to Alice of Abergavenny, but he could never prove it. Anyway, Thackery funded the dig, paid for everything. We found a hoard of Templar coins just outside Lyon. Thackery hired a security company to collect the coins and take them back to Cambridge. But they never arrived.'

'Where did they end up?'

'At a private auction. Thackery refunded the university one hundred and fifty thousand pounds. For which they were very grateful.'

'Do you know how much the coins sold for?'

'Six and a half million. Thackery stabbed Robert in the back.'

'So why trust him again?'

'Believe me, Robert had tried all avenues. Thackery promised Robert he wouldn't do the dirty. He was more interested in having his name associated with the team that found the Splinter of Christ.'

'I take it Robert wasn't going to trust him with handling any artefacts this time.'

'No, he got hold of people he trusted to take anything we found back to Cambridge. But I suspected Thackery would have made money out of the dig somehow.'

'When I spoke to you at the hotel earlier, you said that Robert had an argument with someone on the phone yesterday afternoon. And also he was constantly checking his phone last night. You didn't see any texts he might have been sent.'

'No, Robert had his phone in his pocket. Every time his phone would buzz he would check it, then put it back in his pocket.'

'So he didn't text any response to the messages he was getting?'

'No.'

'What time did you go to bed?'

'It was after midnight. I was talking to someone from Cambridge online. We were talking about the dig.'

'Were you talking through social media?'

'Yes, Facebook. I was sharing a few pictures from the dig.'

Fagan looked at the clock on the wall. 'I think we can leave it there Sarah.'

'What happens now?'

‘We keep trying to find the people who murdered Robert. It may take time, but we’ll find them.’

‘You think there’s more than one person involved in his murder?’

‘It’s looking that way at the moment. But until we’ve more to go on, there’s not a lot I can tell you.’

York nodded before standing.

‘Don’t leave the area for the moment Sarah. We may need to speak with you again.’

‘I’m not going anywhere. I’m going to finish what Robert started. Unless Thackery says different.’

‘Ok, well if you think of anything, you know how to contact me.’

York stood and threw her jacket over her shoulder. ‘I just want to get back to the dig site and find that first marker.’

CHAPTER 9

Nevill Hall Hospital – 2:25pm

Watkins and Brooks had interviewed Spooner and Dayton separately. However, both men had given no useful information that might have pushed the case forward. Fagan drove York and the other two back to the dig site. For the entire journey Fagan had to endure an uncomfortable silence. When he arrived, he checked his messages on his phone. The coroner had messaged Fagan, informing him he had examined the body of Turner and had found some interesting results. After what Fagan called a second lunch, both he and Watkins drove to Nevill Hall to find out more about how Turner had died.

'This is definitely one for the books, I'll tell you that.'

Fagan studied Turner's body. The pathologist had done a remarkable job of cleaning up the wound in his chest.

'Let's start with the dagger, shall we.' The pathologist picked up the murder weapon. 'This dagger is very old. I'd say five hundred years or more.'

Fagan called up the image Thomas had sent him earlier. 'Medieval, to be exact. It's one of four daggers that were stolen in January 2020. They were part of an exhibition which was due to go on display in March the same year. However, because of the pandemic, the whole thing was shelved.'

The pathologist pointed at the blade. 'This has been sharpened. I'm surprised it withstood the process after several hundred years. Whoever did this, knew what they were doing.'

'What about the nails used to pin the victim to the ground?' Watkins asked.

'This is very interesting. I did a little research this morning. Crucifixion was common, as one would expect throughout the Roman empire. The Persians and the Carthaginians also crucified their criminals. However there were different forms of crucifixion. Some people were nailed to two pieces of wood in an X formation and propped up or lay outstretched. Most people are more familiar with the crucifixion of Christ as being the main form.'

'So these are from the Roman period?'

'I'm not sure. I am sending fragments off to a lab at Cambridge University. I have an old friend who is part of the archaeological department. He'll get back to me later today.'

'This friend of yours, did he know Professor Turner?'

The pathologist nodded. 'He was shocked when I told him what had happened. I sent him pictures of these items. He says they are typical of middle eastern spikes used in crucifixions throughout the Holy Land in the middle ages. Thieves who were caught stealing were crucified and put on display on the road to Jerusalem to deter others.'

'Good crime prevention strategy.' Watkins remarked.

The pathologist pointed at the spikes on the table. 'Again, as you can see, these have been sharpened like the dagger, to restore their original potential. This is not straightforward pathology we are dealing with here. Which is why I have taken this up a notch and called on other experts.'

Fagan inhaled. 'As if I haven't had enough of a history lesson today.' He looked at the nails displayed on the table. 'If I were the murderer, and dagger aside, how would I come across nails from the middle ages?'

'There's an entire black market for this kind of stuff. There's been a steady flow of artefacts coming from that region for hundreds of years. Usually ending up in the hands of private collectors. You'll be surprised how much of this stuff comes through the system.' The coroner revealed. 'There was a raid in Cardiff last year. A man had been collecting this stuff for years. Buying it off the black market. His collection was massive. He was caught when the police set up a sting operation. An undercover officer claimed to be a seller and was trying to fence an actual nail from the cross of one of the men crucified with Jesus, the good thief.'

'There's no such thing as a good thief.' Fagan stated. 'Let's recap. Our killer steals these artefacts to murder Turner. Why?'

The coroner shrugged. 'You tell me, I don't think it was a ritualistic murder. But this wasn't a straightforward killing either.'

'I take it the message scrawled on the paper is the victim's blood?' Watkins surmised.

'No, initial analysis confirms that it's pig's blood.' The pathologist handled the parchment. 'Another interesting item. This is genuine parchment from the middle ages. It's been treated with certain chemicals to prevent it from disintegrating. Parchment like this was commonly used from the twelfth century onwards.'

'More history.' Fagan sighed.

'Perhaps that's the whole point of this murder.' The pathologist said. 'The way the victim was laid out, the items used to kill him. This is the type of murder that wouldn't have been uncommon back in the day. Whoever murdered Professor Turner was sending out a clear message.'

'Warning him not to go ahead with the dig.'

The pathologist shrugged. 'Our suspect thought of everything. Including tipping the dagger with poison.'

'Poison?'

'The wounds on his body are typical of stabbing wounds. but, there is a slight discolouration around the mouth. Indicating that he either ate something he shouldn't have. Or, the dagger was tipped with a poison that entered his blood stream. I am waiting on results as to what poison it was. Looks like our killer had a flare for the theatrical.'

'Anything else on the body that stands out?'

'I found several seeds matted into his pubic hair and upper chest hair.'

'They could have blown in during the night when the poor bugger lay dead.' Watkins said.

'No, these seeds were attached to the hair in a way that looks like they rubbed off something else, quite possibly our murderer. I've emailed someone in the hope they can identify what plants these seeds belong to.'

Fagan surveyed the body and the items. 'What kind of murderer are we dealing with here? Someone who hates archaeologists? We've interviewed a few of the team on the dig site. They have all provided watertight alibis.'

'We need to look outside the circle boss.' Watkins suggested. 'Find out who knew about the dig, and more importantly, who knew Professor Turner, but had no connection to this dig.'

'A man called Damien Thackery is funding the dig. Sarah York told me that Thackery and Turner had a history. Thackery double crossed Turner ten years ago on another dig in France. Apparently, they had found valuable artefacts and Thackery sold them to auction. Given what's at stake here and the items found already, there's a hell of a lot of money involved in this project. Sarah said the artefacts found already are worth millions.'

'You think this Thackery is planning another double cross?' Watkins speculated. 'He'll try to get his hands on what they recovered already.'

'It's possible. But why go to all this trouble to dress up his murder, making it look like something else? Plus, Turner's mentor was murdered in the same fashion in 1975.'

'But that would make the murderer old, like Turner?'

'Or, whoever murdered Cuthbert in 1975 is still about and hired someone to kill Turner.' Fagan speculated. 'Making Turner's murder look like a similar murder to Cuthbert's. This case is doing my head in, big time.' Fagan massaged his forehead.

'What about the druids and the metal detector bloke? We've yet to interview anyone from that line of enquiry. I have got the contact details of the chairman of the Abergavenny metal detecting association. That's one of the people that Sarah York said the archaeological team had an encounter with. He works at a DIY store at the back of the BP garage on the Brecon road. There's also the Monmouthshire druid association. They're based in a place called Earlswood.'

'Looks like we're being scattered to the four winds of the county here. We'll talk to this metal detecting guy when we are done here. As for the druids, they're usually pacifists.'

'I don't know about that. The druids were very blood thirsty back in the day.' The pathologist said. 'Human sacrifices and all that stuff.'

Fagan shook his head. 'This goes way beyond the druids and some metal detecting enthusiast. There are much bigger players involved here.' He looked at Watkins. 'We need to keep things as close to our chest as much as possible.'

'I don't think that is going to be possible boss.' Watkins said, glancing towards a flatscreen TV in the viewing room.

A journalist was standing on the side of the road looking back at Skenfrith castle.

Fagan marched into the observation room and turned up the volume on the TV.

'Jenny, what can you tell us about this gruesome murder?' The news presenter asked.

'The body of a man police are naming as Professor Robert Turner was found early this morning, here at Skenfrith castle. He was found naked in the castle keep and had been stabbed with what the police are calling an antique weapon.'

Fagan glanced at Watkins. 'We haven't released any details of how he was found.'

'What about the area where the murder took place?'

'This is a very rural area, popular with tourists and locals who like to come out and enjoy the countryside. We have spoken to some residents here this afternoon who have expressed their shock at such a disturbing incident.'

'What do we know about Professor Turner?'

'Professor Turner was well respected in his field of research. He was head of an archaeological dig in the area. A source has told the local news company that last week a find of significant value was discovered and spirited away back to Cambridge. It is believed the items included a medieval sword and valuable jewellery allegedly worth a lot of money.'

'They know everything about the dig. How the fuck do they know what they found?' Fagan growled.

'One of the team must have blabbed to the media.' Watkins speculated.

'We've just interviewed those bastards. I cannot believe

we're having to drag them back to Newport. Get on the horn and get a couple of uniform to bring Sarah York and the other two in for formal questioning. Also, get a search team over to the Agincourt Hotel. I want a thorough search of Sarah York's room.'

'Think she's hiding something boss?'

'That's what I intend to discover.'

Watkins hurried out of the observation room, barking orders into his phone.

Fagan glared at the TV reporter on the screen. Frustration boiled away. 'Shit!'

Watkins walked back into the room. 'All done, boss.'

'Let's have a quick word with our metal detecting enthusiast.'

'I'll do a more detailed examination of Turner later. I'll let you know if I find anything else.' The pathologist offered.

CHAPTER 10

Baileys DIY – 2:59pm

Russel Smith looked alarmed when Fagan showed him his ID badge. 'What's this all about?'

'We're investigating a murder that took place at Skenfrith castle in the early hours.'

'I had nothing to do with that.' Smith said shakily.

'A witness said that you had an altercation last week with the project leader, Robert Turner.'

'That's the bloke the police found this morning, isn't it? It's all over the news. I didn't murder him if that's what you have come here to accuse me of.'

'We're not here to accuse you of anything Mr Smith. We just want to know what you were arguing about, that's all.'

'Permission to detect on the land. We've had an agreement with that farmer for years. He's let us go detecting there twice a month, as long as he gets forty percent of what we find.'

'Have you found anything interesting?'

'A few bits and bobs. I found a ring several years ago.' Smith fished his smartphone from his pocket and called up a picture of the ring pointing at the insignia. 'It's a letter A.'

'Yes, we can see that.' Fagan remarked, recognising the seal.

'I didn't know what it meant until this morning, which has pissed me off.'

'Why is that?'

'Because that archaeological dig discovered a massive

hoard a week ago. Which means they'll strip the place. Bloody diggers. They always get the best stuff. Finding that chest and sword could have meant early retirement for me.'

'How do you know about what they found?'

'The farmer who owns the field was bragging at the Angel hotel the other night. A mate of mine works there.'

'Is that why you had an argument with Turner?'

'Amongst other things, yes.'

'Other things?' Watkins said.

Smith let out a sigh. 'Metal detecting enthusiasts are always being side lined. We dug up a hoard of Roman gold coins a few years ago in a field near Caerleon. The trouble is, whenever we find something of real value, we have to report it. We can't just go on detecting to find more. The minute we tell the authorities, they shut the area down. In come the archaeologists to strip the place bare. If it wasn't for us metal detectors, half the things discovered over the past several decades would still be buried.'

'Is that what the argument was over? The rights to the site.'

Smith nodded. 'Turner said he had paid the farmer twenty thousand pounds. He promised him more money if they found anything significant, which they obviously did. I did have a bit of a barmy with the farmer over it. He just told me to fuck off. Once again, we've been left out in the cold. I didn't go out there again, and I certainly didn't murder that Professor bloke. I only found out about him when I googled him.'

Fagan snapped his notebook shut. 'Thank you Mr Smith.'

'Another waste of time boss.' Watkins grumbled as they left the DIY store.

'This entire investigation has been a waste of time.

Someone has us running around in circles.'

Watkins looked at his phone that had just pinged. 'The search team at the Agincourt Hotel has found a diary under the mattress in Sarah York's room.'

'I knew that bitch was lying to me.' Fagan seethed.

'You think she had something to do with Turner's murder?'

'No, but she's been keeping secrets. I intend to find out what those secrets are. Text the uniform who found the diary. Tell them to bring it to Newport central immediately. If we take everyone to Newport, then it might loosen their tongues a little.'

Watkins thumbed the screen on his phone.

CHAPTER 11

Newport central police station – 3:57pm

Fagan placed the journal on the table in front of York. 'Care to tell me what this is?'

York glared at it for several seconds before looking at Fagan. 'Where did you get this?'

'Don't play games with me Sarah. You know bloody well where this came from. It was stuffed under the mattress in your room at the Agincourt hotel.'

York struggled with her next line. Her hands shook as she stared at the journal. 'You had no right to search my room.'

'We had every right.' Fagan cut her off. 'Don't you understand? A man was murdered last night. Impaled on the floor and stabbed with a dagger. You need to wake up and grasp how serious this is.' He tapped his finger on the journal. 'Because right now, it looks as if you went into Robert's room to steal this journal.'

'I didn't steal anything, I swear.' Tears tumbled down her cheeks.

'But you must have gone looking for it when you saw Robert had gone out. You noticed the door to his room was unlocked, so you turned his room upside down looking for it.'

'No, you have to believe me!' She insisted.

'Sarah, listen to me. The very fact you have this journal suggests you had something to do with Robert's murder.'

'No, I didn't!' York slammed her hand down on the

table.

Fagan maintained a calm posture. 'When I asked you earlier about a diary or a journal that Robert may have owned, you said he just kept notes.' Fagan pointed at the journal. 'I'd say this constitutes as more than just notes, wouldn't you?' He picked up the journal and thumbed through it. 'I would imagine this would be worth quite a lot in the hands of the right buyer. I mean, look at this. The original owner of this journal, Norman Cuthbert penned his first entry on Wednesday 25th October 1922. That's over a hundred years ago.' Fagan cleared his throat and began to read. 'Just completed a week long trek across the Sahara. The boating lakes of Cambridge now seem a world away. Finally arrived in Cairo. The air is vibrant with anticipation. I will finally meet Howard Carter. A man who is about to change the course of archaeological history.' Fagan pondered the journal's entry. 'A man who will change the course of archaeological history. A pretty powerful statement. Who is this Howard Carter, when he's at home?'

York took a deep breath. 'He was the archaeologist who discovered the tomb of Tutankhamun.'

'Oh really.' Fagan said with a surprised tone. 'I'm no student of history or archaeology, but even I have heard of him. I like to doze off in front of the History channel from time to time. Do you know why most people are familiar with Tutankhamun Sarah? It's not because of the life he led while he was alive. It's because of the shit load of treasure they found in his tomb. That golden mask he wore was priceless.' He turned the page and carried on reading. '4th November 1922. This is it. A step to the boy king's tomb has been found. Had dinner with Howard Carter. What an ambitious individual. This could be the start of my own glorious adventure into the past.' Fagan turned another page. '5th November 1922. All the steps have been cleared away.' Fagan glanced at York. 'They must have worked through the night to dig out all that rubble.'

York stared at the table, nodding.

Fagan continued to read. 'Finally, the door to the tomb's main entrance has been unearthed. An inscription on a stone tablet has been discovered at the entrance. Made a lot of the local labourers jittery. Located a translator.' Fagan paused for a moment. 'Death will come on swift wings, to those who disturb the sleep of the boy king.' He shuddered. 'Gives me the chills just reading it. No wonder the locals were jittery. They're big on religion in that part of the world. It's a wonder this Carter bloke didn't have a full-scale rebellion on his hands.'

York nodded. 'That's what he thought. After all the steps had been dug out, Carter ordered them buried again until he'd cabled his patron.'

Fagan read another journal entry. 'I was with Carter when he cabled Lord Carnarvon. Have made a wonderful discovery in the valley of the kings. A magnificent tomb with all the seals intact. Exciting times. Eagerly await your arrival.' Fagan read through the entry again. 'Who is this Lord Carnarvon?'

'He was Carter's sponsor, or backer. The equivalent to what Damien Thackery is.'

'Oh I see, the money man.'

'Yes, the money man.' She sighed.

Fagan flicked through the pages. 'Fair due to this Professor Cuthbert. He was a very talented artist. These are exquisite. He sketched pictures from all over the world. This journal is packed with detailed drawings of Egyptian buildings, pyramids, locals, wildlife and plant life. All kinds of hieroglyphics and other Egyptian symbols.' He spotted a sketch of two men stood side by side. Signatures were scribbled underneath each man. 'I take it these two are Carter and Carnarvon.'

'Yes,'

'So, this is an autograph book for famous explorers and archaeologists as well.' Fagan mused. 'If this journal is the key to finding the lost treasure of Alice, then it's going to be worth a lot to someone.' He glanced at York. 'Even worth killing for.' Fagan continued to read. '26th November 1922, Carter let me peer into the tomb today, albeit by torchlight. As my eyes grew accustomed to the light, details of the room beyond emerged. Slowly from the mist, strange animals, statues, and gold, everywhere the glint of gold. Truly a magnificent discovery, riches beyond belief.' Fagan closed the journal and sat back in his chair, clasping his hands behind his head. 'Gold, everywhere the glint of gold.' He repeated. 'It all makes perfect sense now, doesn't it? What does the word gold mean to most people? A bit of bling, gold bars, pirate's treasure.' He noticed a gold ring York was wearing on her left hand. 'That's a nice ring. Looks old too.'

York looked down, twisting it on her finger. 'It's second century Roman.'

'I should imagine quite a valuable piece of jewellery for everyday wear. The spoils of being an archaeologist, no doubt.'

'We unearthed it about five years ago at a dig site in Surrey.'

'How did you acquire it?'

'I didn't steal it, if that's what you're thinking.' York said defensively. 'It was all catalogued and then Robert bought it and gifted it to me.'

'He must have been very fond of you.'

'Yes.'

'Do you want to know what I think Sarah? This so-called

fable about the Splinter of Christ is just a cover story. I mean, people love a good story, don't they? This Cuthbert spins a good yarn.' Fagan glanced at the journal. 'Talk of ancient curses and jittery locals. I've had quite the history lesson today. I hated history at school. A load of old dusty books and kings of old. Knights in armour and legends told around the campfire.' Fagan fixed his stare on York. 'You see, you take a dash of history, add a pinch of adventure. In this case, an archaeologist, or two archaeologists who have spent their lives looking for mythical artefacts, sound familiar? I loved *Indiana Jones and Raiders of the lost Ark* when I was young. When I close my eyes, I envision lost treasures, exciting chase scenes, and that music. Da da da daaa, da da daaa.' Fagan leant forward, interlocking his fingers. 'I'm guessing there are two types of archaeologists. There's the type who genuinely like digging in the dirt. You know, like Baldrick from *Blackadder*. And then you have the type who are only interested in one thing, to get rich.' Fagan opened the journal. 'Even Professor Cuthbert says it here. Riches beyond belief. That's what it boils down to, doesn't it? Or do I have to spell it out to you. At the end of the day Sarah, it's always about one thing and one thing alone, greed. Carter, Carnarvon, Norman Cuthbert, Robert Turner and you. You're nothing but greedy treasure hunters. Who will do anything to get your hands on the ultimate score.' Fagan paused. 'Including murder.'

'I didn't murder Robert!' York screamed. 'Jesus, he was like a father to me. You arrogant piece of shit. And I loved him back like a father.'

'Ok then, who murdered him?'

'For the millionth time, I don't bloody know.'

'You must have some idea. Who else knew about this journal?'

'I don't know!'

'You don't know, or don't want to tell me?'

York picked up a water bottle and guzzled.

'What about Thackery?'

'What about him?' York threw a question back before gulping down more water.

'You said earlier that Robert had dealt with Thackery before. And that Thackery double crossed him.'

'He did, big time. Robert vowed never to do business with him again.'

'But he still went back to him, ten years later.' Fagan pointed out.

'Because Robert was desperate. He was utterly desperate. There was no other option. The university turned its back on Robert. He was at the end of his career. Plus, the last few years have been impossible because of the pandemic and the lockdowns. The university was out of money.'

'So what convinced Thackery to front the money for the dig?'

York clammed up.

'Sarah, if you want to help me discover who murdered Robert, you need to tell me everything. I cannot help you if you continue to put up this wall.'

York swilled water around in her mouth. 'Robert showed Thackery that journal.'

'You mean he used it as bait to lure him in?'

York nodded. 'There is far more in the journal than just one treasure hoard. It's packed with clues to other hidden treasures, including Alice of Abergavenny. Chronicled by Cuthbert and Robert. A century's worth of treasure maps.' York took another swig. 'Robert promised Thackery that if he helped him locate the fabled treasure of Alice the vicious, and let him keep the treasure, then he would hand over the journal.'

'So once again, we're back to buried treasure.' Fagan remarked.

'Robert had been studying Alice for decades. The more research he carried out, the more clues he found. Alice's tale starts when she slaughtered seventy prisoners in one afternoon.'

'I'm familiar with the story.' Fagan said, holding his hand up, remembering the lecture Thomas had given him earlier that day.

'Are you?' York asked. 'Let me guess, the story ends after Alice beheaded seventy prisoners.'

'Basically, yeah. I looked her up on the net. Beyond what happened in Ireland there's nothing.'

'But what if I told you the story of Alice continued? A knight of the Templar order witnessed the executions and was impressed with her actions. It is said that he was looking for women like her to go on a quest to the Holy Land. Alice accepted the Knight's offer and travelled through Europe with him. During their journey they amassed over seven thousand followers, mainly women. Widows and wives of men who went off to the crusades. Alice and this knight turned them into a formidable fighting force. A female Templar army called the sisterhood of the Templar knights. Kind of like the Valkyries or Amazonians.'

'Sarah.' Fagan interrupted. 'Before I have another sodding history lesson rammed down my throat. How do you know all this?'

'It's knowledge that was passed on to Robert from Norman Cuthbert.'

'Where did Cuthbert hear the story?'

'Apparently, he was approached by a man a few nights before he was murdered in 1975. It was just after he discovered the four daggers containing the seal of Alice. This man told Cuthbert that Alice kept a scribe with her.'

'I'm afraid I don't speak history Sarah, what is a scribe?'

'A scribe is someone who chronicles everything, kind of like the journalists of their day. This scribe chronicled Alice's journey through Europe, into the Holy Land and back home here to Wales. But Alice forbid the scribe to mention her final location. Cuthbert actually held the scribe's journal in his hand.' York looked at Turner's journal. 'May I.'

Fagan pushed the journal towards her.

York thumbed through the journal. 'This is the last sketch Cuthbert made.'

The sketch was of an ancient book resembling a bible. With Alice's seal on the cover.

'This is the journal that Cuthbert was shown.' York explained. 'When Cuthbert was in Jerusalem in the 1950s, he found a seal that belonged to Alice. There were loads of Templar trinkets being unearthed all over Jerusalem. Cuthbert thought nothing of it until 1967, when he was part of a dig in the grounds of the Agincourt hotel. He came across another seal with Alice's mark. But he was still unable to make any connection with the seal he found in Jerusalem. It was just one of those unsolvable historical mysteries. Until that is, he found the daggers at Tintern Abbey and looked at the journal the stranger showed him. But two nights later he was murdered, and the daggers vanished.'

Fagan recalled the conversation he had with Thomas earlier that day. About the daggers being part of an exhibition at the local museum.

'Look, Inspector Fagan, I know I haven't been totally honest with you. But I don't know who to trust anymore. Especially when it comes to this.' She pointed at the journal. 'Only four people have ever seen this up close. Cuthbert, Robert, myself and Thackery.'

'And now me.' Fagan added.

York nodded.

'Why did you have the journal in your room at the Agincourt?'

'Robert gave it to me last night. He said it wasn't a good thing to be around at that moment.'

'He wasn't wrong about that, was he?' Fagan churned a thought over in his mind. 'Do you think Thackery is capable of murder?'

York inhaled before nodding. 'I didn't give it much thought. I just stuffed it under the mattress.'

Fagan looked at the journal. 'Think about it, this is the holy grail to finding other holy grails.' He smiled at the journal. 'To quote Cuthbert himself, riches beyond belief.'

'It can't stay here and get stored in an evidence locker; it will vanish.' York said. 'And it can't go with me. It will be like painting a target on my back.'

Fagan pressed his hand on the journal. 'I'll keep it safe until we can untangle this mystery.' He pondered the moment. 'Did Professor Turner arrive in his own vehicle?'

'Yes.'

'What car did he drive?'

'A Ford Puma, grey. We drove down here together from Cambridge.'

'Just the two of you in the car?'

'Yes, Robert and I discussed the dig on the way down.'

'How did he seem about the dig?'

'Excited.' York answered. 'It was his last hurrah, as he called it.' She smiled. 'Going out with a bang.'

Fagan tapped the stop icon on his phone.

York stood looking at the clock on the wall. 'Can I go now? I want to get back to the dig before it gets too dark.'

'Yeah sure.' Fagan flashed a brief smile without looking at her.

‘As soon as I think of something else, I will call you immediately.’

Fagan was tapping a number into his phone. ‘That will be very helpful.’

York walked out of the interview room.

Fagan waited a moment before calling Evans. ‘Jamie, I need a favour. I’m about to give you a set of specific instructions. What I don’t want, is you being nosy or asking any stupid questions.’

CHAPTER 12

4:26pm

Fagan marched into the interview room. 'Right then, just for the record, none of you are under arrest. Which is why we are interviewing you both together. Frankly, this is becoming a pain in my arse. So, I suggest you answer the questions we are about to ask and not dick us about.'

'I haven't done anything, anyway.' Spooner protested. 'I don't know why you have dragged us all the way here to be interviewed for something we didn't do. We're wasting valuable time.'

'In a rush to get back, are we?' Watkins said.

'Yeah, it's a very important dig.'

'According to Sarah, you've never been enthusiastic about the dig.' Fagan pointed out.

'That stupid bitch would say something like that wouldn't she. Robert's little pet prodigy.'

'Sarah also told me that Professor Turner was always telling you to toe the line. That you're not a team player.'

'I am when I want to be.'

Fagan sat back folding his arms. 'When you want to be. Is that when you are calling the shots? When I arrived earlier at the dig, both of you looked like you wanted to belt one another. What were you arguing about?'

Spooner and Dayton glanced at each other.

'It's ok fellas, I can sit here all day. I have already let Sarah go back to the dig. It would be a shame if she discovered something significant without you.'

‘We were just arguing.’ Dayton said, rubbing his nose. ‘About archaeology stuff.’

‘Don’t bother wasting your breath, Jay. They’re just plod.’ Spooner mocked. ‘They won’t understand any of what we are doing.’

Fagan glared at him. ‘You’re out here looking for some kind of treasure that may have belonged to Alice of Abergavenny. The splinter of Christ, if I’m not mistaken.’

‘It’s amazing what you can find on google isn’t it.’ Spooner mocked.

‘Us plod aren’t as backward as you think Mr Spooner. I don’t think you are taking any of this seriously. Let me remind you, a man has been brutally murdered. And so far, none of you have been helpful.’

‘We didn’t murder him.’ Dayton stated. ‘That’s what has got everyone jittery.’

Fagan looked at Dayton. ‘Do you have any idea who may have murdered him?’

Dayton shook his head rigorously. ‘No.’

‘How were you both recruited to the team?’ Watkins asked.

‘Turner would pick first-year students every time he went out on a dig.’ Spooner explained.

‘And that’s what you both are?’

Spooner and Dayton nodded in unison.

‘Turner always attracted the wrong attention when he started a new dig.’

‘Wrong attention?’ Fagan commented.

‘You know, environmentalists moaning about destroying the landscape by digging holes everywhere.’

‘Turner had altercations between metal detector enthusiasts and local druids. Did any of you witness any of these arguments?’

‘The druids turned up as soon as we began the dig. It

was almost as if they knew we were coming.' Spooner revealed. 'Whenever they'd turn up, I'd tell them to fuck off. During the first few days of the dig, they would show up and get in the way.'

'Did you witness Professor Turner having an argument with any of them?'

'Yeah, they followed him about everywhere for the first week. I think they got pissed off in the end because they couldn't intimidate us. On one occasion we had to call the police. But by the time you lot arrived they were long gone. Then we had the metal detectors moaning about not being able to get access to the site. Turner had paid the farmer who owns the field where we are digging a shit load of money.'

'Twenty thousand pounds.' Fagan added.

Dayton nodded. 'Yeah, they weren't happy they'd suddenly been booted off the site.'

'Can you at least tell me what you were arguing about when I arrived this morning?'

Both men exchanged glances, but remained silent.

'Jesus, what is it with you two? You're not under arrest for Turner's murder. So you may as well tell us why you were yelling at each other.'

Dayton inhaled. 'We were talking about a diary that Turner kept.'

Fagan knew what they were talking about, but remained tight lipped. 'Diary?'

'A journal he allegedly kept with him when he was at an important dig.'

'Did you ever see this diary?'

'No, it was supposed to be just a rumour. But Turner was the student of another famous archaeologist who was the one that started the diary.' Dayton produced his mobile phone, locating a picture. 'This is the journal that Norman

Cuthbert kept during his time as an archaeologist.' Dayton slid the phone across the table towards Fagan and Watkins. 'This is the only known picture of the journal. This picture was taken in 1973.'

Fagan studied the black and white image of Cuthbert and a young Turner at Stonehenge. The journal he'd taken possession of was tucked under Cuthbert's arm.

'They reckon the journal was lost after Cuthbert was murdered. But rumours over the years began to circulate. Turner took possession of the journal. Cuthbert was an expert in finding archaeological treasures thought to be lost. When Turner carried on having the same luck as Cuthbert, the rumours he had the journal gathered pace.'

'So what was the argument about?'

Dayton glanced at Spooner, who nodded.

'Last night we were having a drink in the Agincourt Hotel.'

'Were you all staying there?' Watkins asked.

'No, only Professor Turner and Sarah York stayed at the hotel. The rest of us are staying at the Premier in Monmouth. It became a nightly thing to have a drink at the Agincourt. Last night, it was just me and David. Robert and Sarah were having a private dinner together. The others had gone back to Monmouth to go on a pub crawl. We got talking about the journal he kept.'

'Go on.' Fagan coaxed.

'That's when we saw Turner walk through the bar of the hotel.'

'He didn't clock you two sat in the bar?' Watkins asked.

'No.' Spooner replied. 'He literally sprinted through the bar towards the main entrance of the hotel.'

'Were there many people about that time of night?'

'No, the place was empty. Even the barman had gone home. We usually order a pile of drinks at last orders.'

'But the main entrance was open?'

'Yeah, the night manager would shut the doors at midnight.'

'What time was this?' Watkins enquired.

'About eleven o'clock.'

'None of you chased after Professor Turner to see where he was going?' Fagan said.

'No.' Dayton answered. 'We started talking about the journal again.'

Fagan realised where the conversation was going. 'Let me guess, you decided to look for it.'

Spooner nodded. 'It was easy to pick the lock of his hotel room. You'll be amazed at what you can learn from YouTube.'

'So you turned his room upside down looking for the journal?' Watkins said.

'Yes.' Spooner admitted.

'You know, you could have saved us a lot of time admitting this from the start. You could both be facing a charge of perverting the course of justice.'

'We didn't murder Professor Turner.' Spooner insisted.

'But you broke into his room looking for that journal. Then said nothing about it when you were questioned earlier. What were you thinking?'

Dayton shrugged.

'If you would have found the journal, what were you going to do with it?'

'We were going to sell it?'

'Who to?'

'We knew there were several interested parties involved with the dig, including a Vatican priest who is due to turn up to the dig tomorrow.'

'Have you been in contact with this priest?'

'Yes.'

'Did this priest offer you a significant amount of money if you got hold of the journal?'

'Yes.'

'How much money did the Vatican offer?'

Dayton and Spooner didn't answer.

'Boys, now is not the time to clam up. How much were you offered for the journal?'

'A hundred thousand quid.' Dayton revealed.

'That's a shit load of money for just a book. Enough to pay off those student loans you're racking up with a bit of change left over.'

'Yeah, because the stuff that the journal contains is worth a lot of money. Turner spent his life looking for mythical treasures. Everything from Excalibur to the lost treasure of Boudica. And then there were the entries that Cuthbert had written.'

'More treasure hunting.' Fagan sighed. 'I'm starting to feel like I'm watching *Pirates of the* bloody *Caribbean*.'

'But none of this explains why you were having a go at each other.' Watkins said.

'We were just pissed off that we couldn't find the journal. It was a stupid argument.' Spooner said.

'I'm guessing you had already assured the buyer you had secured the journal.'

'Yes.' Dayton answered. 'Which is why we were arguing.'

'Talk about a double cross. Looking to steal the journal.'

Spooner nodded. 'It was stupid, I know.'

'And now Professor Turner is dead.' Fagan pointed out.

'We had nothing to do with his murder, we swear. This is totally out of the blue.' Dayton insisted. 'I guess part of the reason we were arguing was out of guilt.'

'It was my idea to break into Professor Turner's room.' Spooner confessed. 'I guess I owe the old man enough to cough up to that.'

'Ok.' Fagan said. 'I think we're done here.'

'Hang on.' Dayton spoke up. 'He did have a massive argument with Lord what's his name.'

'Lord Barry?' Fagan guessed.

Dayton nodded. 'On the day we started the dig, Lord Barry turns up and starts having a right go at Professor Turner. Basically accused him of being a grave robber.'

Fagan glanced at Watkins. 'Thanks for that information.'

'What happens now?' Spooner asked.

'You'll be allowed to return to the dig site. But you won't be able to leave the area. If you remember anything else, you need to contact us. No matter how small a detail.'

Dayton and Spooner stood and left the interview room.

'Jesus Christ, this is giving me a headache.' Fagan complained. 'If I have to hear one more word about buried treasure and journals, I'm going to explode.'

'What do you reckon about their story regarding the Vatican wanting to pay a hundred thousand to get their hands on the journal?' Watkins asked.

'It adds another layer to the mystery. If and when they turn up, I don't care how high up they think they are. I intend to ask them about Turner's murder.'

'You think they had a hand in it?'

'Until I interview whoever they send, then I don't know. But the way Turner was murdered, it's obvious there are powerful players at work here.' Fagan suddenly found himself lost in thought regarding Rebecca and her untimely death.

'You ok boss?' Watkins asked.

Fagan yawned. 'It's just been a long day. Let's grab Brooks and look over this case.'

C H A P T E R 1 3

5:16pm

Fagan stared at the whiteboard, deep in thought. He reflected on the interviews with York, Dayton and Spooner.

Brooks came in and handed Fagan a mug of coffee.

'Jesus bloody Christ, what the hell is that?' Fagan struggled to swallow the coffee.

'It's all they had in the canteen. It's Aldi's budget coffee.'

'I hate anything from Aldi.' Fagan put the mug down, trying to shake off the bitter tasting coffee.

Watkins walked into the room with a box of Greggs confectionaries. 'I love Greggs at this time of day. They always drop their prices. Got all this for six quid.' He opened the box, offering the selection to Fagan.

Fagan grabbed a doughnut, shoving it into his mouth.

'Take it easy boss. You need to be able to swallow.'

Fagan savoured the taste of the sweet jam at the centre of the doughnut. The cheap tasting coffee became an unpleasant memory. 'Ok then.' He said with a mouth full. 'Let's start with the pathologist's report. We know the dagger used in the murder is medieval. A check is being run this afternoon on the spikes used to nail Turner to the floor. What kind of killer are we dealing with here?'

'Someone who likes to read Dan Brown novels.' Watkins answered. 'The way Turner's body has been laid out is exactly the same way the curator of the Louvre museum in Paris was laid out in the *Da Vinci Code*.'

'So you're saying they copied a murder scene out of a fictional novel?'

Watkins nodded as he chewed on an éclair.

'Why?'

'Obviously, our murderer is full of themselves.' Brooks said, glancing at Watkins. 'I saw the film the *Da Vinci Code*. Turner's killer is taking the piss out of us.'

'What do you mean?' Fagan helped himself to a custard slice.

'Whoever murdered Turner is arrogant enough to assume we've no chance of catching them. Meaning they're hidden in plain sight, or they've yet to enter the picture.'

'There is a third possibility.' Watkins offered. 'They could be hell and gone from here. Watching us struggling to identify the murderer.'

Fagan expertly caught a blob of custard that oozed out of his slice. 'What do you think of Turner's dig team, particularly the ones we've interviewed?'

'Spooner and Dayton were obviously out to stab him in the back. Spooner claimed the Vatican offered them one hundred thousand for the journal that Turner kept.'

Fagan nodded, daring to pick up the mug of coffee Brooks had given him. He grimaced, taking a swig. 'They said that a Vatican official is turning up tomorrow. Which means things are about to go up a notch.'

'If the Vatican is about to turn up, then there must be some truth in this so-called Splinter of Christ.' Watkins considered.

Fagan looked at him. 'Are you religious?'

'Not really, but you know what these religious types are like. Have you ever tried to get rid of them when they knock on your door on a Sunday morning?'

'What about the murder weapon? It was part of a

collection of daggers stolen back in January 2020. Why do you suppose our murderer used it on Turner?'

'The dagger is central to this case. There is a web being spun here. Archaeologists, myth and legend.'

'I read part of Turner's journal.' Fagan revealed. 'The original owner was a man called Norman Cuthbert. I looked him up on Google. He was well known in his day. Was at the dig that discovered the tomb of King Tut back in 1922. Cuthbert was murdered in 1975 with a broad sword he found on a dig in Tintern Abbey along with the daggers.'

'So there has to be a connection to last night's murder.' Brooks speculated.

Fagan nodded.

'Trouble is, whoever murdered Cuthbert back in 1975 is probably dead now, or extremely old.' Watkins said. 'Both murders could be totally separate.'

'No.' Fagan picked up the casefile George had given him. 'Turner was at the same dig at Tintern Abbey in 1975. Which means both murders are connected. Not only that, but the former curator at Abergavenny museum, Tony James, was an archaeologist. He was also at the dig. According to my source, who I spoke with earlier. Cuthbert gave James the daggers for safe keeping. A few days later, Cuthbert was found dead at Tintern Abbey with the broadsword sticking out of him. James held on to the daggers and it looks like Turner held on to Cuthbert's journal. There was an investigation, but a few days later, all the evidence vanished and the case was shelved.'

'So we're dealing with a cold case murder from 1975 and the murder of Turner last night.' Brooks remarked.

'It gets better, or more sinister, whichever way you look at it. A few months after the daggers were stolen from the museum, Tony James drops dead of a heart attack. He messaged my contact to say he knew who stole the daggers from the museum.'

'Who?' Watkins asked.

'He never gave up a name.' Fagan rammed the rest of his custard slice into his mouth. 'His daughter contacted the police saying that she suspected foul play surrounding his death. But by then the country was in full lockdown. The police didn't follow up her claim.'

'We could have three potential murders here.' Brooks added.

Fagan licked his fingers. 'Yep. Not only that, James' daughter kept what she believed to be evidence proving that her father was murdered.'

'What evidence?'

Fagan shrugged. 'It's only a matter of time before we talk to her.' He reached for another doughnut.

Watkins snatched the box away. 'You've had enough of a sugar rush for now boss.'

'Which murder do we prioritise?' Brooks asked.

'Turner's for now.' Fagan responded. 'Everything else will require more of a team. Chief Constable Griffiths has already informed me he cannot afford any more investigating officers. Which means we're going to be overstretched on this one. So we'll have to stick to one murder for now. Let's talk about the press. How did they know the details of Turner's death this morning?'

'A leak from our side.' Brooks offered a suggestion.

Fagan looked doubtful. 'Who knew all the details about the way he was found?'

'The first response officers and the CSI.'

'Or the murderer.' Fagan added. 'Sooner or later we would have had to release a statement regarding the way Turner was killed. The killer beats us to it. They contact the press anonymously. Give them the details of how he was murdered. Plenty of cars have driven past the castle today.

The main road wasn't cordoned off, meaning people would have been gossiping about what was happening.' Fagan tapped the screen on his phone. 'The Mail online is leading with this story. Top archaeologist found brutally slain at remote Welsh Castle.'

'I wouldn't call Skenfrith remote. It's on a main road and plenty of people get out there.' Watkins said. 'You know what the Mail is like boss. Any excuse for a bit of gore.'

'Why did our suspect contact the media?' Fagan questioned.

'To throw everyone off the scent.' Brooks answered. 'It's obviously a diversionary tactic to hamper the investigation. If the police are too busy trying to figure out who contacted the press, it gives our killer the chance to put some distance between them and us.'

'Good point.' Fagan scribbled some notes down on the whiteboard.

'What about Turner?' Watkins asked. 'What convinced him to leave the safety of the Agincourt Hotel?'

'Obviously, our suspect must have lured him to Skenfrith castle with the daggers. When he reached Skenfrith, he was murdered.'

'Straight away?' Brooks queried.

'No.' Fagan shook his head. 'A conversation must have taken place regarding the daggers. And let's not forget the dagger appeared to be sharpened. Meaning our suspect had the intention of killing Turner.'

'Premeditated murder.' Watkins offered.

Fagan nodded. 'When I interviewed Sarah York earlier, she claimed Turner had received a message from someone at three o'clock yesterday afternoon. She saw Turner walk away from the group so he could speak to someone alone. York also stated it looked like he was having an argument with someone. But she couldn't make anything out. When they had dinner last night, she said that Turner kept checking his phone.'

'He was in contact with his murderer.' Brooks suggested.

'That's my thinking. So after dinner last night, everyone returns to their rooms and the Premier in Monmouth. Turner then leaves the hotel. Before he leaves, he gives York the journal he kept. She then stuffs it under her mattress. In the meantime Dayton and Spooner are still at the Agincourt hotel. They see Turner leaving and decide to break into his room to look for the journal. Turner drives out to Skenfrith. He is then murdered, stripped naked and laid out on the floor of the castle keep.' Fagan stood back from the whiteboard, summarising what he had written.

'It's a mess.' Watkins said. 'There aren't any suspects.'

Fagan nodded. 'Sarah York said she was talking to someone on Facebook until after midnight. Spooner and Dayton returned to their hotel in Monmouth after they had finished ransacking Turner's room. And finally Turner is murdered.' He glanced at Watkins. 'You're right, it's a mess. Our suspect is not part of the dig team.'

'What about the metal detecting bloke we interviewed?'

Fagan dismissed the notion. 'He didn't strike me as the academic type. Just an enthusiast. And since the daggers are central to this murder, we need to focus on who stole them in 2020.'

Watkins and Brooks exchanged blank looks.

Fagan inhaled. 'It looks like we'll have to find information regarding the thefts of the daggers. My contact Nigel Thomas said he was interviewed by the Abergavenny Chronicle following the break in at the museum.'

Brooks was already scrolling through the Chronicle's

website. 'According to this, the theft took place on January 23rd 2020.'

'Tony James gave an interview to BBC Wales and other local publications on January 24th.'

Watkins was swiping through his phone. 'The Abergavenny Chronicle, The South Wales Argus, Wales Online, Monmouthshire Beacon, a magazine called Archaeology Cymru, and a blog called Welsh nationalist history.'

'The daggers must be important to our suspect, otherwise they wouldn't have stolen them.' Fagan speculated.

'Important enough to use one of them as a murder weapon.' Brooks added.

'It's a weird one.' Fagan sighed, looking at the whiteboard.

'Because we had the lockdown.' Watkins said, staring at his tablet. 'According to this article in Wales on Sunday, the exhibition was supposed to have kicked off on St David's day 2020, which was a Sunday. All the local schools were due to visit the museum the following week.'

'But because of the theft, the exhibition was postponed until the end of March.' Brooks was reading through an article about the theft. 'An article in the Chronicle on February 27th 2020 says that the exhibition was put back three weeks to 28th March. It also says here that the police still had no leads on who could have stolen the daggers.'

'Boris Johnson puts the country into lockdown on March 20th.' Fagan continued. 'Stay safe, stay at home, clap for the NHS on a Thursday night.'

'I hate to say this boss, even though you said we need to focus on Turner's murder, we have to consider all the facts here. Norman Cuthbert, Tony James and Robert Turner were all present at the dig in 1975. Cuthbert was the first to be murdered. The daggers they found disappear before turning up at an exhibition nearly five decades later. The daggers are then stolen, plus the curator drops dead a few months later. Not only that, but his daughter thinks there's more behind his death than a simple heart attack. Then three years later a dig begins outside Abergavenny. Another well-known archaeologist is murdered with one of the stolen daggers.'

Fagan frowned at the whiteboard. 'We're going to have to find out more about the theft that took place at the Abergavenny museum. I'm going to the Angel in a few hours to talk to the current curator of Abergavenny Museum. We also need to contact the media. try to find out how they found out details regarding Turner's murder.' Fagan glanced at his watch. 'Unless someone comes forward with something significant, we'll wrap things up. Perhaps tomorrow we'll have a few more loose tongues.'

CHAPTER 14

The Cantreff Inn– 7:02pm

'Here he is look.' Evans announced. 'Lara Croft.'

'Who?'

'Oh, that's right, you basically stopped living when you left Abergavenny.'

'No, unlike you, I actually got myself a life.'

'It's all over the news.' Simon Edwards looked towards the TV mounted to the wall. 'A murder at Skenfrith castle. The newspapers are going into full details about how he was killed. Pretty gruesome.'

'I thought you lot kept things like that a secret.' Jackie Mills pointed out. 'You know, you're not allowed to tell anyone until all relatives have been informed.' She placed a pint of bitter on the bar in front of Fagan.

'That's the thing. We didn't tell anyone. I spoke to my CO earlier on today. He told me no one breathed a word. And I know none of the archaeology team said anything because they didn't know anything about the way in which his body was found.'

'So, if no one but the police knew how this bloke died, then the only other person who knew.' Evans said.

'Was the murderer.' Fagan finished Evans's sentence before swigging back his pint.

'Well, you've got some real freaky shit going on out there.' Edwards remarked.

'That isn't even half of it. Most of the day, I've been chasing after someone called Alice of Abergavenny.'

'Alice?' Evans smiled. 'Alice, who the fuck is Alice?'

Fagan frowned at Evans. 'That's not remotely funny anymore.'

'Who is she?' Jackie enquired, glancing at Evans, who was still smiling.

'Some local girl that stirred up a fuss a thousand years ago.'

'Well, since I saw you first thing this morning, I have been chock-a-block.' Evans said. 'Especially over the last two hours. I have picked up loads of people from the train station and taken them to the Premier in Llanfoist. All yapping on about buried treasure and the holy grail.' Evans broke into song. *'And, always look on the bright side of life.'* He finished with a whistle.

'That's *the Life of Brian*, you dick.' Edwards corrected him. 'Jesus, you may know everything about *Star Wars,* but you know fuck all about *Monty Python.'*

'What kind of people have you been ferrying about?' Fagan asked.

'The treasure hunter types. I've handled a few metal detectors today. Do you remember that scene in *Jaws* just after that young boy is killed in front of Chief Brody?'

'Yeah.' Jackie answered.

'Every shark fisherman turns up to hunt for it. That's exactly what it reminded me of today, but with treasure hunters.'

'What kind of buried treasure are we talking about?' Edwards asked.

'The holy grail, something called the splinter of Christ, take your pick.' Fagan replied. 'I couldn't get any sense out of these bloody archaeologists today. They were all too busy fighting amongst themselves. Who's going to be the next project leader.'

'So, people think the holy grail is hidden around here?'

Evans said. 'I find that almost laughable. The last resting place of the holy grail is around Abergavenny somewhere.'

'You'll be surprised at what's happened in this town in the past.' Jackie said. 'Our nan said she'd say hello to Rudolph Hess every day when he used to take a walk along the Skirrid. She used to collect milk from the farm. He always used to be accompanied by two guards. He also liked to walk in the castle meadows.'

'Did your nan ever mention the Skirrid mountain?'

'All the time. You know how superstitious she was. Never go up the Skirrid on a misty day.'

'The woman in white.' Fagan remarked.

Jackie nodded.

'Yeah, our mam used to come out with that one.' Edwards said.

'Nan always went on about the jagged bit on the side. She said it was where the devil landed when he was kicked out of heaven.' Jackie explained.

'My mam once told me that the jagged bit was a giant's footprint.' Fagan mentioned. 'This time tomorrow there could be people all over the Skirrid looking for the holy grail, or this splinter of Christ.'

'The search for the cup of Christ, is the search for the divine in all of us.' Evans said in an even tone.

Everyone looked at him.

'look at you, sounding all philosophical.' Jackie remarked.

Fagan shook his head, smiling. 'I'm not buying into that bullshit.'

Evans grinned back at him.

'Come on, which film did you rip that line from?'

'*Indiana Jones and the Last Crusade.*'

Jackie threw a wet beer towel at him. 'And there was me thinking you were having a moment.'

'Jackie sweetheart, I am always having a moment.'

'So, I thought I'd get a few pints in before having to endure another history lesson.'

'Where are you going?' Evans asked.

'The Angel, to listen to some woman waffle on about history, someone called Amanda Rhys.'

'I know her.' Edwards revealed. 'She comes down to the Bailey now and then. Runs the museum, I think.'

Fagan nodded. 'She gives lectures at the Angel once a month.'

'Is she a suspect?' Evans quizzed.

'I don't know until I speak to her.'

'She's quite smart, in her late forties, early fifties maybe. I've seen her jogging down the castle meadows. Bit out of my league.'

'And exactly what is that supposed to mean?' Jackie demanded to know. 'Are you saying I'm somewhere down at the bottom?'

Edwards smiled at her. 'Jackie, my lovely girl, you will always be on top.' He winked. 'In more ways than one.'

Jackie blushed.

'I suppose I better get back to the Bailey. Ladies' darts night can be as brutal as any medieval battle.' Edwards stepped away from the bar, smiling at Jackie. 'I'll see you later.'

'Hold up, I'll give you a lift.' Evans offered.

Jackie wiped down the bar. 'So, how's things with you Fagan? Have you moved all the way from Liverpool yet?'

'Just about. My solicitor text me this morning. I have a buyer for the house. So it's just a case of paperwork and money transfer. Then I'll start looking for somewhere down here. I have already seen something in Midway Lane up at the Mardy.'

'Some nice houses up there.'

'I want to get out of rental ASAP. What with the price of everything right now.'

'Tell me about it. I'm looking at shutting one day a week. I've lost loads of customers. The brewery keep increasing their charges. People are going to Morrisons for their booze.'

Fagan supped from his glass.

'Have you seen Ricky?'

'Yeah, we had a coffee yesterday. It was kind of awkward. All of a sudden I'm a dad to a thirty-seven-year-old. I was sat at home last night thinking about all the things I've missed in his life.'

'And you both still have plenty of time to catch up.' Jackie assured.

'Yeah, but I don't think I can give piggybacks now.'

Jackie laughed. 'I'm sure he'll forgive you for that. Give him time. Any news on the trial?'

Fagan took a deep breath. 'No news yet. An announcement will be made soon. But it will still be a while before it goes to trial. The backlog that covid has caused is ridiculous.'

'What do you reckon the outcome will be?'

'I couldn't tell you Jacks. But if I were to make a guess. Justin might get a couple of years for perverting the course of justice. But Tim, you won't see him back in Abergavenny until he's in his seventies. Speaking of perverting, how's Benny the Bastard?'

'Making another appearance on morning TV tomorrow.'

'Piece of shit.' Fagan seethed.

Jackie placed two glasses on the bar, shooting some Jack Daniels into them. 'Well, here's to justice, and the hunt for buried bloody treasure.'

Fagan laughed, clinking his glass against Jackie's

CHAPTER 15

The Angel Hotel Abergavenny – 7:33pm

Amanda Rhys surveyed her assembled audience. She was familiar with some of the people who had attended that evening. During the five years living in Abergavenny, she had become familiar with all the local history buffs. Many who were retired people looking for something to fill their long days. Amanda never expected any more than twenty people at one time. However, things were different this evening. There were over a hundred people stuffed into the conference hall. Staff had to provide extra chairs as the room filled with people. She sipped from a bottle of local mineral water. Amanda noticed a man sitting at the back. He had moved his chair to create some space around him. A Barbour jacket hung on the back of his chair. He was in his mid-fifties, attractive, wearing a black woollen jumper with casual fitting jeans and a pair of Sketchers. She focused back on the audience and smiled, picking up a clicker from a desk on which sat a laptop.

'Good evening everyone. I would like to thank you for attending this lecture. I have to admit there are more people here than usual. So I will not beat about the bush. A noted archaeologist has been found dead at a local castle. This is bound to attract what many would call as morbid sightseers. In fact, I have had more than my usual number of visitors today at the museum. Asking lots of questions about lost treasures and mythical artefacts. It made me realise the tragic events today at Skenfrith castle have drawn many of you here this evening. The news media has somewhat been graphic describing the manner of his death. Crucified to the floor of the castle keep. Sounds rather barbaric, doesn't it. But let's put aside the way this man was found and focus on what has inspired you to come to the Angel Hotel this evening. What do we think of when we envision an archaeologist? Popular culture has drawn many images of what archaeologists should look like. Most notably, the leather jacket wearing, whip cracking *Indiana Jones*.' Amanda clicked on the device and the familiar theme tune of the Indianna Jones movies echoed around the room. A picture of Harrison Ford appeared on a projector screen. 'We've all seen the films. I mean, Christmas Day wouldn't be complete without an afternoon with *Raiders of the lost ark*.'

Laughter from the audience.

'And then Boxing Day would complete your Christmas viewing with *James Bond*.' She clicked again, and the music switched to the familiar Bond theme.

The laughter grew louder as members of the audience reminisced.

'As time wore on, the image of the archaeologist has changed.' A picture of Jeff Goldblum, Sam Neill and Laura Dern alongside Richard Attenborough. 'And changed again.' The picture switched to the video game character *Lara Croft*. 'But nothing could be further from the truth.' Amanda clicked the device. A black-and-white image of a woman appeared on the screen. Her hair was tied up, and she wore Edwardian garb. 'This is Dorothy Garrod. She is the first recognised female archaeologist. She inspired generations of women to get their hands filthy and start digging around in the dirt.' History is all about the past. We cannot change the way things were, and we cannot erase events that have happened.'

A video played on the large screen of historical events, the Wright Brothers, The Hindenburg Disaster, Hitler shouting at a mass rally followed by footage of London being bombed. Sound accompanied the imagery. A famous war time speech from Winston Churchill, followed by Niel Armstrong making his historical moon landing speech. For a further minute the video played until the end clip of Edward Colston's statue being thrown into Bristol Harbour.

'What a sad world we live in today. When the few try to influence the many. All of us remember that news footage. Edward Colston's statue was torn from its plinth and cast into the murky waters. For history is full of murky waters. When we put up statues honouring the likes of Colston, we don't do it to mock those men and women who suffered because of the slave trade. We erect statues for the good deeds that men like Colston did for the city of Bristol. For all of you who like to travel I recommend the slavery museum on the Liverpool docks. We build museums to recognise all that has happened in history. There are museums to remember it all. From the museum at Auschwitz to the museums chronicling London's dark history. Anyone who has been to the tower of London will have been on the tours. Stories of gruesome executions, torture and other dark deeds. So why do we choose to cherry pick certain moments and blow them all out of proportion?'

The man in the black sweater stood up and grabbed his jacket. He gave Amanda an apologetic look as he turned and left the room.

'Wow! I didn't realise I was that boring.'

The audience burst into laughter.

CHAPTER 16

9:19pm

'Thank you for that wonderful lecture Amanda.'

'You're welcome Gladys, how's the book coming along?'

'I'm finding things a little difficult. I was wondering if you could spare some time.'

Amanda nodded. 'I've got some time next week. I could come by and help you out.'

The woman's eyes widened. 'Thank you dear, I would be ever so grateful.'

Amanda spotted the handsome-looking stranger who ditched the lecture during her opening speech. She glided over to the man propping up the bar.

'Mineral water, please.' Amanda smiled at the young woman behind the bar. 'I rarely have people bail on me on a first date.' She glanced at the man.

He chuckled. 'I'm not much of a history buff.'

'Do I need to return the ten pounds you paid to book a place on the lecture?'

The man shook his head.

The barmaid placed a bottle of mineral water and a glass in front of Amanda. Before she could reach into her purse to pull out her card, the man had already scanned his. Amanda filled her glass. 'Now I'm racked with guilt. I have conned you out of ten pounds and get a free drink. Which in a sign to me you want something.'

The man smiled back and reached into his pocket,

pulling out his ID badge. 'DI Fagan with Gwent police.'

'And how is it I can help you, DI Fagan?'

'I was wondering about your thoughts on what happened at Skenfrith Castle. Since you mentioned it in your lecture.'

'Indeed I did.' Amanda sipped from her glass.

'Did you have anything to do with the archaeology team at the dig at Bont?'

Amanda shook her head. 'I'm a lover of history, not archaeology.' She winked at him. 'I prefer to get my mind dirty, not my hands.'

Fagan suddenly found himself on his back heel. He sensed blood rushing to his cheeks.

Amanda let off an infectious giggle. 'I don't mean that kind of dirty. Those archaeology types assume they are the ones who unearth history. So scholars have something to waffle on about.'

'I didn't think there was that much of a divide between historians and archaeologists.'

'I have had a few unpleasant experiences with archaeologists. I view them as the vultures of history. Picking through the bones of the past. To scavenge lost treasure, all for the sake of getting rich.' She took another sip. 'Still, Professor Turner didn't deserve his fate. To die like that, alone and in the dark, must have been terrifying.'

'I take it you have seen the news?'

Amanda nodded. 'It's been hard to miss. My Facebook account has been pinging all afternoon. The media have claimed Professor Turner was staying at the Agincourt hotel.'

Fagan nodded. 'I'm contacting local experts who might help with the murder enquiry.'

'Sure, anything I can do to help.'

Fagan produced a piece of paper handing it to Amanda.

'The dagger used in the murder was one of four daggers which were missing for nearly fifty years. They were part of an exhibition at Abergavenny museum which was supposed to have happened in 2020. In January of that year there was a break in and they were stolen.'

'Yes, I heard about this. It was before my time. I took over the museum in November 2020. But the museum was still several months from opening because of the Pandemic. This annoying man would show up and bombard me with questions regarding what I knew about the theft.'

'Annoying man?'

'His name is Nigel Thomas.'

Fagan nodded, recalling his meeting earlier. 'I am familiar with Nigel. Used to be in school with him.'

'I can understand local historians like Nigel having their intellectual noses knocked out of joint. Many class me as an outsider.'

'You don't sound like a local.' Fagan pointed out.

'Neither do you, DI Fagan. You definitely have the Welsh twang. But is that a hint of a scouse accent I sense in your voice?'

Fagan nodded. 'I was born and bred in Abergavenny. Moved away when I was twenty, recently moved back.'

'Looking for the quiet life as you wind down you career?' Amanda said.

'You could say that.' Fagan's thoughts turned to Rebecca. An image of her dead body stabbed at his mind. 'But life rarely turns out the way you want it to.'

'Just like history.' Amanda added. 'I am a Cambridgeshire girl. Grew up in a small village on the outskirts of a town called Wisbech. Like this town, my village had its myth and legend. I lived with my grandmother in an old cottage on a junction nicknamed the

Hungate. I grew up with stories of headless horsemen. Mysterious black dogs and cackling witches burned at the stake long ago. So how can I help?'

'I was hoping to enlist someone who could guide me through the minefield, which is local history. Which, at the moment, seems to be at the centre of this murder enquiry. You just mentioned Robert Turner, our murder victim. Did you know him at all?'

'Only by reputation. Famed archaeologist, student of another famous archaeologist Norman Cuthbert. Whom I believe was murdered himself. Quite the Sherlock Holmes mystery you have on your hands, DI Fagan.'

'Reputation?'

'Most archaeologists will tell you they are just that, and nothing more. But others will call them grave robbers. Especially when they dig up people who died thousands of years ago. So they can display their corpses in museums. Along with the treasures that often accompany people from long ago. Turner found himself in hot water all over the world on many of his digs. The press romanticised him as being a modern-day Indiana Jones. While others used to call him quite the opposite along with many other names. That's why I stick to the academic side of history. The things that have been saved and preserved over the centuries. That way I don't have to go digging and disturbing the ground.'

'So you ran the museum from the end of 2020?'

'Yes, during the lockdown the man who used to run it died. When I moved to Abergavenny five years ago, I contacted the museum to ask if there was a position. Unfortunately, there were no posts.'

'What was your last job?'

'I was a lead researcher of history at Cambridge.'

'A bit of a comedown, from the intellectual halls of

Cambridge to a small town museum like Abergavenny.'

'You'd think, but if the pandemic has taught us anything. It's the bustling cities of our nation are no longer hospitable. When the industrial revolution kicked in, large groups of people moved to the cities to find work. Now it seems the very opposite is happening. People are preferring rural areas to populate. The hustle and bustle of our cities is no longer an attraction for many.'

'Sorry, didn't you just say you moved here five years ago?'

Amanda drank from her glass. 'Yes, of course I did. Covid 19 has distorted everyone's sense of time. I moved here three years after my grandmother passed away. When I first arrived here I did try and get a job at the museum. But no jobs were available at that time.'

'Until the curator died.' Fagan mentioned.

'An unfortunate opportunity for me.' Amanda yawned. 'Excuse me, it's been a very long day. People have been asking me questions about buried treasure and religious artefacts.'

'How about I call around at the museum tomorrow? We can talk more about why someone wanted to murder Professor Turner.'

'Don't the police have any suspects yet?'

'We have plenty of archaeologists who are out to stab each other in the back. But, so far no. Which makes this a perplexing Sherlock Holmes mystery.'

Amanda finished her glass.

'Would nine o'clock in the morning suit you?'

Amanda placed her glass down on the bar. 'That would be perfect. See you at nine o'clock sharp.'

Fagan couldn't help noticing Amanda's hour-glass figure as she walked towards the bar entrance.

CHAPTER 17

DAY 2

Abergavenny museum – 09:06am

Fagan and Watkins stepped through the entrance into the museum.

The museum was packed. Many people walking around viewing the artefacts on display. Amanda fought her way through the throng of sightseers, spotting the two detectives standing by the door.

'This way, I have a private office at the back.' Amanda beckoned.

Fagan and Watkins followed her.

Amanda slumped down in her chair. 'Can I make any of you gentlemen some fresh mint tea? It's my own special brew.'

'No, thank you.' Fagan declined.

Amanda got up and walked over to a kettle. 'I never expected madness this morning. I have had to switch my phone off. Every treasure hunter has come to town. I see the mainstream media is continuing their coverage.'

'Yesterday we started off with a murder at an old castle.' Fagan looked toward the office door. 'Today we have a hoard of treasure hunters thinking they're going to strike it rich.'

'It's going to start looking like a gold rush.' Amanda remarked, pouring hot water over a strainer.

Fagan pulled his notebook from his inside pocket, flipping it open. 'I'd like you to tell me everything you know about the treasure of Alice?'

Amanda sipped the hot mint tea. 'It depends where you want to start. Unless you're a true student of history, then you won't know anything. I wouldn't worry about the hoard that have descended on this town. They'll get fed up within a few hours. It's a nice temporary boost to the town's economy and this museum. If you google Alice, the only thing you'll find is a few historical websites telling tales of the terrible deeds she carried out in Ireland. But in certain circles there is a lot more information than amateur researchers can be bothered to look for.'

'What exactly do you know about her?' Fagan asked.

'She was born in the year 1150AD. The daughter of William FitzMiles, a loyal knight of William De Braose. Who was himself favourite with King John. In 1165AD FitzMiles was killed in a failed assault to take Abergavenny castle. Legend states that Alice wept for a week before anyone could even approach her. When a rival family seized lands that belonged to FitzMiles, Alice was reduced to a servant girl to work for the family that murdered her father. In the dead of night in October 1165AD, Alice crept into the bedchambers of the man who killed her father. She stabbed his wife four times through the heart.'

'Ouch.' Watkins said, glancing at Fagan.

'The story is only just getting started.' Amanda continued. 'Alice, being a young girl of radiant beauty, offered her virginity to the lord of the house, as his wife lay dead in the bed next to them. And as they were in the throes of passion, Alice slit his throat.'

'Jesus.' Watkins stated. 'It didn't even get that good on *Game of Thrones*.'

Amanda laughed. 'Many people assume that the middle ages was a time when nothing much happened. In fact, it's quite the opposite. Many events occurred that changed the course of history. You'll be surprised how many values and principles we still stick to today. Most people call them superstitions?'

'So, skipping forward another history lesson.' Fagan said. 'This Alice slaughters a load of Irish a few years later and then goes on a quest to the Holy Land. Along the way she amasses an army and ransacks Jerusalem.'

'Wow, someone has been doing their research, Inspector Fagan. I'm impressed.' Amanda winked at him.

'I have been talking to Sarah York, Professor Turner's assistant. Why is there no mention of Alice in history?'

Amanda frowned. 'Not everything is laid bare on the History channel, Inspector Fagan. There is still much about history we do not know. The story of Alice is one that has been lost to history. Was there an army of women? I believe there was, because I think belief is part of the history we don't know about. And contrary to what I said last night, even archaeologists learn by digging and exploring the landscape, even if it's for financial gain.'

'You seem to have a disdain for archaeologists.' Fagan mentioned. 'Don't you think there are archaeologists out there who are genuinely interested in the past?'

'Yes, but to be honest, they're far and few between.'

'Ok, for argument's sake. Alice has this army. She raids the Holy Land and comes back with a load of treasure. Do you have any idea where she may have hidden it?'

'Now you're asking the question I'm sure everyone is asking.' Amanda looked towards the door of her office. 'Particularly those who have descended on Abergavenny today.'

'How much treasure did she bring back from the Holy Land?'

'After eighteen months of pillaging Jerusalem and the surrounding towns, Alice set out for England. According to scriptures I have read, when Alice fled Jerusalem, she had a caravan at least half a mile long. Laden down with the wealth of the Holy Land. Alice then had to endure the nine-hundred-mile journey to Alexandria. Back then, any journey in the Holy Land was plagued with danger and very often death. One of the reasons the Knights Templar were created. To protect pilgrims on the road to Jerusalem. Alice had stolen so much wealth her army was attacked many times along the route. Mostly by Templars themselves, who saw her actions as an act against God and Christ. There were many splinter groups of the Templars back then. Romantic history states the Templars were one unified army.' Amanda shook her head. 'The sisterhood of the Templar Knights was one of many break away orders. During the journey, Alice herself was captured twice and had to be ransomed for much of the treasure she had stolen. By the time she reached Alexandria, Alice had lost over half her army and three quarters of what she had taken from the Holy Land. She still had a significant amount of treasure. She boarded one of six ships to make the perilous journey back to England, which took a further two years. Along the way Alice lost more treasure and more of her army. By the time she reached English shores just one ship remained. And three hundred loyal followers.'

'That's still a lot of loot.' Fagan remarked.

'Alice's greed cost her most of her army. However, the knight whom she first met in Ireland stayed with her. By the time they reached home, Alice was pregnant with her first child.'

'How many did she have?' Watkins asked.

'Four girls in all. Alice herself lived until she was ninety eight. Which is extremely old for that period. Any average person would be lucky if they lasted beyond thirty five. The scriptures I read in Israel revealed Alice knelt in the spot where Jesus was baptised and drank from the river, thus giving her the gift of long life.'

'A bit like drinking from the holy grail.' Watkins said.

'Yes.' Amanda nodded. 'Legend claims her descendants are blessed with long life. On her deathbed, Alice awarded her daughters with four daggers.'

'Four daggers.' Fagan interrupted, reflecting on what he had learnt over the last twenty-four hours.

Amanda nodded. 'She gave strict instructions that the daggers were to be used when the treasure she had buried under her manor house was under threat. She also left instructions that after her death her manor house was to be destroyed. Her four daughters carried out her last request. However, they made a pact of their own. They left markers to locate the manor house. When any of the sisters died, they would hand over their daggers to the remaining sisters until only one sister was left. Then the last sister would locate the lost treasure and claim the prize. It is said that the daggers, together with a map, will point the way. But you have to be standing within a certain place to know.'

'Something tells me there's a but there somewhere.' Fagan said.

'The last remaining daughter of Alice named Mary was married to a knight.' Amanda sighed. 'Like most marriages of the day, he was an abusive husband. Mary also had a daughter of her own who she gave all four daggers to. She instructed her daughter to bury them at Tintern Abbey and then leave the area. Mary was fearful her husband and the sons she bore him would go looking for the daggers.'

'So she vanished into history.' Fagan finished.

'Yes.' Amanda nodded.

'Does anyone know where Alice of Abergavenny is buried?'

Amanda considered the question. 'People have searched, but have found nothing.'

'And since then, treasure hunters over the years have been looking for this fabled lost treasure.' Watkins said.

'And lost, it will remain.' Amanda pondered the moment. 'I guess there are some things that are best left buried.'

'Try telling that to most of those looking around your museum.' Fagan pointed out. 'So, there are three markers buried around here somewhere. That supposedly point to where this fabled lost treasure is.'

'Yes, but the thing is, these are just stories. Talk of lost treasure will always attract people who have no interest in history. All they want to do is dig holes in the ground and make a mess.'

'Just say one of the markers is found. It could spark a frenzy. I mean, if they exist.'

'I don't think they exist. It's just another tall tale.'

'But the daggers are no tall tale. They were stolen from this very museum in January 2020. Would you know anything about the theft?'

'Not really. It happened before I worked here. I told you most of what I know last night. I had a local security company call on me when I took over to upgrade the systems. They were the company that managed the security system at the time of the robbery.'

'Did they mention anything about the robbery?' Watkins asked.

'No.'

'I'd like their contact details, please.'

Amanda hesitated before nodding.

A knock on the door interrupted the meeting. A young woman poked her head around the door. 'Sorry to bother you, Amanda, but it's getting manic out there.'

Amanda stood. 'Can you excuse me for a moment. I need to take care of that rabble in the museum.'

Fagan let out a loud yawn and stretched. 'What an absolute pile of bollocks this investigation is turning into. Since yesterday morning we have had nothing but myth and legend shoved down our bloody throats. No one seems to be concerned that a man was murdered yesterday morning.'

'What do you want to do? Interview the entire dig team? There's at least fifty of them. It will take days to go through them all. Griffiths isn't exactly tripping over himself to supply us with more men.' Watkins said.

'Ok, let's start with the theft of the daggers. We'll contact the security company later on today. See if they can tell us anything about the robbery. Then we'll have another word with forensics, see if they have anything new about the murder.'

Amanda walked back into the room. 'It looks like I am going to have to close the museum. We don't have the staff to cope with this many visitors.'

Watkins' phone buzzed. He stood and left the room.

Amanda smiled at Fagan. 'So, if I may be so bold. What does a Detective Inspector do in Abergavenny when he's not trying to solve a murder?'

'To be honest with you, not a lot. Abergavenny is a great town. But it's for the young.'

'Inspector Fagan, you have grown old way before your time.'

'It certainly looks that way.'

'Well, there's only one thing for it. Dinner tonight at Aldo's.'

'That's that Italian opposite Tesco, isn't it?'

'It is. They have a great menu there.'

Fagan blushed.

'Not used to having strange women asking you out, I take it.'

'You're anything but strange, Amanda.'

'Well, it's the least I can do for conning you out of ten pounds and a drink last night.'

Fagan grinned.

Watkins breezed back into the room. 'Boss, we have a serious problem. Sarah York just rang. All hell is kicking off at the dig site. Someone called Damien Thackery has just arrived.'

Fagan stood. 'Now perhaps we can get some answers.'

'If you don't mind Inspector Fagan, I'd like to come with you after I have closed the museum.'

'I thought you hated archaeologists.'

'True, but I have just had my schedule cleared for the rest of the day with the closing of the museum.'

'I need the details of that security company asap.'

'Of course, I will e-mail you the details as soon as I close up here.'

CHAPTER 18

Bont – 09:48am

'Bloody hell.' Watkins stared at the chaos in front of him.

Hundreds of people had descended on the dig site and were walking around or digging up large chunks of land.

Fagan spotted Sarah York arguing with a well-dressed man. Their shouts carried on the wind. A few dozen people were looking in their direction. Some were filming the argument on their phones for the entertainment of their followers on social media.

'Where the hell is uniform to manage this lot?' Fagan scowled.

'I'm on it.' Watkins said, pulling his phone from his pocket.

'At least you have one constable on duty.' Amanda pointed towards Brooks, who was standing between York and the well-dressed man, keeping them apart.

Fagan and Amanda trudged towards them.

'I'm going to ask you one more time Sarah, where is that journal that Turner promised me?' The well-dressed man demanded to know.

'For the tenth fucking time, I do not know.' York shouted back.

'But you must have known he brought it with him.'

'I don't know. Robert still kept secrets from me.'

The well-dressed man took a step forward. 'You knew about that journal. Turner spoke to me last week and said you were aware of its existence.'

'Of course I was. I was his closest assistant.'

'I want to know where it is? Either you tell me or you are off this dig site.'

'You haven't got the authority to do that.'

The man pulled out his smartphone. 'How about this then? Why don't I just call the archaeology department at Cambridge? I'm sure they would benefit from a one million pound donation from my foundation. But it will come with strings attached. You are one of those strings I will be cutting, if you don't tell me where that journal is.'

'You don't care about Robert or the way he was murdered. All you give a shit about is that journal and how much knowledge you can gain from it.'

'Come on you two, break it up.' Fagan ordered.

The man stared at him. 'Who the fuck are you?'

Fagan shoved his ID in the man's face. 'DI Fagan, that's who the fuck I am.'

'Great, PC plod to the rescue.' The man rolled his eyes.

'Shut your mouth and tell me who you are.'

Amanda looked at Fagan, impressed with his guile.

'Damien Thackery, I'm one of the main backers for this little venture. Which, if you ask me, is turning into a complete waste of time. I will ask you again Sarah, where is the journal?'

'Drop dead you dick.' York seethed.

'Fair enough. You are off the project.' Thackery thumbed a number into his phone.

'You can't do that. I'm Robert's senior assistant. This site is now under my guidance.'

'Not for long.' Thackery grinned at her.

Fagan grabbed the phone out of Thackery's hand and ended the call.

'Who the fuck do you think you are?' Thackery

screamed. 'Do you have any idea who you are dealing with?'

'A complete twat, from what I've seen so far.'

York smirked at Fagan's insult.

'Listen to me, the both of you. I want to know what the hell is going on here.' He glared at Thackery. 'You just stated you were one of two backers for this project.' He then looked at York. 'You want to tell me why you lied yesterday?'

'I didn't lie to you. I said that Thackery was financing our dig.'

'But he is one of two backers. It's ok, I know who the other backer is. Spooner and Dayton said the Vatican is part funding this project.'

York and Thackery went silent.

'Seriously.' Fagan looked at both of them. 'We're back to keeping secrets now. After all we went through yesterday. Sarah, you're still keeping secrets from me.'

'And me.' Thackery bitched. 'You have until the end of the day to tell me where that journal is. If you don't, then I will have you removed from this dig site.'

'That's very typical of you, isn't it, Mr Thackery? Eliminate the competition.' Amanda spoke.

Thackery glared back at her.

'I was at Cambridge in 2014 when you tried to palm off stolen artefacts smuggled out of Syria and Iraq.'

'I brought those artefacts at an auction.'

'One of many black market auctions that has taken place over the years selling stolen antiquities.' Amanda glanced at Fagan. 'I told Inspector Fagan earlier that I was not fond of archaeologists. But the one thing I detest above all else is a thief. You have a reputation for the type of man who pays others to steal artefacts, then make a profit.'

'And that's exactly what you planned to do here, isn't it

Damien?' York joined the interrogation. 'It's just like ten years ago when you screwed Robert over. And that's why I told him to get another backer before calling you.'

'You manipulative little shit.' Thackery seethed.

York smiled back at him. 'And there is no way you'll be able to screw over the other backers of this project.'

'The Vatican.' Fagan said, looking at York. 'You want to give me a reason why I shouldn't arrest you for perverting the course of justice.'

'What?' York exploded.

'You've done nothing but lie to me since I first met you yesterday. You've filled my head with tall tales about famous explorers and archaeologists. Lost treasure and local legends. It's all smoke and mirrors. Just to get your bloody hands on this so-called lost treasure of Alice.'

'You have no clue what is at stake here, because you're nothing but a flat foot.' York shouted back at him.

'That's it, Sarah York, I'm arresting you.' Fagan was shoved aside by a young woman before he could finish his caution.

'Sarah, we've found it? The first marker.'

'Where?'

'Top left-hand corner of the south wall.' The woman pointed towards the excavation.

'Out of my fucking way.' Thackery shouted at the crowd.

Fagan could barely keep up with the group as they scrambled up the steep field.

'You ok?' Amanda asked.

'Just about.' Fagan panted, stumbling over the rough terrain. 'I'm pissed off with being fucked about.'

'I have to admit even I'm excited about what they could have found.'

Fagan and Amanda fought their way through the crowd of onlookers.

'I was just brushing away some soil and there it was.' The young woman explained.

York looked at the stone tablet that was in the shape of a knight's shield. 'My god this is incredible.' She rubbed her hand over it, smiling.

Thackery looked down at the inscription on the shield. 'What language is this?'

'It's Latin.' York revealed. 'Twelfth century.'

'So that fits the time period that this Alice lived in, doesn't it?'

'Yes, it fits the time period.'

'What does it say?'

'It will take me a few hours to decipher this inscription.'

'Great, Robert would have been able to translate this in a heartbeat.' Thackery complained. 'And now he's dead, we've no chance of deciphering this to tell us the location of the second marker.'

'I said I will decipher it.' York insisted.

'Show some bloody respect, will you.' Fagan chastised. 'A man was murdered last night because of this.' He looked at the assembled crowd. 'You should all be ashamed of yourselves.'

Some of the onlookers peeled away.

'Yeah, that's right, walk away. I mean, it wasn't like any of you gave a shit. Most of you are out here because of Facebook and Twitter.'

More people walked away.

'A man lost his life yesterday. He was brutally murdered. For what? So you can claim your ultimate prize.'

'You think this is the first person to be murdered because of buried treasure?' Thackery said. 'Turner was at the end of his career, desperate for one last big find. Obviously, this dig attracted the wrong attention. There are people who have no intention of sharing the find with others.' He made eye contact with York.

'Oh come on Damien, don't try to lay that bullshit at my door. All you give a shit about is how much money you can make out of this venture. You're just pissed off you can't get your hands on that journal, so you can turn it into one big treasure hunt.'

'If you are one of the main backers on this dig, Mr Thackery, then why haven't you hired protection?' Fagan gestured to the growing amount of people entering through the bottom gate of the field. 'A security company to ensure this site is kept safe.'

'Inspector Fagan is right.' Amanda said. 'You need to secure this site.'

Watkins marched towards the group. 'Sorry, boss, but the chief constable won't spare us any more officers.'

'Shit.'

'If you give me my phone back, I can have fifty people on site within the hour. I'm sure there's a local security company who can oblige.' He looked at York, pointing at the tablet. 'I want that inscription translated asap.'

York stared back at him and nodded.

'Good, then get moving.'

'I suggest we head back to Newport and regroup.' Fagan suggested.

Amanda glanced at her phone that had just buzzed. 'Great, I need a lift. Can you give me a lift back to Abergavenny. I've some things to take care of back at the museum.'

'DI Fagan, can I have a word in private before you go?' York requested.

Both Fagan and York walked out of earshot of everyone.

'I'm sorry I have still been keeping secrets from you. But you must understand there is more happening here than anyone realises.'

'After what has happened over the last twenty-four hours, nothing surprises me anymore.' Fagan stared across the dig site. 'I mean, it's not as happy-go-lucky as Time Team, is it?'

'You were right about what you said yesterday. We are all just greedy treasure hunters. Most of us don't start off that way. There is a certain romanticism about archaeology. Lost treasures and larger-than-life characters.' She looked across at Thackery, who was talking to Amanda. 'But, there are men like Thackery, like Lord Carnarvon, who will only be interested in the wealth that comes with finds like the lost treasure of Alice.'

'I'm sorry Sarah, but if you're looking for a shoulder to cry on, then you've got the wrong person. You're lucky I'm not arresting you for perverting the course of justice. I'm a serving detective, and I have a job to do. And my number one priority at this moment is finding who murdered Robert.'

'That's what I wanted to talk to you about.' York took in a lungful of air. 'I have just received a text from the other partner who is funding the dig.'

'Go on, I'm listening.'

'He's at Newport central police station and wants to speak with you immediately. I sent a text to them yesterday to inform them about what had happened to Robert. They dispatched a special envoy to liaise with the local police.'

'Special envoy?' Fagan quizzed.

York drew closer to Fagan and made sure no one was looking in their direction. She showed Fagan her phone.

'You knew the Vatican would turn up.'

'Yes.' Sarah confessed.

'Boss.' Watkins called out, marching towards them. 'The chief constable just phoned. He wants us in Newport on the double.'

Fagan walked back down towards Amanda and Thackery, who looked as if they were having a heated debate.

'Do us a favour Sean. When we get back to Newport, track down all the media sources that have run the story. Find out if they knew anything about where Turner was staying.'

'Sure.'

CHAPTER 19

Newport police HQ – 10:43am

Fagan stood at the door. Laughter was coming from within the Chief Constable's office. Fagan waited a few moments before knocking loudly.

'Detective Inspector Fagan.' Griffiths greeted as he stepped into his office. 'I Trust you are making progress regarding the murder of Robert Turner.'

'I'm afraid it's slow going sir.' Fagan confessed, making eye contact with the man in priest's robes. 'There is a wall of secrecy surrounding the dig. Everyone seems to be more concerned with finding some lost treasure than helping with a murder enquiry.'

'Greed can be a powerful ally and a potent enemy.' The priest remarked.

'I'll let you get on with the task at hand.' Griffiths brushed past Fagan and left the office.

The priest stood, offering his hand. 'Forgive the intrusion DI Fagan. I am Father Pedro Romano. I am special liaison representative with the Vatican department for stolen antiquities.'

Fagan sat in Griffiths' chair. 'That's quite a mouthful, Father Romano. But I am trying to solve a murder here, not recover stolen property. Can I ask, what exactly is it you claim that has been stolen?'

'I am part of a team that travels the world tracing artefacts stolen over the years. Relating to our lord Jesus.'

Fagan sensed another history lesson was about to be

thrust upon him. 'Let me guess, you are here looking for this so-called splinter of Christ.'

Romano smiled. 'No doubt you are already knowledgeable about this matter.'

'Not by choice, I can assure you. Like every other treasure hunter I have encountered over the past twenty-four hours, you have a tale to tell me.'

'I wouldn't exactly call the splinter of Christ a tale. More like something that happened many thousands of years ago. The story of the true cross has been handed down through the centuries.'

'The true cross.' Fagan ran the image through his mind. As a youngster he would have to endure watching *Jesus of Nazareth*, starring Robert Powell, on Easter Sunday. His parents were not devout Christians. However, there was nothing better than a good biblical epic after a full Sunday lunch. *The Ten Commandments, The Robe and Ben Hur* were all staples of Christmas or Easter viewing.

'I can see DI Fagan, you are a man without faith.'

'I'm sorry, Father, but in my line of work, faith has a minor role to play. I have dealt with many missing children over the past three decades. Thankfully, most are found safe and sound.' Fagan's thoughts turned to his last murder case in Liverpool. The senseless killing of a six-year-old boy. He stared at Romano. 'But sometimes I have seen acts of depravity that defy any explanation.'

Romano nodded without talking.

'Surely a man in your position witnesses acts of evil every day that make you question your faith.'

'I do. But it is the society we live in, DI Fagan. The world is filled with both miracles and things that can only be described as the work of Satan.' He inhaled. 'But I am here to talk about matters of greed.'

Fagan nodded. 'Ok then, Father. What exactly is the

splinter of Christ?'

'It is the holiest of all relics associated with the true cross. It is the part of the cross where the lord Jesus Christ's feet were nailed in place.' Romano paused. 'The splinter contains the blood of Christ and must be returned to Rome.'

'Returned to Rome?' Fagan queried. 'I always assumed this splinter was taken from the Holy Land by this Alice of Abergavenny.'

'Alice and her army marched all over the Holy Land. Stealing artefacts and killing thousands of religious scholars, monks. An army was despatched to take back what she had stolen. Word spread throughout the region of a great caravan laden down with treasure that was making its way to Alexandria. The Templars that were sent after Alice were attacked many times. There were plenty of profiteers who wanted to steal the treasure for themselves. So that they could sell the relics back to the holy church in Rome. Thankfully, many of the relics were recovered and returned to their rightful place. But the splinter of Christ was never recovered and thought to be lost forever.'

'Until?'

'A clue to its location was found in 1975.'

Fagan realised what Romano was talking about. 'A clue. Are you talking about the discovery of the four daggers at Tintern abbey?'

'Yes, you see DI Fagan, I was there in 1975.'

Fagan nodded.

'There are texts within the Vatican archives that tell the story of Alice. During her campaign, one of her female Templars kept a journal of her own. When they reached France and were about to embark on the last leg of the journey, they were attacked. The female Templar stayed behind to ensure Alice's escape. She was captured and brought back to Rome to face the actions of her crimes. She handed over her journal that chronicled her journey through the Holy Land. The journal speaks of Alice slaughtering innocent men, women and children who stood in her path. Her lust for wealth was greater than many of the knights who went out to seek their fortune in the Holy Land. It also revealed information where Alice was heading when she returned to Britain. In 1974, renowned archaeologist Norman Cuthbert visited the Vatican archives to view this ancient journal. It is there he learned that Alice's final destination was this area, as it was her birthplace. The daggers recovered at Tintern were more than just ceremonial. One of them was a key that would open the vault the splinter of Christ was kept in. The four daggers came with a map.'

'A map?' Fagan quizzed.

'Norman Cuthbert drew a copy of the map.'

'I see.' Fagan mused.

'A most unpleasant man. I remember having an argument with him about letting the Vatican have access to the map and the daggers.' Romano paused, remembering the events. 'He burnt the original map right in front of me.'

'So he would have the only copy of the map.' Fagan decided to test a theory. 'Where did he keep a copy of this map?'

Romano hesitated before answering. 'Cuthbert recreated it in a journal he kept during his lifetime as an archaeologist.'

'And you think this journal survived to this day?'

'Yes?'

'How did it survive?'

Again Romano was slow in answering. 'His young

prodigy at the time, Robert Turner, took the journal after Cuthbert was murdered.'

'Have you seen this journal for yourself?'

'Yes.' Romano answered after another brief silence.

'When?'

More silence.

Fagan sensed frustration mounting. 'Look, I get it. This splinter of Christ is important to you. It's important to the Vatican. I should imagine that in the modern world we are living in, more people are turning away from the church.'

'It is of vital importance to the Vatican, to locate the splinter of Christ. It will rejuvenate the church. Not just the Catholic faith, but all faiths.'

Fagan couldn't help smiling at Romano's words. 'I had a similar conversation yesterday. Albeit a little different. Archaeologists interested in buried treasure. And now here you are hoping for a miracle that will bring people back to the church.'

Romano was unimpressed with Fagan's words.

'It's no good looking at me like that, father. It's written all over your face. Let's face it, people are losing faith in the church. Preferring social media, Netflix and the Kardashians. So I'm guessing a minor miracle like finding the splinter of Christ will go in the church's favour. You know, help restore faith in the almighty. After all, the Catholic church has been embroiled in so many scandals you need a miracle to put things right. And you'll do anything to achieve that goal.'

Romano scowled at him. 'What are you suggesting exactly, DI Fagan?'

'A man was murdered yesterday, and no one seems to give a flying fuck about it.' Fagan realised his error. 'Please excuse my language. But you have to look at things from my point of view. All I have had is silence since I was assigned to this murder case. People seem more interested in the pot of gold at the end of the bloody rainbow than who actually murdered Robert Turner. When did you find out that the hunt for the splinter of Christ was about to start?'

'About six months ago. Professor Turner put in a request to look at the text relating to Alice and her exploits in the Holy Land. I met with him personally. He had with him pictures of the map that Cuthbert had copied in his journal. He informed me he was going after the splinter of Christ.'

'Did he say what he was going to do with it?'

'Yes, he told us that this would be his last dig, and that it would be fitting the Vatican should get the artefact.'

'How sure are you that this artefact even exists? We are talking nine hundred years ago.'

Romano grinned at Fagan. 'Unlike you, DI Fagan, I still have faith.'

'Ok, so why do you think Professor Turner was murdered?'

'I suspect there is still an element that has yet to come into play. People have been looking for the splinter of Christ for nine hundred years.'

'So you are saying that Turner's murderer could be someone who has yet to be considered?'

'Look at it this way. Who else has to gain from his murder? And who else will benefit from finding the lost treasure of Alice?'

Fagan could only shrug at the question.

'I am not here as a treasure hunter DI Fagan. I am here as a servant of God. If the splinter of Christ is indeed buried somewhere in the area, then the Vatican has the right to claim what is rightfully theirs.'

'No.' Fagan said. 'Any treasure found on UK territory

belongs to the crown, which is our newly crowned King Charles the third.' He smiled. 'Still can't get used to saying that.'

Romano stared back at Fagan. 'I'm sure, given the significance of this find, His Majesty will be willing to discuss with Vatican officials about this matter.'

'I tell you what, Father. I was just about to head back to the dig site. I'd like you to accompany me. Hopefully together, we will be able to find more answers.'

Romano considered the proposal before nodding.

CHAPTER 20

Bont – 12:49pm

The dig site was a little less chaotic than it was earlier. Thackery managed to hire security in a very short space of time. A number of security personnel were posted at the gate. Barring anyone who wasn't part of the team. All dig team members were required to have their ID badges visible at all times. One man was arguing with a security marshal, trying to push his way past.

Fagan puffed out through his cheeks. 'Right, listen up you three. I have had it up to here with this nonsense. Let me remind you for the umpteenth time, a man was murdered yesterday.' Fagan placed photographs of Turner's body on a makeshift table.

'York couldn't bring herself to look at the photographs.

'Sarah.' Fagan noted she was looking away from the pictures. He pointed. 'Pay attention please. I'm sorry if you find this distressing, but I'm trying to catch a murderer. Like it or not, you will look at these photographs.'

York forced herself to confront the pictures of Professor Turner.

'So far we have very little clue as to who carried out this horrific crime. But I intend to figure this out.' He looked at York. 'Is there anything in Professor Turner's journal that may indicate who the murderer is?'

York pondered the question before shaking her head. 'No, he wrote lots of notes about Alicie's possible last resting place. But there was nothing to suggest who could have murdered him.'

Thackery glared at her. 'So Robert did have the journal with him. And you have seen it. Where?'

'I can't remember.'

'Bollocks.'

'Enough!' Fagan shouted. 'Which brings me to my next question. Is it possible that you have rivals who could have murdered him to stop you finding this so-called treasure?'

Thackery shrugged. 'I have plenty of people who don't like me DI Fagan. The list would be too long for you to go through.'

'I bet it is.' York mocked.

Thackery returned the comment with a hard stare.

Fagan looked at Romano. 'What about you Father. I'm sure the Vatican has made an enemy or two over the past several centuries.'

'Actually, DI Fagan the Vatican was founded in 1929.'

Fagan didn't appreciate another history lesson.

Romano could see the look of disapproval on his face. 'No one is without enemies DI Fagan.' He looked at Thackery. 'Like Mr Thackery just said the list is endless.'

Fagan glanced at Thackery remembering what Amanda had revealed earlier. 'Is it true that you have been involved in stolen artefacts in the past?'

Thackery rolled his eyes. 'Don't listen to that silly bitch who was with you earlier.'

'I'm sure it is only a matter of checking with police records Mr Thackery. So, you'll may as well say something now.'

'I was cleared of any wrong doing.'

'I guess that's what rich and powerful means.' York criticised. 'Pay off everyone to get away with everything.'

'Fuck off.' Thackery shot back.

'You stabbed Robert in the back ten years ago. When

you promised him he could keep the collection of Templar coins.'

'Oh for fuck's sake, I don't have to stand here and listen to this shit.'

'Stop it!' Fagan shouted. 'Ok, what exactly was the deal here?' He looked at Thackery and Romano. 'You are both partly funding this project. What do you both get out of it?'

'We've already told you Detective Fagan. I get the journal and Father Romano gets his little trinkets.'

Romano glared at Thackery. 'The splinter of Christ is no trinket. It is one of the most sort after artefacts in history.'

'If that is the case Father, then why has no one turned up before now looking for it?' Fagan asked.

'Because no one knew it even existed before that dig in 1975. The Vatican always assumed that the Splinter of Christ was lost to history.' When Norman Cuthbert was murdered and the daggers disappeared we assumed that the Splinter of Christ was lost forever.'

Fagan looked at York. 'What is the likelihood of discovering this lost treasure?'

'The odds have trebled. Now we have uncovered the first marker.'

'But you haven't translated it yet.' Thackery complained. 'Which means we're dead in the water.'

'I will spend the rest of the day deciphering that inscription.'

Romano stepped forward. 'If I may, I have access to resources that will speed up this endeavour. If you'll let me view the marker then it might be beneficial to all our parties.'

York considered the priest's proposal before nodding.

'This way father.' Thackery invited.

York shot him a scornful look.

Fagan grabbed York's arm before she followed.

'What is the likelihood of you finding this treasure without that journal?'

'The journal contains the map and other sketches that would have speeded up the process. However the markers will do the same thing.'

'Father Romano told me that one of the daggers is a key that will unlock the vault containing the lost treasure of Alice. How fast do you reckon it will take our Vatican friend here to decipher the stone tablet?'

'He has access to Vatican archives and translators who will speed things up.' York paused looking in the direction of Thackery and Romano. 'What have you done with the journal?'

'It's best if you don't know Sarah. Whoever murdered Robert wants their hands on that journal.'

'So what are you suggesting?'

'The journal must be kept hidden. But if they translate whatever is on that stone tablet it could flush out the murderer. I suspect they want their hands on the treasure as bad as the rest of you. Something Father Romano said made me think earlier. There is another element that has yet to come into play here. As much as I hate to admit it, I'm going to have to play the archaeologist myself. What do you know about that marker?'

'According to the map drawn in the journal, the markers will lead to a point of reference that will point to the location of Alice's manor house. And her last resting place.'

'Do you have any idea what this point of reference could be?'

'No, Alice went to great lengths to keep the location of the artefacts she had taken from the Holy Land a secret.'

'Which brings me to my next question. Everything happened nine hundred years ago. What makes you or Robert believe that there is something out here to find?'

'I guess you could say the same about Howard Carter. What made him believe Tutankhamun's tomb was in the Valley of the Kings? There were always pointers, but at the end of the day it boiled down to faith.'

'Robert must have had a lot of faith in this Alice to believe there is some kind of buried treasure around here. I grew up locally. You hear things about local myth.' Fagan looked over towards the Skirrid mountain. Its distinctive shape dominated the local landscape. 'Where are you from originally?'

'Hertfordshire, just outside Stevenage. My mother still lives there. My dad died of cancer when I was sixteen. When I went to Cambridge I met Robert, who took me under his wing. Just before we came out here I advised him not to go.'

'Why?'

'We'd been sent a series of threatening notes.' York paused to recall the events leading up to Robert making the decision to go ahead with the dig.

Fagan rolled his eyes. 'Jesus Christ Sarah, more secrets. Why didn't you mention this yesterday?'

She wiped away tears. 'My head has been so full of shit since Robert was murdered. All I can do is keep apologising. I know you have a job to do.'

'What notes, Sarah?'

'About six months ago, when Robert decided he was going to try and find the lost treasure of Alice he wrote an article which was published widely in magazines associated with archaeology. Shortly after he published the article he started to receive notes from someone. They would just randomly arrive in the post. 'Only, the notes were written on parchment.'

Fagan stared at York. 'The note we found with Robert's body was parchment. Forensics are still analysing the note.

The note was scrawled in blood.'

York clasped her hand over her mouth. 'God, I wish Robert had listened to me. I never wanted him to get involved with this dig. I thought it was pointless.'

'Why?'

'I thought it was one old man's last hurrah. I never believed in the legend of Alice. There are just too many inconsistencies with the story.' She looked to where Thackery and Romano were. 'But, now maybe there is some sort of truth in all this.'

'Did you go out to the Vatican with him to secure their funding.'

'Yes.' York replied. 'I am very familiar with Father Romano. Another scavenger who just wants to lock up whatever he finds so no one can see it. Robert may not have been perfect, but at least when he found something he made damn sure it went on display so that everyone could enjoy it. He wanted to share his work with everyone.'

'I take it you saw some of the Vatican journals relating to Alice of Abergavenny.'

'Yes, that's what got Robert so excited. He told me that when he and Cuthbert found the daggers there were scrolls with texts found along with other artefacts.'

'Other artefacts?'

'Nails used in crucifixions during the middle ages. Robert said that the Vatican cleaned them out. They just barged in and took everything. Robert said that Cuthbert tried to stop them but there was very little they could do back then.'

'But Cuthbert managed to hang on to the daggers. Until the night before he was murdered.'

'Yes.'

'Did Robert ever mention a map that came with the daggers?'

York stared back at him. 'How did you know about that? Only myself and Robert knew.'

Fagan shook his head pointing at Romano in the distance. He was knelt over the marker reading the inscription carved into it. 'He knew about the map because he was at the dig with Cuthbert and Robert back in 1975.' Fagan thought about what Romano had revealed earlier. He smiled to himself. 'The clever bastard.'

'What?'

'When I was looking through that journal yesterday during our chat. I mentioned that Cuthbert was a very skilled artist. His sketches were very detailed. He drew a copy of the map that accompanied the daggers. That's why he burned the map, because he was able to create an exact copy.'

'Robert once told me a story.' York revealed.

Fagan looked back at her. 'Go on, I'm listening.'

'Cuthbert had a photographic memory. He could draw things in minute detail. Robert was also a good artist but not as good as Cuthbert. When Cuthbert worked with Howard Carter on the Tutankhamun dig he documented everything. Some of his sketches are on display at the British Museum. Exquisite sketches down to the last detail. When they uncovered the main entrance to the tomb, Carter instructed Cuthbert to create a detailed sketch of the seal that had to be broken to gain access to the tomb itself.'

'Let me guess, Carter couldn't wait for Lord Carnarvon to show up so he broke into the tomb.'

York nodded. 'But he was able to recreate the seal for the official opening. He stole a load of artefacts.'

'These notes you said Robert received what did they say?'

'It was the same message every time we received a

note. All sinners will perish.'

'The same message scrawled on the note found with Robert yesterday. Someone was keeping an eye on him long before he came to the dig.' Fagan ran a few scenarios through his head. 'Look Sarah, I get it. You are loyal to Robert. You're not like Thackery or Father Romano. However, you need to trust me. I am not interested in buried treasure or being a part of history. My interest is finding the person responsible for Robert's murder. You need to trust me as much as you trusted Robert. Can you do that?'

York wiped her eyes on her sleeve nodding. 'Ok.'

Shouting could be heard in the distance.

'We better go and see what they have found.' York said walking off.

Father Romano stared at the inscription on the stone tablet. 'This is incredible.' He gasped.

'What?' Thackery stated, frustration was clearly evident in his tone.

'If this reads correctly then Alice was here. This was one of three locations where she hid artefacts she had taken from the Holy Land.'

'What about anything buried here?'

Romano ran his finger along a line of Latin text. 'It says, this dwelling belonged to a knight of the Templar order of Alice. And that a sword guards the holy relics.'

'That would be the sword and chest we found.' York revealed.

Thackery glared at her. 'You should have contacted me and told me what you found.'

'Robert didn't trust you. He knew the moment he would have handed anything over to you, then it would have vanished.'

'I have funded this dig.' Thackery shouted.

'All you want is the journal. You said that yourself. You told Robert he could keep everything else.'

Romano glared at Thackery. 'That was not the agreement we had made. You said the Vatican could have whatever we wanted, including the journal.'

'So you are after the journal as well Father Romano.' Fagan said. 'You told me the journal contains a copy of the map that came with the daggers. Because the map is the last piece of the puzzle. That's why Cuthbert burnt the map. You had already taken most of the items associated with the dig at Tintern Abbey in 1975. But he kept the daggers and the map.'

'The Holy See has been searching for the splinter of Christ for centuries. It is one of our most sacred relics.'

'Oh spare me the sob story.' Fagan hit back. 'This is bugger all to do with holy relics. It's all about finding buried bloody treasure.'

'Never mind any of that.' Thackery interrupted. 'Does it say where the second marker is?'

Romano looked back at the tablet and continued reading the inscription. 'It says here, the worthy shall seek and find the shield of Joseph of Arimathea.' Romano stepped back from the tablet. 'So it's true?'

'What?' Thackery's face turned purple with rage.

'One of the artefacts Alice stole from the Holy Land was a shield belonging to Joseph of Arimathea. It's supposed to have been a shield made out of bronze.'

Fagan shrugged looking at the inscription. 'Who was he?'

'Joseph of Arimathea was supposed to be the man who was charged with the burial of Jesus after the crucifixion.' York explained. 'He is the source of many legends involving holy relics. Literally every legend that has been created about anything associated with Christ came from this man.

The Holy Grail is one of the most recognisable legends. along with various parts of the cross which was dismantled following the crucifixion.'

'Including the Splinter of Christ.' Romano added. 'Joseph of Arimathea fashioned a shield that contained another part of the cross. It is said he marched across Europe to spread the word of God, and educate the people.'

'I've heard this bedtime story.' York said. 'Apparently Joseph is said to have taken the holy grail to Glastonbury where it mysteriously disappeared.'

'Yes, this is all very interesting. But where does it say this so-called shield is?' Thackery's impatience was at boiling point.

Romano read more of the script. 'This text speaks of someone called Hubert-De-Burgh and resides at castle white.'

'Even I know that one, it has to be White Castle.' Fagan said.

'Hubert-De-Burgh was the lord of the three castles in this area.' York said. 'There's Skenfrith Castle, White Castle and then Grosmont Castle.'

'But surely archaeological teams have been through there already.'

'The shield isn't in the castle.' Romano said staring at the inscription. It's just outside along the wall that looks upon sunrise.'

'The wall that faces sunrise.' York stated.

'Well even an idiot can figure that out.' Thackery said dialling a number on his phone.

Fagan sensed his own phone buzzing in his pocket.

'Boss, I'm about to visit the security company who supplies equipment for the museum.' Watkins said.

'Hold off until I get there.' Fagan instructed. 'I want to

speak with them myself.'

Romano and Thackery were already leaving the site.

'Do me a favour Sarah.' Fagan asked. 'Is there any way you can stall those two?'

'I'll try but I have to leave later on. I need to go to Stevenage regarding a personal matter.'

Fagan nodded. 'Ok, we'll meet back tomorrow.'

CHAPTER 21

Bowman's security solutions – Abergavenny – 1:32pm

Fagan smiled at the man, who shook his hand. 'Wow, look at you! Michael Bowman running his own security firm. Didn't you work for that double glazing company?'

Bowman nodded. 'They went under years ago. I heard you were back in town. Or rather, I read it in the Chronicle when they arrested Tim Davis for the murder of Rebecca. Must have been a nightmare for you.'

Fagan nodded. 'It was.'

'So, you're a detective Inspector now. Isn't it funny how things turn out. I always thought that stint in Usk would have led you down a different path.'

'More like sobered me up.' Fagan said. 'This is Detective Sergeant Watkins.'

Bowman shook Watkins' hand. 'So what brings you to my humble abode this afternoon?'

'We were hoping we could talk to you about the robbery that took place at the Abergavenny museum a few years back.'

'Let me guess. The missing knives or whatever they were.'

'Those are the ones.'

'I knew that would come and bite me in the arse at some point.'

'What?'

'I bet that little shit has been shooting off his mouth again.'

Fagan shook his head, perplexed at what Bowman was saying. 'I have no idea who you are talking about Mike.'

'Shit.' Bowman seethed.

'Let me just bring you up to speed. One of the daggers stolen in 2020 was used in a murder.'

'Oh yeah, I saw the news earlier. Poor bloke.'

'It's important you tell us anything that might be helpful in this murder investigation.'

Bowman nodded. 'I occasionally employ criminals that are on early release. I get a government grant for helping newly released prisoners. We employed Ross Smith a few years ago. He's a local boy. A bit of a reputation for being a druggie.'

'How old is he?' Watkins asked.

'About thirty-seven, I think. The same age as my boy. I'd walk the dog in the park and see Smith, usually stoned out of his face. He was jailed in 2017 for possession. Got eighteen months. The parole board sent him my way. I took him on and all was fine for a while. Then we were doing a job at the town hall in Pontypool when he was caught red-handed stealing a collection box. So, I had to boot him out. I was thinking about sacking him before that incident. It wasn't long after he was out of clink when he started back on the drugs again. He was harmless enough. But very unreliable.'

'What about the break-in at the museum?' Watkins asked.

'It happened while Smith was working for us. I thought nothing of it at first. I remember the council questioning us about the matter. I nearly lost the bloody contract. I have contracts with Herefordshire council, Torfaen, Caerphilly, Monmouthshire and Newport. I'm currently working on signing a contract with Powys council. If I get that, then I can sell the business and retire. Powys is the largest council in Wales.'

'Did Smith confess to the burglary?'

'In a nutshell, yeah.'

'In a nutshell. So he never actually admitted it?'

'Not at first.'

'Go on.' Fagan said.

'During the lockdown, Smith knocked on my door at three in the morning. He said he needed money.'

'I take it you told him to fuck off?' Watkins guessed.

'Initially yes.' Bowman replied, shifting in his chair.

'What do you mean, initially, yes?'

'He threatened me. Said if I didn't hand over a grand he would tell Monmouth council. He was the one who broke into the museum. And that I knew it was him, but didn't say anything.'

'He was blackmailing you?' Fagan said.

Bowman nodded. 'I flew at him, wanted to kick the shit out of the little prick.'

'Let me guess, you handed over the money?'

Bowman inhaled, nodding. 'I didn't see any other choice. Smith was rabbiting on about telling everyone I had contracts with. I was terrified. Smith may have been a druggie, but he wasn't stupid. When we went into lockdown, I nearly lost everything. It's all very well the government putting everyone on furlough, but it turned out to be a disaster for a lot of local businesses around here. Most of which have collapsed thanks to the pandemic. Anyway, he bragged that some bloke had paid him five grand to break into the museum.'

'Five thousand pounds?' Fagan looked at Watkins.

'I always thought Smith had taken the stuff from the museum and sold it on. Until he boasted he'd broken in and then handed those daggers to this bloke.'

'I don't suppose he went into any details about this

man?' Watkins asked.

'Not really. Smith couldn't tell one face from another because most of his time he was off his head.'

'Did you see him after you gave him the thousand pound?'

'Yeah, last year. I gave him another thousand pound just to keep him quiet..'

'When was the last time you saw Smith?'

'Last week in Morrisons. He was in the alcohol aisle as usual. He said he'd be calling me soon. For more money.'

'You should have done something about him Mike.' Fagan said.

'If I would have told you lot, you would have ignored me. And I didn't think the little shit was worth it. Once this deal with Powys council is done, I'll give it a year until I have my feet firmly under the table. Then sell the company on. I have already had one offer of two million.'

'Nice amount to retire on.' Fagan said.

'I've done my bit for king and industry. I want to spend more time at my villa in Spain.' He looked at Fagan. 'So, why did you decide to return to the fold?'

'Wanted a change of scenery.' Fagan replied. 'Found myself missing Abergavenny.'

'Give it six months and you'll be pissed off you moved back.'

'Maybe.' Fagan responded. 'So where does this Ross Smith live?'

'Up at Old Tavern way, by the school in a block of flats. Number thirty-three, I think. Once I have sold up, I won't have to give that little shit any more money.'

Fagan stood. 'Thanks for your time Mike. Let us know if you remember anything else.'

'Will do.'

C H A P T E R 2 2

1:56pm

Fagan yawned, staring at the road ahead. The car crossed the roundabout near a Waitrose supermarket, continuing towards a bridge that crossed the river Usk. The Bridge Inn was on his left. He recalled the times heoff went there with Rebecca when they were young.

'So what do you think?' Watkins asked, yanking Fagan back to the present.

'I reckon this whole murder investigation is a load of bollocks. Since yesterday we've been given the runaround. And now the Vatican has turned up on soe kind of holy quest.'

'It's kind of cool. Almost feels like we're in a Dan Brown novel.'

'What do we know so far? Renowned archaeologist is found murdered on the grounds of a castle. His death is dressed up to make it look like something out of those books you read. We have another archaeologist who has lied to us, time and time again. A ruthless businessman who doesn't give a shit about who dies. Then we have Father Romano who is out to claim the ultimate prize.' Fagan made a mental list of everyone he had spoken to over the last forty-eight hours. 'Did you get hold of the druids Annie at Skenfrith mentioned?'

'Yes, the Monmouthshire druid association. The leader of their little band admitted he had a few cross words with Turner and his assistant Sarah York. He's provided a watertight alibi.'

'I might have a word with Lord Barry.' Fagan considered.

'Who?'

'My contact mentioned him yesterday. He said that Tony James gave an interview with the BBC and several newspapers about the exhibition. Barry had an argument with James about the daggers going on display.' Fagan suddenly had an idea. 'Do me a favour. The museum curator died in May 2020. Apparently from a sudden heart attack. See if we can obtain coroner's report on his death.'

Watkins nodded. 'You think this lord Barry might have something to do with the theft of the daggers?'

'I won't know that until I speak to him. Just strikes me as a little odd, this Lord Barry having an argument about the daggers, then the curator dropping dead a few months after. It's like Father Romano pointed out earlier. There is another element we are not seeing here. So far, all the suspects have been people from out of town.'

'So, what, we look closer to home?'

Fagan nodded. 'Someone knows about Alice of Abergavenny. And has some kind of local connection. But what that is, I simply don't know.'

Watkins manoeuvred the car into a parking space.

Fagan got out of the car and looked about. The block of flats where Smith lived in was built in the mid-sixties. A three story red brick building with three large flats on each floor. Behind the flats were fields stretching all the way to the foot of the Deri mountain. The sound of a barking dog drifted across from a garden. Litter was strewn all over the place in the carpark. A black rubbish bag was torn open with its contents exposed.

'I fucking hate people who don't recycle their food waste.' Watkins complained, looking at a mouldy loaf of bread that had been torn from its packaging. 'I'm huge on recycling. My girlfriend just chucks everything into black bags. It does my bloody head in.'

Both men walked down a path to the main doors. 'What number did Smith live at?'

Watkins flipped open his notebook. 'Thirty Three.'

Fagan pressed a button on the panel. Several seconds passed before he pressed it again.

'If he's the local druggie, what are the chances he's too off his face to answer the door buzzer?' Watkins considered.

Fagan pressed the buzzer for the third time. 'We'll give him a little while.'

Both men waited patiently.

'Bugger this.' Fagan pressed the service button. Eventually, the door clicked, and both men slipped through.

Smith lived on the top floor.

As the climbed the stairs, Fagan noticed discarded syringes. 'Watch your step.' He warned. 'The last thing you need is a needle poking through your shoe.'

Watkins shifted his position, avoiding a used syringe.

When they finally reached number thirty three, Fagan stopped at the door, pressing his ear against it.

The sound of a whimpering dog could be heard. The glass window on the door was filthy. However, Fagan could make out the outline of a small dog standing in a doorway. He knocked on the door loudly.

The dog's whimper became a furious bark as it attacked the door.

'Should we call an ARV to deal with the dog?' Watkins asked.

'Looks like a Jack Russel, and by the sounds of the bark, an old one. Shouldn't be a problem.' The dog stopped barking and returned to the doorway. It began whimpering again.

The door to another flat opened. A young woman emerged with a pushchair with a young child. A rolled up cigarette was hanging between her lips. A young toddler also appeared out of the doorway. He clung to his mother as soon as he spotted the two strangers standing nearby.

Fagan produced his ID badge. 'DI Fagan with Gwent police.'

'What's that prick done now?' The woman complained. 'This fucking shitbox is full of druggies. I have emailed the council so many times to have them thrown out.' She gestured to a syringe near her door. 'It's not fucking fair. They don't give a shit if anyone has kids.'

'Do you know the individual that lives in this flat?' Watkins asked.

'Yeah, Ross Smith, fucking waste of space. His dog has been howling for hours.'

'When was the last time you saw Mr Smith?'

'This morning, maybe. He was having an argument with his mate, Darren Stephens. Another fucking druggie. They were standing out here screaming.'

'Do you know what they were arguing about?'

'Haven't got a fucking clue. But if it was those two, it was probably about drugs.'

'Are there other residents who live on this floor?' Fagan asked, looking towards the door of another flat.

The woman shook her head, sucking on her cigarette. 'Been empty for a few weeks. Knowing the council, they'll move another druggie into the flat.'

'Thank you madam.' Fagan said politely.

The woman squeezed past Fagan and Watkins. Her young son clutched his mother's coat.

Fagan waited until the woman had manhandled the pushchair down the stairs before he knocked loudly again.

The dog began another furious assault on the door. Fagan could hear it panting. He looked through the window.

'Stand back.' Fagan instructed, before hammering his foot against the door.

The door gave way immediately.

'Not bad for an old copper boss.' Watkins quipped.

Fagan was already regretting his actions. Despite the door being relatively easy to kick in, his leg throbbed.

The dog in the hallway snarled at the two men standing in the entrance. Too tired to launch another attack, it lay down and looked towards what appeared to be the kitchen.

Watkins followed Fagan's lead, slipping on a pair of blue latex gloves.

The dog remained where it was. It was elderly and was too tired to fend off the strangers who had entered the hallway to the flat.

Fagan pushed open a door to reveal a room that was sparsely furnished. A filthy looking bathroom was on the opposite side.

Watkins scanned the floor for discarded syringes.

Fagan stared at the dog that was facing the entrance to the kitchen. Its panting had stopped. Fagan edged towards the doorway. An odour he was all too familiar with filled his nostrils. The scent of death was a unique odour. Slowly, a pair of legs came into view, followed by the rest of the body that lay face down. A pool of blood spread out under the man's body.

'Jesus.' Watkins gasped, standing on tiptoe, looking over Fagan's shoulder.

Fagan studied the body. 'It doesn't look as if he put up much of a fight.' The t-shirt the man was wearing had a gash sliced through the material. The blood had stopped pumping out of the wound.

A filthy worktop contained a kettle with two mugs. Along with piles of washing up, packaging and rotting food that was mixed in with the stench of a decaying body.

Fagan stepped back from the doorway. ‘Call this in.’

CHAPTER 23

2:25pm

'Can I have your attention, ladies and gentlemen, please!' Fagan shouted over the din.

Residents had been evacuated from the building while forensics searched the flat where Smith lived. Fagan and Watkins were now dressed in white forensic jumpsuits.

'When are we going to be allowed back in?' A man shouted.

'I'm afraid you won't be allowed into your properties for some time.'

'That's bollocks. It's not like he died in my flat.'

'Who says someone is dead?' Fagan asked, knowing full well the residents weren't all that stupid.

'I think it's obvious that Smithy is dead. Or you wouldn't have all those coppers in white jump suits wandering about on the stairs.' The man pointed at the building that had a glass front exposing the staircase. Forensic officers were scouring the staircase. Gathering anything that might aid them in their investigation.

Fagan knew he could not sugar-coat anything.

'Is it Ross Smith or not?' The man demanded to know.

Fagan inhaled. 'We have found a body at number thirty-three.'

'Then it's him. He was the only one who lived there.'

The residents who were present nodded.

'It was only a matter of time before that dull fucker overdosed. He was off his face most days.'

'Just hurry up with CSI Abergavenny in there.' Another resident called out. 'I don't want to miss *Emmerdale.*'

Fagan glared at the woman. 'Seriously, that's all you can think of right now is a bloody soap opera.'

The woman showed no sympathy. 'It ended on a cliffhanger last night.'

Another resident looked at her. 'Haven't you ever heard of catchup, you fucking retard?'

'Fuck off, weirdo. Everyone knows you're a pervert with that camera outside your door.'

'It's there to monitor twats like you who do nothing but scrounge off the system. Pisses me off when the likes of you make out you're working class when you don't even work. I work my arse off every day on the factory floor so that my taxes can pay for your handouts.' The man spat on the floor. 'Fucking benefit class scum.'

'Well, I'm not standing out here all night long.' A scruffy-looking man complained. 'I've got things to get on with.'

Fagan stared at the man. 'I'm sure Facebook can take a back door for a few hours, sir. Do you have a phone you could entertain yourself with?'

The man waved an ancient phone in the air. 'I fucking hate staring at a small screen. There'll be a generation of people with eye problems in another twenty years.'

'Look, officers will take your names and just give you a quick interview.' Watkins said.

The air filled with the voices complaining residents.

Fagan looked at the man who had a CCTV camera outside his front door. 'Let's start with you, shall we?'

The man stepped forward willingly.

Fagan led him away from the din of shouting residents. 'Did I hear that woman say you had a camera outside your door?'

'Yeah, it's there to keep an eye on people like her.' The

man pointed to the woman he had insulted. She was heckling a uniformed officer who was trying to get some sense out of her.

'Name?' Fagan barked.

'Ryan, Ryan Butler.'

'Which number to you live at Ryan?'

'Number thirty on the second floor.'

Fagan jotted notes on his pad. 'What did you mean when you said you used it to monitor people?'

'Don't take any notice of what that stupid cow said. Fucking benefit class, always acting like they're victims.'

'Let's not turn this into a political debate shall we Ryan.' Fagan noticed the expensive smart phone in his hand. 'Can you link up to the camera outside your front door with that?'

The man smiled and activated the app that controlled the camera. 'Always happy to help the police.'

'Did you know Ross Smith?'

'Not really. I kept away from him. I barely acknowledged his existence when he was not high as a kite. Fucking hate the druggies in this town. They fucking leave needles everywhere in the flats. Mostly by my front door.'

'I suspect you're not popular having a CCTV pointed at the hallway.'

'People complain, but I don't give a shit. I have even had a few cameras destroyed. The dull fuckers who break them don't realise everything is uploaded to the cloud.'

'Did Ross Smith ever cause any trouble in the block?'

'Not really, just fucking annoying with his drug habit. A mate goes there every day and do whatever these crackheads do all day long. I have lived here for over ten years. It used to be a decent block. Everyone used to have jobs. Real friendly neighbours and all that. But then the council moved these benefit class in. They don't give a fuck about anything but themselves.'

'What footage have you got from the last few hours?' Fagan said, cutting him off. The man seemed obliging enough to help. But Fagan sensed a hatred embedded within him. Hatred to anyone who didn't work and relied on the benefit system.

'Here we go.' Butler said, pointing at the screen. 'There's that stupid bitch I was arguing with earlier. She's going out for her cheap wine and discount rollies.'

'Discount rollies?'

'The ice cream man sells more than just ice cream. I can't stand the bloke. Always giving the kids free bubble-gum. They stick it to the handrails on the stairs, fucking disgusting stuff. But he also sells cheap fags and other items, if you catch my drift.'

'Drugs?' Fagan stated.

The man nodded. 'Been doing it for years. I have tweeted local police loads of times about it. But you've turned a blind eye.'

Fagan realised this man was also prejudiced towards the police.

'Here we go.' Butler pointed. 'That's Smith's drug partner. They're always getting off their faces together. Wouldn't be surprised if they get up to other stuff as well.'

Butler annoyed Fagan with his constant criticism of everyone. He had encountered people like Butler loads of times. The type that worked all day for a minimum wage and then look down on those who they classed as lower lifeforms. It was the sign of the times, modern Britain today. 'One of your neighbours who lives on the top floor next to Smith said that it all kicked off this morning. And that he was arguing with another man.'

Butler nodded. 'It kicked off big time.' He pointed at the screen. 'There he goes, Darren Stephens on his way up for his daily fix.'

Fagan frowned. Butler seemed to relish putting people down.

'And here they are, twenty minutes later. Bloody arguing outside my door.'

Fagan watched the video of the men arguing about drug-related issues. It was obvious Stephens owed Smith money for drugs he brought a few weeks previous. Both men seemed high, too high to punch each other. Stephens stormed off, leaving Smith alone in the corridor. He looked up at the CCTV camera before sticking his middle finger up before speaking. 'I'll ave you, Butler.' Smith sneered at the camera.

Fagan smiled briefly at the reference to the popular 1970s sitcom, *On the Buses*.

'There's not a lot after that. Just an Amazon delivery person.' Butler revealed. 'The woman who lived on the same floor and then you lot.'

Fagan watched a person in a jacket and baseball cap rush past the camera. The courier was carrying a box with the distinctive Amazon logo on it. Whoever it was kept their head down, making sure not to show their face. The figure was aware of the camera. Fagan also noted he or she wearing gloves.

'That Amazon delivery person took their time.' Butler pointed out. 'They must have been a good ten minutes delivering their parcel.'

Fagan continued to watch the video as the courier came into frame again, hurrying past the camera. This time having their back to the camera. Fagan also notice the courier no longer had the box. 'I need you to send a copy of this video to Gwent police.'

'Yeah sure.'

Watkins exited the main entrance of the block of flats.

A few of the residents heckled him as he walked towards Fagan and Butler. 'Boss, CSI wants a word.'

Fagan nodded, glancing at Butler. 'I don't suppose you know where this Darren Stephens lives?'

Butler nodded. 'In one of the flats, by the chippy. Don't know the number, but someone is bound to.'

'Thanks.'

'So how long are you going to be? I need to get online and tell everyone about this.'

Fagan shook his head. 'First, Mr Butler, you will not spread gossip through social media. As for how long we're going to be.' Fagan shrugged. 'About as long as a piece of string, I'm afraid.'

Butler frowned.

Fagan and Watkins returned to Smith's flat. A CSI was photographing Smith's body. The flat felt cramped with so many CSI officers searching the place. A CSI appeared out of the living room.

'What have you got?'

'Your typical drug habitat.' The CSI answered. 'Local drug enforcement officers will be happy. There's enough crack in that living room to supply the town's addicts for months. Smith was both an addict and a supplier by the looks. There's also nearly eight grand in fifty-pound notes. But that's not the best part of this. If you'll follow me to the kitchen, I have something very interesting to show you.'

Fagan followed the forensic into the kitchen. The photographer stood over the body, taking detailed pictures of the deep stab wound at the base of Smith's spine.

'Give us a moment will you Ted.' The CSI asked.

The photographer stepped out of the kitchen.

The CSI knelt down by Smith's body, pointing at the wound in his back. 'A very nasty way to die. Poor fucker didn't stand a chance. All it took was one thrust of the dagger.'

'Dagger?' Fagan said.

The CSI nodded, running his finger down the wound. 'This tear is approximately ten inches long. It is very similar to the wound on Professor Turner's body. If you look closely, you can see black flecks on the wound. It's a similar wound found Turner's body. The black flecks are from the blade of the dagger that has been sharpened to carry out this murder.'

Fagan looked around the kitchen. A blooded piece of kitchen towel was scrunched up.

'As you can see, the murderer wiped the blade clean on the towel.'

Fagan studied the way Smith's body had fallen. He was facing the cluttered worktop. 'He was entertaining the murderer.'

'How do you mean, boss?' Watkins asked.

Fagan looked at the two mugs on the worktop. A jar of coffee and a battered-looking sugar tin sat next to the mugs. Fagan took a step forward. 'The murderer entered the flat and engaged him in a conversation. Long enough for Smith to offer his killer a cup of coffee.' Fagan looked towards a small circular glass top kitchen table. Like the worktop it was cluttered with rubbish. The Amazon box the courier had was on top of the rubbish. A space had been cleared on the table to make room for something. One of two kitchen chairs had been placed against the wall. The other chair was tucked under the table. 'Whoever murdered Smith was sitting here.' Fagan pointed to the chair. 'The moment Smith turned his back on his killer to make the coffee, they struck.' Fagan walked from the kitchen into the hallway, looking towards the front door. 'There's no chain on the door, meaning Smith just opened the door. Plus, if Smith was off his head, he wouldn't have been able to put up any kind of fight. It would have been very easy for the murderer to have gained access to this flat.' He stepped back into the kitchen. 'It has to be the person captured on the CCTV camera downstairs. The one carrying the Amazon box.' He pointed at the box sat on the table.

'Containing the dagger.' Watkins guessed.

Fagan nodded.

'It makes little sense, boss. Why take the dagger? Why not just leave it in the victim?'

'Because Smith is collateral damage.' He looked at Watkins. 'I don't have all the answers just yet, but I am beginning to create a picture here.'

'Are you at least going to tell me what you're thinking?'

'Not until all the pieces of this puzzle are in place.'

'Do you have any idea who the murderer is?'

'I have a list of suspects, but no proof.'

Watkins pointed back towards the kitchen. 'What has Smith got to do with this?'

'I think that whoever murdered him didn't want him identifying a major player in this crime. And his murder, although unplanned, was necessary to stop him from talking. What did Bowman say earlier? Some bloke had paid Smith five grand to break into the museum.'

'That's a lot of money, especially cash.' Watkins pointed out. 'Five grand isn't exactly an amount you can draw out from the cashpoint at Morrisons.'

'No it isn't.' Fagan said. 'Let's bring Thackery in for questioning. We're not going to arrest him. It's just a routine enquiry.'

'He should be at White Castle now, looking for another clue to that buried treasure. I'll bring him in.' Watkins turned and left the flat.

Fagan returned to the kitchen and looked down at

Smith. 'Poor bastard didn't have a clue that what he did a few years ago would lead to this. Druggie or no druggie, he didn't deserve to die like this.'

'I also found something else that I found on Turner's body yesterday.' The CSI pointed to the victim's tracksuit bottoms. 'Remember those seeds I found?'

'Yeah.'

'If you look, there is a similar seed on the victim's clothing. I'll phone the lab later on to see what kind of seed it is.'

Fagan nodded and took a last look at the body before leaving the flat.

CHAPTER 24

Newport Central HQ – 3:13pm

'Thank you for coming down to speak with us, Mr Thackery.' Fagan said politely.

'What exactly am I doing here?' Thackery asked.

'We just want to ask you some questions regarding an incident a few hours ago.'

'What incident?' Thackery said nervously. 'I have been nowhere else but at the dig site. So whatever you are about to accuse me of, you better be prepared to be fucked by a very expensive lawyer.'

Fagan studied Thackery's tone. 'First of all Mr Thackery, we are not here to accuse you of anything. But, an incident has occurred within the past few hours in Abergavenny. What I would like to ask you is, did you know a man by the name of Ross Smith?'

'No, who the hell is that?' Thackery answered quickly.

'Mr Smith was found murdered at his flat on Old Tavern way.'

'Why has any of this got to do with me?' Thackery shrugged. 'I don't know who this bloke is you just mentioned. As I just said. I have been at that bloody dig site for the last several hours. I'd appreciate it if you would let me get back there before they find the second marker.'

'Why the rush?' Watkins asked. 'You are one of the backers for the dig. I'm sure you are kept up to date on everything.'

Thackery glared at him. 'I just want to get back to the

site before that prick from the Vatican finds the second marker. I'm already pissed off that Turner has already hidden stuff from me.'

'Are you referring to the sword and chest he found?'

'Yes, I am.'

'Sounds to me Mr Thackery, that you're the kind of man that doesn't like to be conned. But is quite happy stabbing others in the back.'

Thackery rolled his eyes. 'Oh, here we go. I bet that bitch Sarah York has been slagging me off about what happened ten years ago, hasn't she? Turner knew what I was like when he made the deal with me. I suppose she hasn't mentioned that Turner kept some valuables he found at that dig. The Templars were just as bad as everyone else. They plundered the Holy Land for all kinds of things. You two need to brush up on your history sometime. Turner lied to me from day one about this dig. It's clear that all he wanted was my money. Shithead thought he could sneak things away under my nose.'

'That shithead you just referred to was brutally murdered.' Fagan pointed out. 'Did he deserve that as well?'

'No, he did not. Look, I know where you are going with this.'

'And where exactly are we going, Mr Thackery?' Watkins asked.

'You think I had a motive to murder Turner. I may be an arsehole sometimes, but I am no murderer.'

At last, something we can all agree on. Fagan thought. 'What exactly are your plans regarding the dig, Mr Thackery? I thought you were only interested in the journal that Turner kept.'

'Of course I am.'

'Why is that exactly?'

'Because it contains other maps and clues to other lost treasures, including.' Thackery stopped.

'Including what Mr Thackery?'

Thackery drew a breath. 'I take it both of you have heard of Tutankhamun?'

Watkins and Fagan nodded.

'Last November marked one hundred years since they discovered the tomb. For several years, archaeologists have been banging on about several other chambers that have yet to be discovered. Apparently, one of those chambers could contain his wife, Nefertiti.'

Come on, another bloody history lesson. Fagan frowned.

'When Turner's mentor, Norman Cuthbert, accessed the chamber with Howard Carter, they found a stone tablet that instructed how to find this hidden chamber. Carter asked Cuthbert to sketch the tablet in detail before it was destroyed. Carter knew it would only be a matter of time before he would lose control of the dig. That's why he destroyed the tablet. He thought he could return to the dig with new information about the hidden chamber. But he never did. His backer, Lord Carnarvon, died not long after they had discovered the tomb. There's been a lot of talk about the curse of the mummy and all that crap. Carter died penniless. That's not how I'm going out.'

'But you're not an archaeologist, Mr Thackery.' Fagan pointed out. 'You wouldn't have just been able to go there and start digging up Tut's tomb.'

'No, but the information in that journal is worth millions to the right buyer.' Thackery paused. 'A few years back, when Turner first showed me the journal, he showed me the tablet that Cuthbert had sketched. Archaeologists think there is a hidden chamber or even several chambers undiscovered. They would contain treasures that even Carter wouldn't have been able to imagine. Engineers having been allowed into the tomb with ground penetrating radar and believe there are other chambers that could be packed with treasure.'

'You just mentioned that Turner showed you the journal a while back. Exactly when was this?' Watkins asked.

Thackery thought for several moments. 'I reckon summer 2019, maybe early autumn.'

'And that's when he came to you for funding for the dig out at Bont.'

'Yeah, it took a while to organise, but when we got the go ahead, covid hit. So that was it for the time being. Game over. I tried to start up the dig last year, but there were still too many restrictions in place. It wasn't until several weeks ago we could get things going.' Thackery inhaled. 'Now that Turner is dead, there's no way I'll be able to get my hands on that journal. I bet that stupid bitch of his has hidden it away, so that she'll be able to claim it all.'

'Is everything about profit to you, Mr Thackery?' Fagan asked.

'Yes, it is. Let me tell you something. It's every man for himself these days. You have to be ruthless in everything you do.'

'What was the deal you made with Romano?'

'Just that he could have the splinter thing he's been going on about for the last few years.'

'But he was also interested in getting his hands on Turner's journal. How were you both going to share the information?'

'We were going to break down the journal. The bits that contained any reference to religious artefacts the Vatican was going to keep. And the other stuff like King Tut's tomb belonged to me.'

'Let's get back to why we called you down here.'

Watkins said. 'You maintain that you have no idea who this Ross Smith is.'

'No, I don't know why you've bothered dragging me down here.'

'The reason we've dragged you down here, is because we've reason to believe that Mr Smith was murdered with the same type of dagger as Professor Turner. Only, the murderer took the dagger with them.'

Thackery shifted in his chair. 'I have no idea who this Smith bloke is. So if you don't mind I want to get back to the dig. If you have any more questions for me, then you'll have to tell me in advance. I am not saying anything else without my solicitor.'

Fagan considered the information Thackery had given. 'Ok, thanks for speaking to us Mr Thackery.'

Thackery looked startled momentarily. 'That's it? You drag me all the way down here to ask me a couple of questions.'

Fagan smiled. 'We're just making sure no stones are left unturned.'

Thackery stood, throwing his jacket on. 'Yeah, well, I have more important things to do.'

'We'll arrange transport back to the dig site.'

Thackery acted as if he was the only one in the room. He turned and marched towards the door.

'He's full of shit?' Fagan said as soon as he was out of earshot.

'Well, it's obvious he didn't murder Ross Smith. So that just dumps us back to square one.'

Fagan hated the fact that Watkins was right. 'None of it makes sense. What are we missing here? All the prime suspects who would have wanted Turner dead are right in front of us. It's almost like a classic whodunit. You have a greedy businessman, a priest who just wants to get his hands on some mythical treasure. And to top it all off, you have the ambitious assistant who wants to jump into Turner's shoes. And let's not forget Dayton and Spooner and their deal with Romano.'

Watkins' phone vibrated. 'This is Watkins. Ok, well.' Watkins listened. 'It was a long shot, anyway.' He ended the call. 'That was Brooks. They have arrested Darren Stephens. The trouble is he's too off his head to give a viable interview.'

Fagan shook his head dismissively. 'It's not Stephens, it has to be the Amazon delivery driver. We'll get hold of uniform and get them to knock on every door within view of that block of flats. To see if anyone has CCTV cameras facing that building. Call Brooks back and tell him to get down here for a briefing.'

CHAPTER 25

3:56pm

Fagan stared at the incident board. Normally, in most murder cases he had worked over the years, there would be a lot more information available. However, a lack of suspects made it impossible to make any educated guesses on who the killer could be. 'I don't believe this. I find it hard to grasp that we have two dead people, which at first glance have no connection. So questions. What connects the murder of a renowned archaeologist with the murder of a local drug addict?' He looked at Brooks. 'What do we know about Smith?'

'Thirty-eight-year-old Ross Smith. Has a string of offences as long as your arm. Started out small time. First offence was shoplifting from Farmfoods when they used to be opposite Tesco. Two GBH charges against a past girlfriend. Three convictions for possession of illegal substances, before his first imprisonment for intent to supply.'

'When was that?' Fagan asked.

Brooks checked his notes. 'In 2012, Smith served twenty months of a four-year prison sentence. Was jailed again towards the end of 2017 possessing class A substances. Released in May 2019, again, on good behaviour.'

Fagan looked at Watkins. 'Shortly after his release, Bowman employed him for several months until he got caught stealing a collection box. Bowman fires him. Sometime later Smith confesses to Bowman that he broke into the museum.'

'Someone who paid him five grand.' Watkins added.

Fagan scribbled notes down on the whiteboard. He stepped back, conjuring the image of a jigsaw puzzle in his mind. 'For a moment, let's focus on the murder weapon. Believed to be one of four daggers stolen from the local museum in January 2020. The daggers were part of an exhibition which was due to kick off at the end of March of that year. Boris Johnson puts the country on lockdown on March 20th. Everything shuts down, including the museum.' Fagan checked his notes on his phone. 'The name of the museum curator was Tony James.'

'The man who dropped dead in the middle of his living room.' Brooks mentioned.

Fagan looked at Brooks. 'What do you know?'

'I was the officer who found him.'

'Ok, spill the beans Brooks. Everything you can remember.'

'It was May 2020. His daughter made the call to the police station. She was worried she couldn't get an answer from her dad when she knocked on his door.'

'Didn't she have a front door key to her father's property?'

'No.'

'Where did he live?'

'In an old cottage on Chain Road.'

'That's at the foot of the Deri, off the beaten track a bit.' Watkins said.

'I used to run along that route at school when they made us do cross-country. Perfect place for a murder.' Fagan said.

'That was my thinking at the time.' Brooks revealed.

'Explain.'

'The bloke died suddenly. The coroner concluded he

had a heart attack.'

'But you thought different.' Watkins concluded.

Brooks shook his head. 'No, but his daughter was convinced he was murdered. She pestered us for a few weeks after his death. She was convinced that someone was in his house when he died. I said I'd look into it.'

'Did you?' Fagan asked.

'I didn't get the chance. The police were down to the bare minimum. The autopsy on James' body was basic. The coroner said he died of a massive heart attack. When I spoke to his daughter, she said he'd been for his yearly medical a few weeks before we went into lockdown. His doctor had given him a clean bill of health. She also presented evidence to the police.'

'Where is it?'

'The police refused to take it for fear of catching covid. As far as I'm aware, she held on to it.'

'Was James buried or cremated?'

'Cremated.'

'Shit.' Fagan cursed.

'Everyone was cremated during the early days of lockdown.'

Fagan scribbled James' name on the board and put a question mark next to it.

'What do we have here? One dead museum curator. A dead archaeologist and a local drug addict.' Watkins said, staring at the whiteboard. 'The CSI claimed that Smith could have been murdered by one of the other missing daggers.'

'But why murder the curator? If the daggers had already been stolen a few months earlier.' Brooks questioned.

Fagan recalled the conversation he had the previous day with Thomas. 'Because James text someone. Saying he knew who stole the daggers. But James never text back to say who stole them. Let's not forget we have Lord Barry, who we have yet to speak with. He had an argument with James about the daggers a few months before the exhibition was going ahead. Plus, we know Lord Barry had an argument with Professor Turner about the dig. We're also nowhere near proving that James was murdered because of those daggers.'

'You don't suppose it was lord Barry who paid Smith five grand for information about the museum's security, do you, boss?'

'It's another line of enquiry.'

'You realise Lord Barry is in his nineties.' Brooks said. 'My daughter visited his manor house at Skenfrith earlier this year with her school. My daughter said they walked around the ruins of an old abbey.'

Fagan felt his heart sink. 'Ok, but it's still a line of enquiry I'm going to follow. What about Turner's vehicle?'

'It's still missing.'

'Shit.' Fagan seethed. 'Every time we think we've got a hold on this, it just slaps us back in the face.'

'So do we call it a day?' Watkins said.

Fagan looked at him. 'Why, you have somewhere to be, do you?'

'No, but you said it yourself. This case is doing our heads in.'

'I can keep going on this if you want sir.' Brooks offered. 'I'll dig out the case file involving the death of James to see if I may have missed something.'

'Ok, but don't leave it too late.'

CHAPTER 26

Aldo's Italian restaurant – 7:45pm

Fagan savoured the last fork of spaghetti. 'That's the best Italian food I've had in a while.'

Amanda smiled. 'I do an even better lasagne.' She winked.

'I love lasagne.' Fagan said. 'I used to eat at a restaurant in Liverpool that made superb lasagne.'

'I make my own with all locally sourced products, mushrooms, homegrown tomatoes and peppers, goose grass.'

Fagan recoiled. 'What an earth is goose grass?'

Amanda giggled. 'It's a plant that grows everywhere. It sticks to your clothing.'

'Ah, I think I know what you mean.'

'Abergavenny has a great selection of restaurants these days. The food festival has opened this town up. It's known as the Hay festival for food.'

'I have read a few articles about the food festival over the years. Had been meaning to come back before.'

'So why did you move back to Abergavenny?'

'I guess I missed home. Plus over three decades serving with Merseyside police finally took its toll. The pandemic has taken so much away and changed the police force beyond recognition. When I first joined up, it was a different force. It was emerging out of the Sweeny era.'

Amanda laughed. 'I loved John Thaw as Inspector Morse.' She looked at Fagan. 'So, what kind of Detective

Inspector are you? Are you the Jack Regan type? Or are you the more reserved Inspector Morse?'

Fagan smiled. 'Actually, I always thought of myself more as Columbo.'

'One of the few American detectives I love to watch.'

'I even brought the same colour trench coat as Columbo. And I still have it.'

'I used to watch *Murder she Wrote* with my grandmother. I fancied myself as a bit of a Jessica Fletcher type.' Amanda looked out of the restaurant. Shoppers were walking in and out of Tesco directly opposite. 'Must be quite a change for you, coming from a big city to a small town.'

'You'd think, but people are people wherever you go. I came home to serve out my remaining years in relative peace and quiet. I guess I'd fallen in love with the idea that Abergavenny would have less crime and more of a community spirit. The last thing I expected was an old flame from over thirty-five years ago turning up dead.'

'The body in the park?' Amanda questioned.

Fagan nodded.

'You caught the killer though. That has to count for something.'

'I suppose, but in doing so, I have exorcised a few ghosts.'

'You'll be surprised how many small towns harbour ghosts. No town is perfect. Besides Liverpool couldn't have been so bad. You stuck it out for over thirty years.'

Fagan nodded. 'Liverpool is a great city, full of great people. But like other cities around the UK, it's also seen a rise in violent crime.' Fagan picked up a glass of red wine, savouring the taste. 'What attracted you to Abergavenny?'

'My love of history more than anything, I suppose. This area is a rich source of historical events. From the reformation, to Hitler's right-hand man, Rudolf Hess, being imprisoned here during the war. You'll be surprised how many people have watched the History channel, but still have no idea he spent over three years at Maindiff Court. I researched him when I first moved to Abergavenny. No records remained at the hospital. I spoke to the daughter of a guard that was assigned to him for over a year. Her father would tell her what an ordinary man he was.'

'Ordinary, save for the fact he was Hitler's right-hand man.'

Amanda finished her glass of wine.

'May I?' Fagan offered, picking up the bottle.

Amanda smiled back. 'You may?'

Fagan poured.

'I take it the life of a Detective Inspector is a lonely one.'

'What makes you say that?' Fagan poured the remaining wine into his glass.

'First and most obvious, you're not wearing a wedding ring. And secondly, you're out on a date with me, so you're unattached.'

'Is that what you're calling this, a date?' Fagan winked at Amanda.

She drank from her glass, maintaining eye contact.

'I have had a few relationships in the past. I was with another DI for over ten years. But in the end, the job came first for both of us. We drifted apart. When I moved back home, I thought that old love could be rekindled.' Fagan stared at his glass. Rebecca's face became as clear to him as the day he left her. 'But sadly, people move on with their lives. What about you, Amanda? I'm sure there were plenty of suitors in Cambridge.'

'Good lord no. Well, I had a relationship, but it ended badly and basically left a nasty taste in my mouth.' Amanda finished the last of her wine. 'I guess we're both the same in many ways. Not wanting to weigh our lives down too much.'

'Maybe.' Fagan considered. 'But sometimes I wonder what my life would have been like if I had never left Abergavenny.'

'Why did you leave?'

'I had no choice. Back in the day, I was a very bad boy. It was either leave or spend most of my life behind bars.'

'Do you believe in fate?'

'As in destiny and all that.' Fagan shook his head. 'I've encountered a lot of people over the years who have done shit things. People do stuff because they want to do stuff, including murder. Not because of some message from a higher power.'

'Speaking of which, how is the big case going?'

'It's not going anywhere. We have questioned people, but no one is in the frame.'

'Someone must have had good cause to murder Professor Turner.'

'My DS mentioned someone called Dan Brown yesterday. He said the way Turner was laid out was like something out of one of his books.'

Amanda nodded. 'I was reading a press report earlier. Now that you think of it, this resembles something out of the *Da Vinci Code*.'

'I have no clue what you're talking about. I have never seen the film or read the book.' Fagan confessed.

Amanda laughed. 'Don't worry, I won't hold it against you. In the *Da Vinci Code* the protagonist Robert Langdon finds evidence that Jesus may have had a bloodline. I'm a bit of a Dan Brown fanatic.'

'I thought Jesus died a virgin.'

'That's what people with faith will tell you. But in Dan Brown's book, Mary Magdelene and Jesus were supposed to have done the dirty and had children. And that a bloodline made it to modern day.'

Fagan digested the information. 'What do you like to do in your spare time, Amanda?'

She seemed thrown off by the question. 'I uh, I'm a bit of a forager?'

'Forager?'

Amanda smiled. 'My grandmother was a herbalist. She was very much into her natural healing remedies. The countryside where she lived in Cambridgeshire was rich in plant life. She taught me everything about natural medicines. I loves living in this part of the world. The surrounding valley offers an abundance of foraging opportunities. You would have thought with the cost-of-living crisis people would be out foraging, but they're not. I rarely rely on the supermarkets for any kind of vegetable. I grow almost everything I need at home.'

'People haven't got time to grow their own. Social media is far more important than digging in the garden. We live in a shallow society of whingers who want life handed to them on a plate.'

'Wow, that's quite an opinion you have there, Detective Inspector Fagan.'

'I guess because I have worked all my life, I don't have much of an opinion of those who don't work. Many of the crimes I dealt with back in Liverpool happened in communities with high unemployment. I have met many people who have never worked. Sometimes second or third generation families who do nothing but scrounge off the system.' Fagan paused. 'You mention your grandmother. What about your parents?'

'They died when I was a baby. Car accident.'

'I'm sorry.'

Amanda shook her head. 'I have no memory, so there's

nothing to miss. When my grandmother died in 2017, I was devastated. My entire world seemed to crumble. She was everything to me. All of a sudden, Cambridge became bland. There was nothing left for me.'

'Still, bit of a leap from Cambridge to Abergavenny.'

Amanda nodded. 'It was, but I don't regret it. Monmouthshire is rich in myth, legend and natural beauty that most seem to ignore. I like to go walking on the mountains locally. When the pandemic hit, it was chaos. Suddenly, people wanted to see the great outdoors. Mostly for the first time in their lives.'

'A lot of things were suddenly taken away. You couldn't jump on a plane and go abroad anymore. You couldn't just hop in the car. You had to stay at home. I used to work with a DI who was used to going to India every year with her husband. They holidayed in the UK. She absolutely loved it.'

'There are some people who have reconnected with this country. But now that things are more or less back to normal, people have returned to old habits.'

Fagan nodded. 'More or less, people are creatures of habit.'

'What about you, Marc? Do you have any interesting pastimes?'

Fagan smiled broadly. 'As a matter of fact, I like jigsaw puzzles. They help me when things become out of focus.'

'How about this? I will cook lasagne for you tomorrow night. I am due to give another talk at the Angel at eight thirty. I should be finished by eight. Perhaps you can come around to my place tomorrow evening and I'll show you how good locally sourced food tastes like.'

Fagan was taken aback by the offer. 'I would love to.'

'Great, you can pick me up at the Angel around half-past nine.'

Fagan nodded enthusiastically. 'What are you talking about tomorrow night?'

'I am going to do a talk on Alice of Abergavenny.'

'Should be another good turnout for you.'

'She was a fascinating character, with all her dark deeds.'

'Sounds like you admire her.'

Amanda looked at Fagan. 'Perhaps. She did terrible things. But in those times, terrible things were part of everyday life. There was no idiot woke brigade to lecture us on how we should live our lives.'

Fagan glanced towards the entrance.

A man walked into the restaurant, looking around. He spotted his target and marched towards a table near the back.

'Detective Inspector Marc Fagan?' He enquired.

Fagan looked up at him. 'That's me.'

'I'm a freelancer working with the Sun. Can you tell me if you have any regrets about the wrongful arrest of Ben Nelson regarding the murder of a local woman?'

Fagan briefly glanced at Amanda. 'Any information regarding that matter is to be handled through the press office in Newport. Not a restaurant in Abergavenny.'

'So this means you will not admit that Mr Nelson's arrest pushed him to try to take his own life?'

Fagan suppressed the urge to get up and punch the gutter journalist. 'Mr Nelson was a suspect in a murder enquiry and was subject to a lawful questioning by the police.'

The journalist flipped open a notebook. 'One Rebecca Jenkins, fifty-four years of age. Wasn't she an ex-girlfriend of yours?'

Fagan almost choked on the last of his wine. 'A girlfriend from almost forty years ago.' He glanced at Amanda again, who had an unsettled expression.

'You've also got a history with Mr Nelson. Weren't you charged with assaulting him twice in the 1980s? The second time you put him in the hospital.'

'So let me get this straight. You have the bloody nerve to wander in here out of the gutter and harass me about an incident that took place decades ago.'

The journalist seemed to ignore Fagan and carried on with his attack.

'Don't you think you should resign after pushing Mr Nelson over the edge, resulting him attempting to take his own life, and streaming it live online?'

'Check your facts. I didn't push anyone into anything. Mr Nelson's arrest was within the boundaries of the law.'

'Is it true that you were jailed between 1983 and 1985 following a violent assault which left a man disabled?'

'A man who has since been arrested and is currently awaiting trial for murder.'

'Why haven't the police issued an apology to Mr Nelson concerning his false arrest?'

'Because he wasn't falsely arrested.' Fagan was tired of the journalist's constant badgering. 'At the time of his arrest, Mr Nelson was a suspect. After being interviewed by local police he was released without charge.'

Amanda slid her chair back. 'I have to meet someone later on. So I'll leave you gents to it.'

'Are we still on for tomorrow?'

'Yeah sure.' Amanda replied half-heartedly.

The journalist smiled at Fagan. 'Ruined your night, have I?'

Fagan squared up to the gutter trash. 'Must be a slow news day for the Sun if they employ morons like you who throw accusations at people they don't even know.'

'I know plenty about you, Detective Fagan. Quite the

hard man back in the day. Prison must have toughened you up.'

'I'll tell you what prison taught me. It taught me to stay out of trouble.'

'Weren't you commended in the Aron Miller case? You were the Detective that broke the parents. After breaking Liam Miller's nose in that punch up during that press conference.'

'I didn't break anything. I operated within the confines of the law. That resulted in putting the sadistic killers of an innocent child away for a long time. But journalists like you don't see things like that. You just want the lowdown on innocent people so you can make their lives a misery.' Fagan barged past the man.

CHAPTER 27

The Cantreff – 8:55pm

'Hey Indiana Jones, over here.' Evans shouted from the lounge after spotting Fagan walk into the bar area.

'He doesn't look too happy.' Edwards remarked.

'You ok Marc.' Jackie asked, holding an empty pint glass.

'Treble brandy.' Fagan demanded.

Evans and Edwards glanced at each other.

'Rough day?' Jackie enquired, expecting to get her head chewed off. She placed the brandy down on the bar.

'I'll give you one fucking guess.'

'Benny?'

'Benny fucking Nelson.' Fagan bolted his glass in one go.

'I take it you've seen the interview then?' Jackie said.

Fagan looked at her. 'No, but I've just had a twat of a tabloid journalist ruin a perfectly good date.'

Evans smiled. 'You didn't waste any time, did you Fagan. You haven't been home long and you're already getting yourself laid.'

Fagan cast Evans a frown. 'It wasn't like that.'

'It never is.'

'I had to stop myself from punching his bloody lights out. Making out that I was some kind of violent thug.'

'You kind of were back in the day.' Evans shrugged.

'You're not helping Jamie. You know that, don't you?' Jackie scalded him.

'What interview?' Fagan asked.

Jacking reached for a tablet she kept behind the bar and

activated it. 'He was on the sofa with Isaac and Lucy this morning. The twat has already uploaded it to his YouTube channel.'

Fagan tapped the play icon.

'Our next guest has a harrowing story to tell. This is Ben Nelson. For years, Ben has been the target of vicious bullies in his hometown of Abergavenny in south Wales.'

'Vicious bullies.' Fagan exclaimed. 'Is he having a fucking laugh?'

'Ben, please, in your own words. Tell us about your experiences.'

'Thanks for having me, Lucy and Isaac.' Nelson glanced at the camera, flashing a grin.

'Cocky twat.' Fagan stated.

'For years, the people of Abergavenny have both mentally and physically abused me. I have lived in the town all my life. My family has been the subject of constant ridicule and harassment. My father had a heart attack because of the stress he suffered because of people's horrible behaviour. I was left all alone. But it didn't stop people from carrying on with the abuse. If there was ever a crime in the town, I was always the one who was accused of it.' Nelson wiped a tear away with a handkerchief. 'I have tried to live a normal life in the town, but people just won't leave me alone. I could never find work because my reputations seems to follow me wherever I go.'

'Can I ask Ben, why haven't you moved away?' Lucy asked.

'I love where I live. I grew up in Abergavenny. Why should I move away? I have done nothing wrong. There are people who have been spreading rumours about me for years. Accusing me of being the town's pervert.'

'A few months ago, Ben's life took a turn for the worst when he was arrested and accused of murdering a local woman. Ben, tell us about when you were arrested. What was it like?'

'It was my worst nightmare Isaac. The police just turned up at my house and dragged me away to be interviewed. I was held for twelve hours and questioned repeatedly about a murder I didn't commit.'

'What a load of bollocks.' Fagan seethed, pausing the video. 'We released him without charge. Then the next day, when we arrested him for having that shed up at the allotment, he suddenly wanted to confess to Becky's murder. Just to deflect attention away from what we had found.'

'Speaking of which, did you at least charge him for what he had in that shed?' Edwards asked.

'I spoke to my CO last week about it. He said they were still assessing the material they found at the shed.'

'But he had child porn in there?' Jackie stated.

'Not according to the evidence presented so far. And now that his wife is no longer in the country, we can't even question her about whether Benny was pimping her out.'

'Justin was paying to have sex with her. Surely that's enough.'

Fagan shook his head. 'Justin has clamped up on us.'

'Why?' Evans asked.

'I think he's been leaned on by that fancy solicitor Nelson has representing him. Promised an early release, probably. Justin didn't aid in the murder of Becky, but he helped with the disposal of her body. I'm guessing Nelson's solicitor has already brokered a deal. Part of that deal involves Pike not mentioning a word about Nelson pimping out his wife. We have traced the number plates of all the vehicles that were caught on your CCTV.' Fagan looked at Evans. 'But so far, no one has provided any kind of information that proved useful.' Fagan hit the play icon again.

Nelson continued with his lies. 'My wife, who is pregnant with our first child, has had to go back home to Indonesia for her own safety. This has had a profound effect on my mental health.'

The camera switched to a tearful TV presenter.

'Jesus, he's laying this on thick, isn't he?'

'Fucking wanker.' Evans stated.

The TV presenter looked at the camera with a grim face. 'After Benny was falsely accused of a murder and released without charge, he returned home. He then tried to take his own life, streaming it live on social media. Benny, what was going through your mind?'

'I just wanted to end it all. A lifetime's worth of ridicule finally caught up with me. I felt trapped. Like there was no way out. I contacted my wife and said goodbye to her. Then I took a bottle of antidepressants I had been taking for years. They say hindsight is a wonderful thing, but that's not what I was thinking about at the time. All I wanted to do was make the pain go away.'

'These antidepressants, they were there to help you through the daily trauma you have to face.'

Nelson nodded. 'Without them, I wouldn't have been able to carry on.'

'During your arrest Ben, there was a police officer who interviewed you. You had a personal connection with this man.'

'Yes, but for legal reasons, I am not allowed to name him.'

Fagan clutched the tablet, glaring at the screen.

'The detective inspector who interviewed me knew me from my childhood. On two occasions he assaulted me resulting in me spending time in hospital. He is one of the people who made my life a total misery. When I was led into the interview room, it just all came back when I saw that man sitting there.'

'You lying twat Nelson!' Fagan yelled at the screen.

'And what do you want to say to the people of your home town?'

'I just want to let everyone know I have never been a threat to anyone. My family has had to carry the burden of being ridiculed for decades.'

'There is also a petition online to urge the government to act regarding the detective who interviewed you.'

'Yes, it already has twelve thousand signatures. I am hoping to get to a hundred thousand for the authorities to act. To look into the conduct of this detective.'

'Ben, thank you for joining us on the sofa this morning. If any of you have been affected by a lifetime of bullying, please go to our website and click on the link. After the break, cooking with Hilary.'

Evans handed Fagan his phone. 'Since that interview this morning, there's been another ten thousand signatures added to his shitty petition.'

'He's trying to get you booted off the force?' Edwards said.

'They can't boot me out unless there's overwhelming evidence to show misconduct. I did nothing in those interviews that would come anywhere close. Nelson is going for the sympathy vote here. He's using his social media presence to gain support for his twisted little lies.'

'Can't you lot do anything about it?' Jackie said.

Fagan studied the government webpage. 'Welcome to the world of democracy, Jacks. My only saving grace at the moment is that I don't have a social media presence. I can only imagine the nasty little trolls hard at work trying to track me down.' He handed Evans his phone back.

'So what happened to Ross Smith?'

'We found him dead in his flat earlier. That's what happened. We have arrested a suspect, but it will be tomorrow before we will be able to question him.'

'Darren Stephens.' Evans said. 'It's been the talk of the town all day. First that bloke at Skenfrith, now this.'

'Do you know Stephens or Smith?'

Jackie nodded. 'They're both regulars in here. Not every day. Usually when they get paid their dole. Darren puts a fortune in the bandit. They usually sit outside and smoke a spliff, have a couple of pints.'

'Spliff?'

Jackie nodded.

'Look, I know we go way back, but I am still a serving police officer. I can't protect you. So if anyone comes in here when I'm in here and you know they're smoking something they shouldn't be, then you have to keep them out. Trust me Jacks, I've seen too many good officers booted out of the force over the years because they turned a blind eye to family members or close friends doing things they shouldn't have been doing.'

'Ok.' Jackie promised.

'There's no way Darren killed Ross. They were lifelong mates.' Evans remarked.

'He didn't.'

'Then who did?'

'We don't know. The CCTV footage we have is useless. Can any of you think of anyone who'd want to kill him?'

'No, Ross was mostly harmless.' Jackie said. 'He's served time for drugs and everything, but there was no one in this town who hated him that much to want him dead.' Jackie said. 'It's a tragedy what happened to Ross. He was very clever.'

'Clever?' Fagan stated.

'Ross had one of those photographic memories. Before

he got into drugs, he used to captain the pub quiz team. For about five years in a row this pub was Abergavenny's undefeated pub quiz champions.' Jackie pointed to a dusty trophy cup behind the bar. 'Ross had a good job and everything. When his mam died, he went downhill.'

'We think his murder had something to do with the murder out at Skenfrith.'

'What?'

'It's a long story. Until we interview Darren tomorrow, we won't know anything more.'

'Why do you think Ross' death is connected with what happened at Skenfrith?'

'He was apparently paid five grand to break into Abergavenny museum. Some items were stolen, connected with this murder investigation.'

Jackie looked at Edwards wide eyed.

'What?' Fagan noted the look on her face.

'Ross came in here a few years ago. Spreading a lot of cash around. I thought he was back into selling drugs, so I chucked him out.'

'The week after that he was skint again.' Edwards said. 'Moaning about how everyone had taken advantage of him because he had that cash.'

'I know it's a longshot, but did anyone know the man who ran the museum before Amanda Rhys?'

'No, but I know his daughter, Sally. She's a couple of years younger than us. She was devastated by his death. I remember seeing her last year. She said he didn't die in natural circumstances.'

''She thinks he was murdered?' Fagan quizzed.

'She didn't use the word murdered. But because of covid they wouldn't let a doctor do a proper examination of the body. They said it was just a heart attack. He was cremated a week later.'

Fagan scribbled in his notebook. 'Where does Sally live?'

'Up at the Mardy where they built those new houses. I'll text you her number if you need to speak to her.'

'That would be great, thanks Jacks.' Fagan smiled to himself.

'I know that look.' Edwards said, pointing at him. 'You've suddenly realised who the murderer could be.'

Fagan maintained his smile. 'At this moment in time, I am not at liberty to comment on anything.'

'So what did that journalist say to you?' Evans asked.

'He was just sniffing. He probably watched Benny's interview. Being a typical freelancer for the Sun he added two and two and came up with seven.'

'I have a more important question. Who was your date tonight?'

Fagan shrugged. 'Just that woman who runs Abergavenny Museum.'

Edwards smiled. 'She is quite smart. A little too smart for you Fagan.'

'Trust me, I've had some pretty smart women in my time as a copper.'

'Are you seeing her again?'

'As a matter of fact she's invited me over tomorrow to her place.'

'She sounds like a fast mover.' Jackie winked at Fagan. 'So how's the big case going out at Skenfrith?'

'It's not. So far, everyone we've interviewed has a watertight alibi.'

'Have you interviewed everyone?'

'Just about. I'm going to pop in on Lord Barry tomorrow.'

'He's a bit of a weirdo.' Evans said. 'I took a wrong turn one day. I was searching for some cottage in the middle of nowhere. So I knocked on his door to ask for directions. He gave me a right ear bashing for trespassing on his property.'

'I've had plenty of cases like this where there seems no obvious suspects. But usually the killer makes a mistake. Tell you what though, the Vatican has sent a priest to the dig site at Bont.'

'No way.' Evans stated.

Fagan nodded. 'He arrived earlier today. Looking for this so-called splinter of Christ.'

'Do you know who you should talk to?'

'Who?' Fagan sighed, knowing full well Evans was going to say something ridiculous.

'Karl, the conspiracy theorist.'

Fagan thought about the name before twigging. 'Karl Huntley, that pleb who believes in aliens?'

'Bingo.' Evans declared. 'He's a self-published author now. Got a hundred thousand followers on YouTube.'

'I remember that time we went to see *Close Encounters of the Third Kind* with him. He was banging on about aliens for months.'

'He may be a bit out there, but he's well up on his conspiracy theories.'

'It couldn't hurt.' Edwards said. 'Help you look at things from a different angle.'

'I'm not having aliens shoved down my throat.'

'He's not that bad. Karl actually makes a lot of sense about stuff.'

'Yeah, and I bet he's one of these anti-vaxxers.'

'He's not actually. I was talking to him online during the pandemic. He said that some of the conspiracy theories floating around were stupid and harmful.' Evans checked his smart watch. 'He'll probably talk to you now if you want me to call him.'

Fagan considered Evans's proposal. 'Ok, but the moment he starts talking shit, I'll arrest the both of you for wasting police time.' He glanced at Jackie and winked.

'If that doesn't work, go home and do one of those jigsaws. You said it helps you when you have a difficult crime to solve.' Jackie suggested.

'Perhaps I will, after a pint.'

CHAPTER 28

9:45pm

Fagan was already regretting the decision he made an hour earlier. Sitting in what Karl Huntley called his office. Fagan stared at a large poster on the wall. A flying saucer hovering over some trees with the slogan, *I want to believe,* printed in large letters.

Huntley smiled at Fagan as he entered the room with a tray of coffee and biscuits. 'Do you believe?'

Fagan glared back at him.

Huntley held up his hands submissively. 'Ok, I get it. You don't want to talk about UFOs and aliens. What are you here to talk about?' He glanced at Evans, who was sitting in front of a computer playing a classic eighties arcade game. 'Jamie was being cryptic when he called.'

'I take it you heard about the body found at Skenfrith yesterday?'

'Yeah, it's been all over the news. Some Cambridge archaeologist bloke. There's been a lot of chatter on social media about it. I drove by the dig site earlier today at Bont. There's security out there. Have they found anything interesting?'

'A sword and some chest packed with jewellery. But that was back last week.'

Huntley listened enthusiastically.

'We've had a Vatican official turn up today.'

'Why?'

'The Vatican is part funding the dig.'

'Wow, really.' Huntley seemed excited by Fagan's revelation.

'Apparently, something called the splinter of Christ is buried out here somewhere. It's supposed to be part of the cross that Christ was nailed to.'

'Well, if the Vatican has sent someone, there must be some kind of truth to it all.'

'You don't think it could be some centuries old conspiracy.'

'There are loads of conspiracies about the bible. Too many to count.' Huntley picked up a tablet and searched. 'Loads of references on Google to this splinter of Christ.'

'The priest I spoke to earlier said that the splinter has the blood of Christ on it.'

Huntley looked up. 'Interesting, if you're into grail legend and that kind of stuff. The blood of Christ has a lot of meaning. But if what that priest said is true, then the possibilities are endless. However, you have to be a believer to truly benefit from this. If, for argument's sake, this splinter does contain the true blood of Jesus. Then the Vatican will bend over backwards to get their hands on it.' Huntley glanced at Fagan. 'Even murder an archaeologist.'

Fagan inhaled. 'The priest only showed up today.'

'You sure about that? Have you checked his travel records with Interpol? It will all be there to see. Getting his hands on something that may contain the blood of Christ could have huge implications for the Vatican. Let's face it, no one is turning up to church these days. If the Vatican finds something like this, then it will give them a boost. Not to mention a medical cure for every known disease.'

'What do you mean?'

'The bible speaks of Jesus healing the sick with a touch of his hand. Think about it, the blood of Christ has healing properties. Don't tell me you've never seen *Indiana Jones and the last Crusade?'*

'Yeah, but that's just a film.'

'I know that, but the actual blood of Christ could be priceless to the Vatican.'

'You don't believe in that kind of stuff, do you?'

'No. But there are plenty of people who still believe in god.' Huntley stared at the poster on the wall of the flying saucer.

'But you believe in aliens.'

Huntley pointed at the poster. 'UFOs are different. It's not a matter of belief. The fact that we know there are other planets is direct evidence life exists elsewhere. You see, that's the thing. People assume that faith covers just about everything, including aliens. Let me ask you this. How do you know God exists?'

'I'm not really a believer of God or anything like that.'

'The reason the Vatican has sent an investigator all the way to Abergavenny is they are sure that there is truth to the story. Which usually means they have something locked away in that vast secret library of theirs.'

'Secret library?' Fagan dared to ask.

'Don't even get me started on that. The Vatican has been keeping secrets since the time of St Peter himself. Again, if you're a true believer in all that. As for what they keep. It's been the subject of books, films and TV documentaries. Ancient Aliens on the history channel are always going on about the library containing accounts of alien encounters over the centuries. There are those who believe the Vatican has dirt on just about every politician that has ever lived. From kings to presidents. They reckon the archive holds the wealth of Ancient Rome just before it fell. The Vatican doesn't just deal with religious matters. They have a science division that does all kinds of research you wouldn't associate with the Vatican. If they believe this splinter of Christ is covered in his blood, then they can use it for medical research. Cure just about every known disease. Or they could just hide it away like the rest of their dirty little secrets.'

Fagan inhaled.

'Were you hoping for some kind of breakthrough coming to see me?' Huntley smiled.

'This is one of the most unusual murder cases I have had to deal with. Someone had a motive to kill this man.'

'Do you have any other suspects?'

'We have interviewed a few people today. But they all have watertight alibis.'

'Then you need to think outside of the box. Consider possibilities you'd never usually go near.'

Fagan smiled at the poster. 'Like aliens.'

'We all have to have a hobby. Didn't your dad work at the old ammunition factory at Ty-Affan?'

'Yeah, he did. Why do you ask?'

'Got a man working on the inside there. They don't make ammunition anymore. They're into something a little more exotic these days.'

'Exotic?' Fagan repeated.

'Next generation drones. My contact has been working there about five years. He reckons he's seen weird shit there. Strange objects have been sighted over where the factory is. You can't get near it these days. It's fast becoming known as the Area 51 of Monmouthshire.'

Fagan glanced at the poster again.

'Not the homecoming you envisioned I should imagine. Especially with what happened to Rebecca.'

Fagan shook his head.

'Looks like Benny Nelson has it in for you. Creepy little shithead. People call me weird because I'm into aliens. Benny Nelson is downright weird. I remember the hammering you gave him up the Chevron. Probably deserved it.'

Fagan nodded. 'He did.'

'Well sorry I can't be of more help to you. There's definitely something out here worth looking for. Don't give up. The murder of that archaeologist has attracted a lot of attention. That's when the murderer usually makes the mistake.'

'There was me thinking I was the detective.' Fagan looked at Evans. 'Jamie, I'm off.'

'Ok.' Evans replied without looking back at Fagan.

CHAPTER 29

Llanfoist – 10:27pm

Fagan sat down in his comfortable chair, mulling the case over in his mind. He reminisced about his previous life in Liverpool and the cases he was involved in. He recalled a case from the early nineties. A serial killer on the loose in Merseyside targeting prostitutes. As quickly as the case developed. It soon came to a dead stop when the killer, for reasons unknown, stopped killing.

His thoughts turned to the case in hand. He thumbed the screen on his phone after Googling Alice of Abergavenny. There was very little information about her. The woman wasn't as well-known as Tutankhamun, so she didn't have much of an online presence.

Fagan mulled over what he had learnt about Alice. A woman scorned, losing her father before plotting a bloody revenge. Losing her lover in a medieval battle. Beheading seventy prisoners. The images swirled around Fagan's mind like an epic film. A member of the Knights Templar offering Alice a path to glory. Raising an army as they made their way across Europe. Then the march into the Holy land, more killing. More throats slit and decapitated corpses. Raging battles on horseback. Alice leading her army of medieval warriors. Banners fluttering in the wind. Men and armour smashing together, the sound of screams and clashing swords. A nine hundred mile trek across bleak desert. Constantly under attack and having to be ransomed twice. Then returning home, triumphant with the Splinter of Christ as the main prize. Home is where the heart is. Fagan smiled as he remembered a scene from one of his favourite films, *Robin Hood Prince of Thieves*. Kevin Costner jumping off a boat and kissing the sandy shores of Dover, declaring he had returned home. Hundreds of years had passed and people were still looking for the Splinter of Christ. That was dedication, that was faith.

Fagan had told his friends he didn't do social media. However, several years previous Fagan had created a fake profile on Facebook. It was part of an initiative by Merseyside police to view suspects online profiles. Fagan logged on to his fake account and trawled through the newsfeeds. He tapped in a name and looked through the profile. A typical profile, drenched in selfie images and filters. The odd cat picture. But nothing out of the ordinary. As it should be, if you are a murderer wanting to stay hidden in plain sight. Fagan found himself looking through his friend's profiles. He started with Evans. A profile packed with Star Wars memes and film trailer links. Edwards's profile was different. He'd mainly stick to pub landlord matters. Discussing the impact of covid and the cost of living crisis on the pub industry. Displaying pictures of people in the pub. Each picture told a tale, happy faces at parties, sports presentations and quiz nights.

Fagan tapped in Jackie's name. Her main profile picture tugged at his emotions. Jackie and Rebecca cuddled together. A message written at the bottom of the image. Miss you every day hun, xx. Fagan stared at the image for a few minutes. Remembering his childhood in Abergavenny.

He had attended junior school and secondary school with Evans, Tyler and Edwards, and Graham Walker, George's son. Fagan remembered the day the headmaster gathered the school together. 'It is with great sadness that

I have to tell you that Graham Walker passed away yesterday.' Fagan inhaled, suppressing the grief that welled up from deep within. 'I swear, Graham, I'll get that prick, Nelson, for what he did to you.' He whispered.

He typed in Rebecca's name before trawling through her newsfeed. Dozens of people commenting on her page regarding her murder. Lots of heartless trolls. Facebook had yet to police Rebecca's page. He scrolled down further, spotting a picture taken back in the eighties, in Cardiff. Fagan remembered it as if it were yesterday. Rebecca's smiling face.

She looked at Woolworths store. 'Come on, let's see if they have one of those photo booths.'

Fagan smiled back at her. 'You paying? Because I just run out of money spending it in the food theatre. I'll be glad when the YTS money goes up next year.'

'I've still got five pounds.' Rebecca teased. She grabbed his hand and led him into the shop.

Fagan reached for his wallet. He pulled out a faded colour photo of the pair of them in the photo booth. A tear trickled down his cheek, remembering the good times. Then the darkness kicked in. Fagan punched in Nelson's name. His profile was packed with endless garbage about miscarriages of justice. Fagan was mentioned more than a few times. Nasty little trolls offering to end his life. Fagan knew there was nothing he could do. Facebook was a law to itself. He logged off the social media platform and put his phone down. His kindle was on a small coffee table. Fagan picked it up and entered the name and title, Dan Brown, *The Davinci Code*. He then pulled the lever on his recliner and began to read.

CHAPTER 30

DAY 3
6:27am

Fagan opened his tired eyes, slowly adjusting to the sound of his telephone. Watkins' contact number displayed on the screen.

'Boss, there's been another murder.'

'What?' Fagan managed to say, shaking off a deep sleep.

'A body has been found at Grosmont castle. Forensics aren't even out there yet. The body was found about an hour ago.'

Fagan yawned. 'I'll pick you up in ten minutes and we'll head out there.'

'I should warn you boss, Herefordshire police are attending the scene.'

'Ok, be ready when I pick you up.'

Grosmont Castle – 7:17am

'We're waiting on more officers from Hereford.' The uniform said as he scrutinised Fagan's badge.

'There's no need. This is a Monmouthshire jurisdiction.'

'But it was called in to Hereford.'

'Look, I'm not going to stand here and get into a pissing contest about who's patch this is. I need to see the body.' Fagan stared up at the uniform, who was considerably taller.

The uniform conceded and let Fagan and Watkins pass.

'Who found the body?'

'A local, out walking her dogs first thing.' The uniform replied. 'She lives in one of the cottages at the front of the castle.'

'Tell her someone will be along to interview her soon.'

The uniform peeled off.

Fagan and Watkins made sure they were properly suited up for a crime scene. Unlike two other uniforms that were wandering about the castle like enthusiastic tourists. After a chastising from Fagan the uniforms retreated. Both detectives walked across the bridge that spanned a dried-up moat.

Watkins looked about. 'Another remote location, boss.'

'I was just thinking that.'

As they walked into the castle grounds, Fagan spotted the naked body of a man straight away.

'Jesus, he's been murdered just like Turner.' Watkins stated.

'Our killer certainly has a flare for the dramatic.' Fagan sighed.

The man was in a similar position to Professor Turner. He was naked, with his arms and legs outstretched. A dagger was buried in his chest. His hands and feet were pierced with nails. A rosary was draped around his neck.

Fagan recognised the man. 'Here lies Father Romano.'

Watkins looked about. 'Why would he have been all the way out here? It doesn't make sense. Skenfrith castle is miles away.'

Fagan studied a map on his phone. 'It's only five miles. It's a relatively small area.' He looked down at Romano's corpse. 'Dagger number two, by the looks.'

'Two down, two to go. You don't reckon there's going to be more of these murders?'

'I bloody well hope not. Jesus, our killer seems to be one step ahead of us with this.' Fagan Scanned the immediate area of the body. 'No parchment this time. The killer could have been in more of a rush.'

'Why murder Romano?'

'He was here for the splinter of Christ. Someone didn't want the Vatican getting their hands on that artefact.'

'Still, murdering a Vatican investigator is going to cause one hell of a shit storm.'

'Of course it will. That's why the killer struck again. Our murderer wants to throw everyone off the scent. The only way to do that is to create more controversy. Whoever murdered Turner and Romano is hoping it will be enough to stop the dig.'

'So that they can find the treasure instead.' Fagan surmised.

What's the betting the media will somehow find out about this, just as they did with Turner?'

'Exactly.'

'But this isn't going to go away in a hurry.' Watkins pointed out. 'Two people have now been murdered in the same fashion.'

'Plus, we have another two murders. One in 1975 and the murder of Ross Smith yesterday. This puzzle is growing larger by the day.'

'The Chief Constable is going to pull out all the stops now and give us a decent size team to crack this.'

Fagan looked around. 'That track we just walked up was wide enough to get a vehicle up here.'

'Yeah, looks like it.'

'So a vehicle would have made a lot of noise, navigating the rough terrain. Lots of gear changes. I suspect the woman who found Romano isn't the only village resident with a dog. You'll find in areas like this most people own a dog.'

'Unless the vehicle used was electric.'

It was an idea that had escaped Fagan's train of thought. 'Fuck!' His voice rebounded off the walls of the castle.

'Besides the tyres on the gravel track, an electric vehicle would have hardly made a sound.' Watkins added.

Fagan surveyed the immediate area. 'There are two houses with a clear view of this castle. Let's see if anyone of them have CCTV.' Fagan closed his eyes momentarily. 'What was Romano doing out here at such a remote location?'

'Makes no sense. The other dig sites are miles away.' Watkins said.

'Something must have lured Turner out of that hotel the other night. Something important enough for him to have faced his murderer.' Fagan stopped talking.

'What?' Watkins noticed the expression on Fagan's face.

'They both knew the murderer. They knew them well enough to be in their company.'

'We know both Thackery and Romano were funding the dig.' Watkins pointed out. 'And they both knew Turner.'

Fagan pointed at Romano's body. 'Now Romano is dead. Which makes Thackery the last man standing.'

'Thackery only arrived yesterday. He couldn't have been here the night Turner was murdered.'

'Shit, it all falls apart the moment we try to connect anything.' Fagan groaned.

'There has to be a suspect we haven't considered yet.'

'But who?' Fagan almost stamped his foot like an angry child.

'We have yet to interview Lord Barry.'

'We'll interview him later. Brooks pointed out yesterday that Barry is elderly. So it's just a case of eliminating him from our enquiries.'

'Boss.' Watkins looked towards the entrance to the castle grounds. A small army of CSI officers fanned out across the field.

The CSI supervisor who had attended Turner's murder was clutching a forensics kit. Another CSI accompanied him, armed with a camera.

Fagan crossed the moat again to meet them at a gate. 'It's the same MO as the other night with Turner. The victim has been crucified and stabbed.' Fagan let the snapper pass.

'I'll start knocking on doors boss.' Watkins offered. 'See if anyone heard anything last night.'

The CSI looked around. 'This murderer of yours likes historic locations, don't they?'

Fagan nodded

'Another remote location. Quiet, no one to hear you.'

'We think they may have used an electric vehicle to get up here.'

'It's a possibility, reduced noise. No revving engines to disturb anyone with pets. Come on, let's take a look, shall we.'

Fagan accompanied the forensic across the bridge. They approached the body of Romano. Fagan explained he knew the victim, and that they had had a lengthy chat about Turner's death the day before.

The snapper circled the body, taking pictures from multiple angles. Another two forensics joined them.

The CSI studied the way the body was positioned. 'It's similar to Turner.' He pointed to where the nails had been driven through each palm. 'Although I would say this is slightly different. Our killer could have been in a rush.'

'Do you think they were disturbed?' Fagan queried.

'Not likely. It looks as if they still had time to carry out their work. But the nails aren't as deep in the ground as they were at Skenfrith castle.'

'Jesus, whoever did this must be a piece of work.'

'They've got a lot of balls, I'll say that.' He looked at the snapper. 'Are you finished?'

The snapper nodded.

The CSI looked at the other two that had just arrived. 'Let's pry these nails and remove the dagger before we turn him over.'

It took a few minutes to remove all the nails. The CSI gently pulled the dagger from Romano's chest.

The snapper documented everything. Photographing each action the CSI carried out.

Romano was rolled onto his front. The snapper took more photographs.

Fagan pointed at the priest's back. 'It's similar to what happened to Turner.'

The CSI nodded. 'If both were stabbed in the back, then it indicates they trusted their killer enough to turn their back on them.' He pointed at Romano's forehead. 'There's no branding this time. Meaning the murderer was alone. Unlike last time when there could have been two of them. Both men are elderly and slim. So it would be easy for our killer to man handle their bodies.' The CSI looked towards the foot bridge. 'Looks like the shit has finally hit the fan.'

Fagan turned, spotting Chief Constable Paul Griffiths in full forensics garb.

'Good morning sir.' Fagan greeted.

Griffiths looked past Fagan at the body on the ground. 'Jesus, it's just like the other one.'

'Yes sir, same MO. So far, there have been three murders. I believe they are all linked.'

'Even the body found in that flat in Abergavenny yesterday?'

Fagan pointed at the dagger that had been placed in an

evidence bag. 'That dagger is one of four stolen from Abergavenny museum in January 2020. In May of that year, the museum curator died of a heart attack. It is my belief he may have been murdered. And if that's not enough, we have a cold case from 1975 in which another archaeologist was murdered. He had links to Romano and Turner.'

'What exactly are we dealing with here, DI Fagan, a serial killer?'

'It's looking like that. Someone who has murdered multiple times over the past few years. This is all connected with the missing daggers.'

'What exactly are they searching for at this dig?'

'Some fabled lost treasure. Religious artefacts, take your pick. The thing is, we've yet to produce a credible suspect. All the people we've interviewed so far seem to be hell bent on keeping secrets. I've had to go off the rails on this one, sir.'

Griffiths shot Fagan a hard stare.

'A journal belonging to Robert Turner, seems to be at the heart of all this.' Fagan glanced at Romano's corpse. 'He had made a deal with two of the dig team to buy the journal for one hundred thousand. Turner had also made a deal with Damien Thackery. Turner promised to hand over the journal after this dig was completed. I found out yesterday that Thackery and Romano had also made a deal to divide the journal between them.'

'What's in the journal that's worth that much money?'

'I'm no archaeologist sir, so I wouldn't know. I have taken possession of the journal and it's in safe hands.'

Griffiths inhaled. 'Very well, DI Fagan, the ball is in your court. What do you need?'

'I need a major incident room for a start. Setup in Newport central. I need more officers, a competent CSI team. We need a family liaison officer to coordinate with

Ross Smith's family. This is huge. Three murders in three days. Plus, another possible murder carried out two years ago. And a murder carried out almost fifty years ago.'

Griffiths nodded. 'I'll get the ball rolling and push the panic button with the Home Office. Anything else?'

'A latte with two sugars.' Fagan grinned at him.

'Don't push it.' Griffiths marched off.

'Fagan.' The CSI called out. 'Over here, I've found something?'

Fagan returned to Romano's body.

The CSI pointed at Romano's head. 'There, it's matted into the victim's hair.'

Fagan moved in closer. 'Shit, that's the same seed found on Turner and Smith?'

'I looked it up last night. It's known as galium aparine. You can barely see it. It's a small seed off a larger plant.'

'And there is no way it could have blown in off the wind.'

The CSI shook his head. 'No.'

'What did you just call the plant this seed came from?'

'Galium aparine. It grows all over. It's known by most people as sticky willy or goosegrass.'

'Or kisses.' Fagan said, smiling. 'Shit, they've been under our noses the whole time.' His phone buzzed. 'DI Fagan.'

'Detective inspector Fagan, it's Charles Decker.'

'Up early, Doctor Decker.' Fagan remarked.

'I carried out another post mortem on Turner. He was in the advanced stages of bowel cancer.'

'How long did he have?'

'Weeks maybe, perhaps a few months. Until I get medical records, I can't be sure.'

'What about Ross Smith.'

'Smith had a shit load of cocaine in his bloodstream.'

Ok, thanks for letting me know.'

Watkins walked back into the field. He had interviewed several residents who lived in the row of cottages located near the castle. The woman who had discovered the body was of no help. She was more concerned about the stress it had caused her dogs than the actual man who had been murdered. Watkins spotted Fagan marching across the bridge. 'I'm afraid none of the houses have CCTV.'

Fagan looked back towards Romano's body.

Watkins noted the expression on his face. 'You ok boss.'

'I need a favour from you.'

Watkins nodded. 'Sure.'

Fagan relayed what the CSI just revealed, adding a set of instructions. Watkins took everything in.

Fagan checked his watch. 'It's coming up to a quarter to eight. If you set off now, you can be there before midday. Ask around, see what you can find out. There's a detective chief inspector with Cambridgeshire CID. I worked with her several years ago, DCI Penny Farthing.'

Watkins smirked. 'You sure that's a real name, boss?'

Fagan nodded. 'It is. Drop my name, tell her I'm calling in a favour. She'll give you everything you need.'

'Sure thing, boss. You going to be ok handling all this without me?'

'Griffiths has decided to give me a full team. Now get going. I need that intelligence as soon as possible.'

Watkins spun on his heels.

CHAPTER 31

Newport Central police HQ – 9:36am

Fagan walked into the incident room, checking his phone. He mused at the message Watkins had just sent him. He had already arrived in Cambridge and had made contact with DCI Farthing.

The room was packed with a collection of uniform and plain clothed officers. Many had been drafted in from all over Gwent constabulary, which comprised officers of from Monmouthshire, Newport, Blaenau Gwent, Caerlssacly and Torfaen.

'Right, you lot, shut your gobs and listen up.' Fagan called out over the din of chatter. 'Thanks for all coming here this morning. I know some of you have been drafted from important work. But time is of the essence. I am the SIO on this case. My name is DI Marc Fagan. All communication will be directed through me. Each one of you has been given a casefile that will fill you in on what we are dealing with here. In just over forty-eight hours there have been three murders within the Monmouthshire area. Our killer seems to have a flare for the dramatic. All three victims were stabbed.'

'Perhaps you should call Sherlock Holmes in for this one guv.' A plain clothed detective remarked, smirking back at Fagan.

Laughter rippled through the incident room.

'What's your name?' Fagan glared at the man.

'DS Dave Padfield.'

'Well DS Padfield, Mr Holmes is not available. And I think Benedict Cumberbatch is too busy playing a bloody wizard. So I'd appreciate it if you wouldn't throw anymore shitty little comments my way.'

Padfield seemed to shrink at least ten inches as eyes focused on him.

'With all due respect, sir, isn't this a large team for this investigation?' A young female uniformed officer remarked. 'Some of us are fresh and don't have the experience with a murder case like this.' She held up the casefile she had been given.

'Then consider this a learning curve.' Fagan gestured at the whiteboard, which was packed with pictures of the victims and scribbled notes. 'The first victim is Professor Robert Turner. A noted archaeologist working out of Cambridge university. Professor Turner was here with a team digging for something called the Splinter of Christ.'

The room suddenly lit up with smiles.

'Right, this isn't a bloody *Indiana Jones* film or a Dan Brown novel. This is a murder investigation. What I want from each one of you is a hard investigation. The killer seems to be one step ahead of us. They have planned these murders, making sure they have us running around in circles. You will all be divided into teams. I want people interviewing friends of Ross Smith, the second victim who was found yesterday. I'll be interviewing his closest friend later on today. An FLO is already with the family and is advising them. I want you interviewing Smith's wider circle of friends, anyone who knew him. Which means a door-to-door chat with everyone else who lived in the other blocks of flats near where the victim lived. Anyone unfamiliar he may have had contact with prior to his death. Every stone needs to be kicked over if we are to have a quick result with this case. Some of you will research this Splinter of Christ.

See if we can get any information about it we don't already know. Any of you who have an interest in history may find this fascinating. I want to build enthusiasm with this case. I want officers looking into poisons and other local plants. You all have the report the pathologist has prepared. Check to see if there are any old investigations regarding poisonings. I also want someone to check with Interpol.' Fagan pointed at the picture of Father Romano. 'I want to know exactly how long this man has been in the UK. I want a team going out to the dig site and interviewing members of the dig who have yet to give statements. The tiniest bit of information could be vital to cracking this wide open. The deputy scene of crimes officer is Andrew Brooks. My usual man is on a special assignment. He won't be back for several hours.'

Brooks looked back at Fagan with mild shock.

Fagan smiled back at him. 'Sorry mate, you've been bumped up.' Fagan scanned the room. 'Some of you may think that such a large team is overkill on this investigation. But it is important we catch the killer as soon as possible before they strike again. Assembling a big team is a show of force. I am hoping it will deter the murderer from killing again. I want full media coverage on this, I need a volunteer to be a media liaison coordinator. I want you contacting all the major nationals and news networks. As for my role in this, I will be interviewing all the leading suspects regarding these murders.' Fagan sighed. 'Although we are short on those at this present moment. One of you will be my co interviewer.' Fagan made eye contact with a young female police officer who was doing her best to stay out of sight. 'Police Constable Stacy Flynn, front and centre please.'

Stacy hesitated before stepping out from behind several officers.

'You will be conducting interviews with me. Brooks will

start organising you into teams. I want to draw on all of your collective knowledge. You'll be surprised what you are capable of when you put your mind to it.' Fagan glanced at the clock on the wall. 'You have until three o'clock until the next briefing, so get stuck in, heads down and arses up.'

Everyone scattered, muttering amongst themselves.

A female officer dressed in civvies approached Fagan, smiling. 'Marc Fagan, the boy I snogged in the dugout at the Mardy playing field all those years ago.'

Fagan had to do a double take before he recognised her. 'Wow, Liz.' He searched his memory but failed to come up with a second name.

'Used to be Fletcher, now Mrs Teller.' She replied, putting Fagan out of his misery.

'Nice to see you've joined the cause.'

'Well, it's just detective sergeant Teller. I haven't the ambition to climb the ladder.'

'Not everyone wants to aim for the stars in this job.'

'Jackie messaged me a few months back, saying you were back in Abergavenny. I'm so sorry about Rebecca. That must have been so hard on you.'

Fagan nodded. 'Yeah, it was.'

'I can't believe Tim would do something like that.'

'I found it hard to digest when I had to arrest him. So, are you based in Monmouthshire? Only we have yet to cross paths.'

Liz shook her head. 'I'm stationed at Caerphilly. Looking at early retirement. Find myself a cushy job to last me for the next ten years.'

'It's kind of why I made the move from Merseyside police. Had enough of the big city. I wanted something smaller and less chaotic.' Fagan looked around the room. 'This is just the same as Merseyside.'

'Crime is crime, wherever you serve.' Liz remarked.

'So what team do you want to be part of?'

'I was hoping to Be the MLO.'

'The media liaison officer, sure. Talk to young Brooks over there and tell him I have just appointed you.'

'We should catch up some time.' Liz suggested. 'I'd love to hear about your time in Liverpool. I expect we've got a few interesting stories to swap.'

Fagan nodded before looking at Stacy. 'I need to brief this young lady. Would you excuse me.'

CHAPTER 32

9:49am

'I appreciate you letting me be your backup.' Stacy said. 'You didn't have to go out of your way.'

Fagan smiled. 'Don't worry, I'm not giving you the special treatment because you're Ricky's girlfriend. I was in a senior officers' team briefing a few weeks back and your name came up. Your CO seems to think you've got potential as a serving detective. He says you're a quick study and can often see things missed by others. But he's also a little miffed that you seem to be holding yourself back. You've been in the force for over seven years, but you're still in uniform. I read about that drug gang you helped crack last year. Superb work on your part.'

Stacy released a snort of derision. 'Fucking Ukrainians posing as helpless refugees. When Russia invaded the Ukraine last February, the drug gangs were the first to take a hit. So the moment the government opened up the borders, in came all the crap. The media only focussing on the families that had been displaced by the war. Anyway, a body turned up under the Transporter bridge in Newport. It was a local dealer. Part of an Ebbw Vale gang. A lad called Gavin Jones. The police already had him under surveillance, but he suddenly dropped off their radar. He was a major player in valleys drugs. Jones had been shot at point blank range through the head. The weapon used was Russian. The team didn't spot it at first until I did a ballistics check on the bullet they dug out of his skull. They thought that a gang from Merthyr was responsible for his killing. There had been a few disputes on the Gurnos Estate over the past three years. I didn't believe any boys from Merthyr were capable of cold-blooded murder. The fact the gun was Russian rang all kinds of alarm bells with me. So I made a list of all the recent Ukrainian refugees the Welsh government had given asylum to. Low and behold, I came across two names. They were brothers. Claiming to have lost their parents during the Russian invasion. But after an Interpol check, I discovered they were part of a Ukrainian drug cartel distributing heroin across Europe. I did a little surveillance of my own one night.'

Fagan smiled. 'You went off grid.'

'Yeah.' Stacy admitted, hanging her head.

'Do you know how many times I have gone off grid to get the job done? More than I can count. We can't always rely on protocol to guide us. There's still such a thing called gut instinct. Or as the Americans like to call it, a hunch.'

'So I tracked them to a warehouse in Cardiff. They were about to be integrated into a larger gang that had been operating in South Wales for over twenty years. At the time my CO was hopping mad with me.'

'You made him look like a right wanker, I suspect.'

Stacy smiled 'Yeah, I did.'

Fagan looked at her. 'You don't enjoy treading on toes.'

'Not really.'

'If something is missing from a case, I welcome anyone who wants to tread on my toes. Just because I have been in the job over thirty five years doesn't mean I don't need my wings clipping from time to time. Don't feel guilty because you've made a senior officer look like a dick. In my career I have seen plenty of officers promoted to jobs they had no right being in. My deputy scene of crimes officer, who I sent to Cambridge this morning, brought up a point about an electric vehicle being used in the murders. It's one of those things I didn't see. This is why I want you in on the interview. Perhaps you'll spot something I will miss.'

'I'll do my best.'

'Why did you decide to join up?'

'I grew up in Newport.' Stacy revealed. 'The wrong side of Newport, unfortunately. My dad was a dealer, and expected his kids to carry on the family tradition.'

'Your mother?'

'Off her face most of the time. My dad got her hooked the moment they met. My grandparents wanted nothing to do with us.'

'Must have been hard.'

'Very. I never wanted to be a part of that culture. My dad tried to get me hooked on drugs when I became a teenager. He used to say to me, it was the only way to get me used to the harsh realities of life. So I decided I wanted to learn about life in my own way. I ran away from home, purposely got into trouble with the local police. I was hoping they would send me into foster care. But it never happened. When I was sixteen, I went to visit my grandparents. They took pity on me and gave me a home.'

'What about your father?'

'My grandad had to take out a restraining order on him.'

'Well, you did the right thing getting out.'

'I realise that now. I didn't want a life on drugs. I saw many of my friends from school take that path and it didn't end well for them.' Stacy paused. 'My mam eventually died of an overdose.' She wiped away a tear. 'I was devastated. When I moved in with nan and grandad, we all worked so hard to get her away from that twat of a dad of mine. But in the end the drugs won, and she stayed. My grandparents are good people. It was just bad luck their daughter ended up with someone like my dad. When mam died, we were all devastated. I went to confront my dad about it, but he didn't give a shit. So I quit my job and joined the police. The first thing I wanted to do as soon as I finished my training was go after my dad and brothers. They were already on the police radar in Newport. But people were too afraid of them.'

'I take it you weren't.'

'No, definitely not. They were finally brought down, and I had to testify against them. I remember looking at my dad in court. For the first time in his life he was actually sorry. He's currently serving a twenty-five-year prison sentence. My brothers are serving fifteen years each.'

'It took a lot of courage to do what you did. It must have been hard turning on your own family.'

Stacy shook her head. 'That's the thing. I never classed them as my family. To me, they were just a bunch of dealers who deserved what they got.'

Fagan checked his phone to see if Watkins had anything new to report.

'He doesn't hate you. You know that, don't you, Ricky.'

Fagan was on his back heel. 'When I came back home to Abergavenny, I thought I had a clean slate. The last thing I expected was discovering I had a thirty-seven-year-old son I didn't know about.' Fagan blew out through his cheeks. 'When his mam was murdered, it devastated me in ways I never thought possible. I guess I still held a torch for her.'

'When Ricky found out that Tim wasn't his real father, it was like a release for him. He knew deep down that he wasn't. I remember when you first called round the flat. There's a picture of Ricky and his mam. When I looked at it, I clocked straight away.'

Fagan smiled. 'Like I just said, you see things missed by others. Listen, let's focus on the job for now. Grab yourself a coffee. Spend half an hour with the case file. The man we'll be interviewing is Damien Thackery.' Fagan checked his messages again. 'His lawyer will be in this interview. If I didn't know better, I'd swear he knew he would be arrested at some point. Google him, find out as much as you can.'

Stacy nodded. 'Understood, guv.'

CHAPTER 34

10:25am

Damien Thackery drummed his fingers on the table as Fagan and Stacy walked into the room. He glanced up at the attractive uniformed officer who was accompanying the DI.

Fagan activated the camera and tapped the record icon on his phone. 'Interview with Mr Damien Thackery. Present in the room is Mr Thackery's solicitor, Ryan Bridges. Interviewing officers are Detective Inspector Marc Fagan and Police Constable Stacy Flynn.'

Stacy scrutinised Thackery's manner.

'Could you tell us where you were last night, Mr Thackrey?' Fagan asked.

'I was at my hotel.' He answered abruptly.

'Which hotel?'

'I'm staying at the Celtic Manor.'

'Nice place.' Stacy remarked. 'But I suppose a man with your kind of money can afford that type of accommodation.'

Thackery stared back at her. 'I've stayed in far better hotels.'

'Still, nice golf course. I hear the owner has applied to host the Ryder cup again for 2025.'

'Golf doesn't interest me sweetheart. It's a sport for those who can't be bothered to get physical.'

Stacy's eyes narrowed. She hated being called sweetheart, except by her boyfriend.

'When did you last speak with Father Romano?' Fagan asked.

'Yesterday at the dig. He was there until late last night. We were looking for the second marker.'

'I would have thought it would have got too dark to work.'

'I had some portable lights brought in with some generators. I also had a security team there all night protecting the site. After the fiasco yesterday with every tom, dick and harry turning up with a spade and a metal detector, I didn't want to take any chances.'

'What time did you leave the dig site?'

Thackery inhaled. 'About a quarter to eleven.'

'A bit late.' Stacy remarked.

'I just want to find the second marker. This dig has already cost me a lot of money.'

'Not to mention three lives.' Fagan added.

'Look, I had fuck all to do with any of these murders ok.'

Fagan made eye contact with Thackery's solicitor. 'Bit handy you having your solicitor with you today, Mr Thackery.'

'After I have been interviewed twice regarding crimes I have not committed, I thought it would be better to have a lawyer I trusted, rather than a poor excuse for a duty solicitor you would have given me.'

'What did you discuss with Father Romano last night?' Stacy asked.

'We discussed this splinter of Christ he wants to get his hands on.'

'So you didn't know he had made a deal to buy Turner's journal?'

'What?' Thackery looked at Fagan and Stacy. 'Impossible.'

'Why?'

'You know why. Turner said he would give me the journal as soon as they had found what they were looking for.'

'But then you added that you and Romano were going to divide the journal between you. After Turner had handed it over to you.'

'Yes.'

'Would it interest you to know that Father Romano had offered two others on the dig team one hundred thousand for the journal?'

Fagan's revelation seemed to anger Thackery. 'Fucking archaeologists, they're all back stabbers. Who were the two he was going to pay?'

'David Spooner and Jay Dayton.'

'Them two arseholes, as thick as thieves. Doesn't matter anyway, the journal is long gone. I expect that bitch of an assistant has tucked it away somewhere so that she can use it to find that hidden chamber in Tut's tomb in the Valley of the Kings. I wanted to front all the money for the dig, but Turner wouldn't have it.'

'I suspect Professor Turner approached the Vatican because he knew you couldn't stab them in the back the way you did with him ten years ago.'

'Are we back to that old chestnut again?' Thackery groaned. 'It's water under the bridge.'

'Do you know what time Romano left the dig?'

'Yes, he left the same time as me. We all did. There were a couple of mini buses to pick up the team that had stayed with the dig.'

'What time was this?'

'Like I just said, around eleven. I made sure the security team stayed in the castle grounds.'

'I take it Sarah York left in one of those buses?'

Thackery nodded.

'What about Father Romano?' Stacy asked.

'He was still there after everyone left. I asked him if he needed a lift somewhere, but he said someone was picking him up. I gave him a lift to the main road. That's where he said he was meeting his lift.'

'But you saw no one picking him up.'

Thackery shook his head. 'No, I didn't see a soul. I thought it was odd that he wanted to be left alone in the middle of nowhere.'

'What route did you take back to your hotel?' Fagan asked.

'I followed the mini buses back to Monmouth. Then got on the dual carriageway towards Newport.'

'What time did you arrive back at your hotel?'

'Around twenty-past eleven. I remember checking my phone. It didn't take me long to get back to the Celtic Manor.'

'Did you notice any other vehicles on the road when you left the castle?'

'Not that I recall.' Thackery paused.

'Mr Thackery, is there something you remember?' Stacy asked.

'After I had dropped off Father Romano, another car turned off towards the castle. It was coming from Abergavenny way. I remember because whoever it was had their full beams on. But I didn't think anything of it, so I floored it to catch up with the mini buses.'

'Have you ever been to Abergavenny before?'

Fagan gave Stacy a sidewards glance. 'No.'

'Are you familiar with the local area?'

'No, this is my first time here.'

'Exactly where are you going with this line of questioning?' Thackery's lawyer asked.

Stacy ignored the question. 'Then how do you know the

road led to Abergavenny?'

Thackery shifted in his chair before shrugging. 'I don't know, probably my sat nav told me.'

'Probably?'

'Look, I had fuck all to do with that priest's murder. I followed the buses back to Monmouth, then headed down the dual carriageway back to my hotel. I even had a late night drink. That place is bristling with cameras. Probably picked me up a dozen times.'

'Detectives, my client has just stated he had nothing to do with Father Romano's murder. He has cooperated fully with your murder enquiry. I'm sure everything checks out and that the Celtic Manor hotel will confirm he returned at the time he said he did.'

Fagan ended the interview. Thackery and his solicitor left the room.

'Something definitely off about that bloke.' Stacy commented.

'We have another two of these interviews to do. We'll take a short break. The duty solicitor is yet to turn up.' Fagan's phone buzzed. He looked at the message, smiling. 'Nice one, Watkins.'

'Guv?'

Fagan shook his head. 'It's nothing. Can you do me a quick favour?'

'Sure.'

'Run a check to see how many registered electric vehicles are in Abergavenny? I need a list printed out.'

'I'm on it.'

'Thanks Stacy.' Fagan said as she left the room. He then hit the speed dial. 'Sean, what have you got?'

CHAPTER 35

White castle - 11:41am

'This is all we bloody need.' Fagan grumbled, looking up into the inky grey sky. Rain started to fall steadily as they made their way towards the team that were digging along the perimeter wall of the castle.

In the distance Damien Thackery's voice cut through the rain as he barked orders at the dig team.

Stacy popped a large umbrella she had the good sense to bring from the police station.

Sarah York spotted Fagan and Stacy approaching and peeled herself away from the dig team.

Thackery shouted after her before spotting the two police officers.

Even at that distance, Fagan could make out his foul language after spotting him.

'Any luck?' Fagan asked.

York threw her hood over her head. 'It could be days, even weeks, before we find anything. We had a representative from the National Trust here this morning. You missed a brilliant argument between him and our benefactor.' She looked back at Thackery. 'They want us to stop digging in light of what happened to Robert.'

'Did you know, Sarah? That Robert had advanced bowel cancer.' Fagan asked, tentatively recalling what the pathologist had told him earlier.

A look of grief flashed across her face. 'Yes.' She nodded.

'Do you know how long he had?'

'He saw a doctor about three months ago. Robert was given less than a year. He refused chemotherapy despite me begging him to undergo the treatment. He was stubborn, I'll give him that.'

'Is that why the university refused funding for his dig?'

York nodded. 'Robert took the dean of the university into his confidence. But he just used it as an excuse to shove Robert out of the door. They'd been friends for years. Robert couldn't understand why he was denied funding. That's why he turned to Thackery and the Vatican. I remember him having an argument with James Slattery, the dean of Cambridge, about the funding. Slattery explained times were changing. The archaeology department was undergoing a massive overhaul. Ground penetrating radar technology made it possible to scan the ground and make 3D recreations of buildings. Slattery told Robert this was the way forward for archaeology at Cambridge.'

'I take it he was none too happy about this decision.'

'He was fuming with Slattery, who told him the only way to sanction the dig was to secure private funding. To be honest, Slattery was annoyed when Robert went back to tell him he had found a backer. At first, Slattery denied Robbert anyone from the archaeology department. But then Robert made the call to the Vatican. That's when Father Romano visited the university. Damien Thackery also turned up to offer his support. Slattery crumbled and said Robert could have one last team.'

'One last team?' Stacy stated.

'After the dig was over, Slattery told Robert he wanted his resignation in writing. He also gave him just six weeks to find something significant. It just wasn't long enough. Robert knew we could be in the area for a year.'

'But you found the first marker quite quickly.'

'Robert really pushed the team. After about a week arguing broke out.' York looked toward Spooner. 'He caused most of the arguments. Forever influencing the rest of the team. Robert complained to Slattery about the poor team he had given him.'

'It sounds like this dig was being sabotaged at the highest levels at Cambridge.' Fagan suggested.

'That's exactly what Robert thought. So time was against him, in more ways than one. He was feeling a lot of pain from the cancer. Used to swallow a whole packet of pain killers every day. I begged him to slow down, but he wouldn't listen. In the end he became hostile towards me.' York composed herself. 'On the night he was murdered, he apologised to me about the way he had been.'

'Did he say anything about meeting up with whoever murdered him?'

'No, and that really annoyed me. When we were having dinner that evening, he brought the journal with him. He said he was passing his legacy on to me. And that I was to continue the work he and Cuthbert had started. He read through the journal and showed me the tablet Norman Cuthbert had drawn.'

'The tablet that gave instructions on how to find lost burial chambers in Tutankhamun's tomb.' Fagan explained.

York stared back with a puzzled expression.

Fagan gestured to Thackery. 'Damien spilt the beans. He wanted his hands on that journal so that he could auction off information. After, he was also going to break up the journal and share it with Romano.'

'Typical of that bastard.' York said.

'What else does that journal contain?'

'Maps to dig sites all over the world. After Norman Cuthbert had been in Egypt for over two years, he decided he wanted to see more of the Middle East. He travelled all over collecting information on dig sites in Iraq, Syria, Iran, Saudi Arabia and Afghanistan. He spent ten years cataloguing different sites. He would start a dig, find something of importance, then bury it. But not before he knew where to dig when he returned. Cuthbert then went to South America. To the jungles of Mexico. He visited Peru and documented the lost civilisations. Before making his way up to north America and exploring the Native American culture and on to Canada. In 1960, he came across settlements in Newfoundland that suggested the Vikings had a settlement there. It sparked a whole new argument that Europeans had settled on the north American continent at least five hundred years before Columbus. Norman Cuthbert was one of the greatest archaeological influencers of the twentieth century. He inspired the likes of Robert to carry on.' York fought back the tears. 'And now it's about to come crashing down. I received a call from Slattery this morning. He said, considering what happened to Robert. He was giving me just one week to make a significant find.'

'Before he pulls the plug on everything.' Stacy finished.

York nodded, looking at Spooner in the distance. 'No thanks to that twat, who happens to be the dean's grandson.'

Fagan sensed frustration rush through his mind. 'You didn't mention that before Sarah. All you said is that he was from a family with money.'

'I know, another lie. No, it wasn't a lie, it was just information I withheld.'

'It's the same bloody thing Sarah.' Fagan seethed.

'I know, and all I can do is keep apologising.'

'Is Spooner part of the revamp to the archaeology department?'

'Yes, as soon as Robert would have retired, then Spooner was to be given the department.'

'But he's only a first-year student.'

'That's what Cambridge is all about these days. The powers that be don't care about the opinion of the more experienced. Scholars like Robert are seen as dinosaurs. Well past their sell by date.'

'That explains a lot.'

'The day before Robert was murdered, David Spooner had a go at Robert. He said that his time was at an end and all his work would be erased to usher in a new age of archaeology. An age of wokeness, wiping away the hard work Robert and Norman Cuthbert accomplished during their careers.'

Stacy looked to where Spooner was. 'Sounds like a right twat.'

'Did you have any dealings with Father Romano yesterday?' Fagan asked.

'We had a brief conversation about what happened to the journal. He asked me if I knew where it was.'

'But you didn't reveal that Turner had given it to you?'

'No.' York replied. 'I think he was angry that Spooner and Dayton could not find the journal when they broke into Robert's hotel room.'

A young woman sprinted towards them. Her eyes filled with excitement. 'Sarah, we've found it. The second marker.' She pointed towards a group huddled around a small area near the castle wall.

They hurried over.

Thackery glared at York. 'Please say you can decipher this. Now that Father Romano has shed his mortal coil, you are our only hope.'

York stared at the decaying bronze shield. 'My god, this is the actual shield that belonged to Joseph of Arimathea.'

'Who gives a shit who's shield it is.' Thackery mocked. 'What does it bloody say?'

Sarah ran her finger over the inscription on the shield. 'It talks of a table where Satan dined as our lord Jesus sacrificed himself. The dagger and the scroll will point the way to the shard of the true cross.'

'What's that supposed to mean?' Thackery asked with growing frustration. 'What scroll?'

'I don't know.' York answered, glancing briefly at Fagan.

'What do you mean, you don't fucking know?' He shouted.

'I have seen texts, but none of them mention any table where Satan dined.'

'For fuck's sake!' Thackeray cursed.

Fagan examined the shield. Underneath the Latin text was a detailed etched carving of a dagger. He smiled to himself. 'Listen, we have to leave. A murderer is still at large.'

Stacy noted the expression on Fagan's face. 'You know what it means, don't you guv?'

Fagan said nothing until they reached the car. He started laughing to himself.

'What is it?' Stacy asked.

'I know what the devil's table is. And I know where it is.'

'You do?' Stacy smiled at Fagan.

'They haven't got a bloody clue.' Fagan chuckled.

'So what is it, and where is it?'

'It's a rock formation on the side of the Skirrid mountain. We used to play there as kids. I also remember an indentation on the top of the table shaped like a dagger.' Fagan called up an image Nigel Thomas had e-mailed him a few days earlier of the daggers on display at the museum. He pointed at one of the daggers. 'This one has a distinct shape, which is like the indentation on the devil's table. I haven't been up there in decades, but I bet it's still there.'

'Why didn't you tell those lot?'

'Why should I?' Fagan snorted. 'Ever since Turner was murdered, his team has done nothing but bicker and trample on the poor man before they even bury him.'

'But what about the other murders?'

'I have a theory.'

Stacy looked at him for several moments. 'You know who the killer is?'

Fagan smiled back. 'Until Watkins gets back from Cambridge, I can't prove anything.'

'So what next?'

'We piece this all together. We'll do a quick interview with Darren Stephens. Then interview the daughter of the former curator at Abergavenny museum. We'll also pop in on lord Barry to see what he knows. Then we gather the team back together and see if we have a clearer picture.' Fagan started the car, still smiling to himself.

CHAPTER 36

Newport central police HQ – 12 51pm

Darren Stephens looked dishevelled. He bit into a yellow stained nail. His hands were shaking and he was sweating buckets. The effects of having no access to drugs for the last twenty four hours.

'Darren, you know why you are here today don't you?' Stacy asked.

'Yeah.' He answered in a husky voice.

'You can relax, we are not arresting you in connection with the murder of Ross Smith or anything like that.'

'Neither are we going to question you about the large quantity of cocaine found in Mr Smith' flat. Or the large quantity of money found.' Fagan added.

Stephens seemed dazed.

'As you can see Detective Fagan, my client is in no fit state to be put under pressure during this interview.' Smith's solicitor stated.

'And we are not here to put Mr Smith under pressure. He's not under arrest. All we want to know is the last time Darren spoke to Ross.' Fagan looked at Stephens. 'Do you understand Darren?'

Stephens placed his trembling hands on the table in front of him. 'Yeah.'

'Ok, so we have a witness yesterday who saw you arguing with Mr Smith. They said that the argument was quite intense. Can you tell me what the row was about?'

Stephens sniffed. 'Nothing.' He shook his head.

'Nothing.' Fagan repeated. 'It must have been something Darren. I mean, who argues over nothing these days. There's always something to argue about.'

Stephens swallowed. Despite sweating profusely his mouth was bone dry. He picked up a bottle and drank greedily.

Fagan's patience started to thin. 'Look Darren, I know this is difficult for you mate, but Ross was murdered yesterday. He didn't deserve that did he. You were the last one to see him alive. There is no evidence linking you to his death. In other words you didn't do it. But you have to help us out here. Did you see anything unusual when you visited him yesterday.

Stephens wiped his mouth, sniffing. 'The money.'

'The seven and a half thousand pounds found in the living room?' Stacy said.

Stephens nodded. 'Yeah.'

'What about it?' Fagan asked.

'It wasn't drug money.'

'Ok, this is good Darren. Can you tell us what you mean by that?'

Stephens inhaled. 'Ross got it from someone.'

'Did he say who that someone was?'

Stephens shook his head, swilling a mouthful of water. 'No.'

'So what was the argument about?'

'He owed me money.'

'How much?'

'Three hundred quid I leant him last month. He said he wasn't going to give me any of the money he had been paid.'

'Did he say where the money came from Darren?'

'Some bloke paid him ten grand a couple of days ago. Ross said it was to keep his mouth shut.'

'But he didn't say who this man was?'

'No, he just said he bumped into him at Morrisons last week.'

Fagan remembered a conversation he had the day before. 'He didn't mention Michael Bowman did he.'

'No, this was some other bloke.' Stephens looked at Fagan. 'I knew that Bowman was paying Ross money every now and then.'

'But he didn't say a name.'

'No, but he did say this bloke had paid him money before.'

'Did he say when?' Stacy coaxed.

'A few years ago maybe, I can't remember.'

'He didn't mention Abergavenny museum did he.'

Stephens nodded. 'Yeah, something to do with a break in there. Ross told me he was paid five grand to break into the museum and steal some stuff.'

'This is brilliant Darren. This will help us a lot in our investigation.' Stacy smiled at him.

'Do you know who murdered him?' Stephens asked.

'Not at this time.' Fagan answered. 'But we're going to do everything to catch the individual who did.' Fagan sat back in his chair glancing at the clock on the wall. 'Ok, I think we're done here. You can go Darren, thanks for your help.'

Stephens and his solicitor left.

'Well that adds another piece to this puzzle. Whoever murdered Turner, Smith and Romano paid Smith money to keep him quiet.'

'Before murdering him.' Stacy shook her head. 'Seems like a long shot guv. Plus whoever paid Smith must have had money to burn.'

Fagan smiled. 'Jesus.' He clicked his fingers before producing his phone. 'Andrew, do us a favour get a warrant to look through Damien Thackery's credit card record will you. As soon as you have something let me know. Also get in touch with security at Morrisons, see how long they keep security footage for.'

'Do you think Thackery killed these men?'

Fagan shook his head. 'No, but I bet that shithead has been lying to us about his involvement in all this. We'll go and interview the daughter of the museum curator to find out if there is another link.'

CHAPTER 37

Abergavenny – 2:13pm

'We appreciate you speaking to us Sally. I know this must be difficult for you.'

'To be honest, I thought Jackie was having some kind of morbid joke when she said the police might be calling to talk about dad.' Sally Parsons said.

'Your dad's name came up in a conversation I had with Nigel Thomas a few days ago.'

Sally smiled. 'Dad and Nigel were good friends.'

'I'm sorry if I am making you relive your experience Sally. But I need to know more about your father's death.'

Sally inhaled. 'He died in May 2020.'

'You were the one who found him?' Stacy said.

Sally struggled with her emotions, but remained dignified. 'Yes.'

'Are you able to recall the moment? It's ok you can take your time.'

'During lockdown, we would keep in regular contact. Our mam passed away five years ago. Dad took it hard. They'd been married for over sixty years. I would phone him at least three times a week. Every other Sunday, he would come around and have lunch with us. Dad was part of our bubble when the country shut down. When the lockdown started to ease, my daughter and son-in-law would bring their two children round.' Sally smiled. 'Dad thought the world of them. On May 3rd I phoned him to have our usual chat. His phone went to voicemail. I assumed he was out walking. Dad lived in Chain Lane. He'd walk up the Deri mountain regularly. I would go with him now and then. I tried his phone again in the evening but he still didn't answer.'

Fagan could see Sally was getting upset recalling the events. 'If you want to take a rest, just say.'

Sally composed herself before continuing. 'I should have gone round there to check on him. Dad sometimes went silent. But he'd usually phone me the day after. I think sometimes he wanted time alone to think about mum. The next day when I phoned him, he still wasn't answering. So I went round there to see if he was ok.'

'Did you have a key to your dad's property?' Stacy asked.

'No, dad was really independent. Even though he was eighty-three, he was very healthy and fit. So there was no need to keep an eye on him. He would see people every day. It wasn't like he was a recluse.' Sally took a breath. 'I decided to call on him, just to make sure he was ok. I went to his house and noticed the car was in the driveway. That's when I started to dread the worst. After trying his doorbell a couple of times I went around the back to look into the kitchen.'

'But you didn't see anything.' Fagan added.

'No, and the curtains had been drawn in the living room. I couldn't understand. Dad hated the curtains drawn, even at night. His house was enclosed, so it wasn't like people could walk past and look through the window. That's when I became concerned and called the police.'

'How long did the police take to arrive?'

'Over an hour, maybe two.' Sally sounded disgruntled. 'I rang the police and told them I couldn't gain access to my dad's property. They told me it would be quite a long wait for a police officer to attend.'

'I'm so sorry they took so long Sally.' Fagan sympathised with her.

'The police said they had been dealing with other issues. One of them mentioned that covid was causing a lot of problems. He did sound quite apologetic.'

'What happened then?' Stacy jotted notes in her pad.

'One of them smashed the window to the back door. They told me to wait outside.' Sally closed her eyes. 'Within a few short minutes, they came out and phoned an ambulance. Before they could stop me, I rushed into the house. That's when I found him. They had to drag me outside. I then called my two sisters to tell them what had happened. They arrived within twenty minutes.'

'You strike me as a close family?'

Sally nodded. 'We were as close as anyone could be. If anything, the pandemic had made us closer. One of my sisters was rushed to hospital with covid. She was very ill, on a ventilator. We thought we were going to lose her. Dad was in pieces. Anyway the day he was found, the three of us went to the hospital with dad and sat with him for a while. It was awful because we were all blaming each other at first. Saying we should have gone around there to look in on him more often. We've all made up since. At the end of the day, there was nothing we could have done. He was gone.'

'I take it you went back to the house?'

'Yes. I was the first one there. The police were still there. They'd even called a man to fix the window they had broken earlier. When I arrived, the paramedic told me it was likely that dad had suffered a massive heart attack and keeled over. He tried to assure me it would have been very quick, and that dad didn't suffer or anything like that.'

Stacy scribbled away furiously.

'Then everyone left and I was alone. My sisters came

over later that day to help me sort things out.'

'When the police left, and you were alone in the house, did you notice anything odd?'

Sally nodded. 'For a start, there was the broken mug in the living room. I picked it up and noticed tea leaves at the bottom. Thing is, dad wasn't a tea drinker.'

'Did he drink coffee?'

'No, and that's the other thing that got me thinking. He would start his day with a glass of orange juice and some dried toast. Dad was a creature of habit. He would have the same routine. Get up at seven o'clock, get the morning papers and then have his breakfast. He'd usually be done by eight thirty. Then he would spend most of the day reading. He would go out for a walk in the afternoon. It's what kept him fit. He became so fed up with the lockdown. He'd been running the Abergavenny museum for so long.'

'So you found a broken mug on the living room floor? What did you do after?'

'I went to see if everything was in order in the house. I grabbed the broken mug from the living room and went into the kitchen. That's when I spotted the other mug on the worktop with a tea strainer. It really made me think. Dad didn't keep teabags, even for guests. He had the odd visitor, but he was very particular who he let in to the house. The only person I can think of who he would invite in was Nigel Thomas, who lives out in Llanover.'

'Nigel told me you went to speak with him after your father died. He told me you had raised concerns about the nature of his death.'

Sally nodded. 'When I saw the other mug with the tea strainer, I knew someone had been in the house at the time of his death. That's when I went looking to see if anything had been disturbed.'

'What did you find?' Stacy asked.

'I went into his office. The first thing I noticed was that the key to the office door was in the lock. He never kept it like that. He always kept a key in a small jar in the kitchen. When I opened the drawer of the bureau, I noticed that someone had been through it. Dad kept everything meticulous. But someone was definitely in the house when he died. That's when my sisters turned up. I remember us having an argument about it. They said I was being paranoid.'

'How close were you to your dad, Sally?' Fagan asked.

'I was the closest. I shared a love of history with him. When I was young, he would take me to all the museums.' Sally smiled, recalling childhood memories. 'The day after dad died I was in the back garden checking that everything was in order. I was thinking about the day before, about the bureau being disturbed. Dad was a stickler for recycling. He kept everything in order. I noticed the lid on the waste bin was hanging off. So I went to put it straight. That's when I noticed a pair of disposable gloves in the bin. Someone had piled a load of rubbish on top of them. But because they were bright blue, I noticed them straight away. Dad hated the lockdown. He hated having to wear masks and gloves everywhere. So he would order everything online and get his shopping delivered. The man would leave it at the back door. He didn't keep any kind of PPE.'

Fagan and Stacy glanced at each other.

'I fished the gloves out of the bin. Then I took them to the police station. I also took the cups and teas strainer. But the police didn't want to know. It was during the darkest days of lockdown. They said because of the pandemic, they were dealing with serious cases only. I guess a man found dead, alone in the middle of his living room, didn't warrant as serious.'

Fagan inhaled. 'Sally, what did you do with the disposable gloves?'

'I kept them. And I kept the broken mug and tea strainer.'

'Thank you.' Fagan sensed a wave of relief engulf him.

Sally got up and left the room for a few minutes before returning with two bags. The first containing a pair of blue disposable latex gloves. And the other containing the broken mug and the tea strainer. 'I made sure I wore gloves before I picked anything up.'

'This could be a vital clue in helping us find out what happened to your dad.'

'Dad always taught me to question everything. Within a week of him dying, he was cremated. Only me and my sisters were allowed to attend the funeral. Dad was very popular, so many people wanted to say goodbye.' Sally wiped a tear away.

'You just said your dad used to take you to museums. Did he ever mentioned the exhibition at the museum he was showcasing just before the lockdown?'

'Do you have all afternoon? I can go into loads of detail about that. Me and Nigel helped him organise it.'

Fagan sat back in the comfortable armchair. 'Tell me everything.'

'The exhibition was the pride and joy of his life's work. He collected everything.'

'So you knew about the daggers he had?'

Sally nodded. 'You could say they were a bit of a legend in our house. We all grew up at the house in Chain Lane. He mounted the daggers in a display case on the wall of the office. He built the case especially for them.'

'What did he tell you about them?'

'Dad was an archaeologist when he was in his younger days. He wasn't a globe trotter or anything like that. He worked in Caerleon many times on the Roman settlements in that area. Dad also helped with iron age earth works in Pontrilas up the road. He's worked in Wiltshire at Avebury. His main job was with land registry, mostly for Monmouthshire Council. When he retired in 1990, he took over the museum.'

Fagan smiled, but had little interest in listening to a biography. 'Did he say how he came across the daggers?'

'Yes.' Sally replied. 'He said they were given to him by his former lecturer from Cambridge.'

Fagan's eyes widened. 'Would that be Norman Cuthbert?'

Sally nodded. 'Dad studied under him in the 1960s. In 1975, dad answered an ad in the paper for researchers needed on a dig at Tintern abbey. He used to say that he was chuffed to be working at Norman's side again. They started to dig where the original abbey was built. It wasn't long before they found some artefacts, including the daggers.'

'Did your dad ever say what the other artefacts were?'

'A medieval sword, a knights Templar shield and iron nails bought back from the Holy Land during the crusades.'

'Did you say iron nails?'

'Yes, dad said there were dozens of them. Dad used to tell me the same story over and over. He said a few days after they made the discovery, a Vatican priest arrived in Tintern. He demanded to see the daggers and a scroll that came with it. The scroll was supposed to be a map showing the final resting place of Alice of Abergavenny.'

'Do you know if the priest saw the daggers?'

'No.' Sally replied. 'When they found the daggers Norman gave them to dad straight away for safe keeping. He told dad to keep them until the priest had left the site. Lord Barry also turned up, demanding to see the daggers.

Dad reckons there were people on the dig site who were either in contact with the Vatican or in touch with Lord Barry. Dad always used to say there was so much interest in the daggers and the scroll. He also said he witnessed an argument between Lord Barry and the priest.'

'What happened?' Stacy asked.

'Barry had a go at the priest. He said the Vatican had no right just turning up and demanding that artefacts from the dig should be handed over to them. But then he had a go at Cuthbert and told him that the artefacts belonged to descendants of Alice of Abergavenny. On the day they discovered the daggers, Norman decided to give them to dad.'

Fagan clanked at Stacy. Cuthbert must have known they'd attract attention from other parties.'

'He told dad to just leave the site with the daggers and contact him after the attention had died down. The next day, dad received a phone call from one of the dig team. He drove to Tintern and saw the body of Norman Cuthbert. He'd been stabbed with the same sword they had found a few days previous. That's when the police turned up. They took everything away. Dad said the priest left along with Lord Barry.'

'Did your father say anything else about what happened?' Fagan questioned.

'Dad always believed Norman Cuthbert was murdered. But he could never decide if it was the Vatican priest or Lord Barry. The police interviewed everyone about the murder. They questioned dad, but he never said a word.'

'Do you know if Lord Barry was interviewed by the police?'

Sally shook her head. 'Dad never mentioned.'

'He kept the secret for a long time.'

'Yes. I remember when he told us the story of what

happened at the dig. We were just in our teens. He built the case for the daggers and mounted them on the wall.' Sally smiled. 'Dad used to love telling the tale of how he acquired the daggers. He used to dress up the story and make it sound like an Agatha Christie murder mystery. I used to love hearing the story over and over.'

'What about the exhibition he was due to showcase in 2020?'

'It was his pride and joy. It had been forty-five years since the events at Tintern. Dad didn't think anyone would make a connection. He did an extensive interview with the BBC for a documentary. He had interviews with several local newspapers and an archaeology magazine. Me and Nigel Thomas helped him organise the exhibition. I remember him being so excited.' Sally paused. 'Then that awful break in happened, and the daggers were stolen.' Sally paused again. 'It tore dad to pieces.'

'Did he ever tell you about any suspicious activity around the museum before the break in?'

'No, but just after he had made the exhibition public, Lord Barry turned up at the museum and had a rant at him. He ordered dad to hand over the daggers.'

'But your dad refused.'

'Yes.' Sally nodded. 'A few days later the break in occurred and dad was heartbroken. It's hard to believe that a few months after that, he died.'

'Did he ever have any suspicions as to who stole the daggers?'

'He was convinced Lord Barry was involved. By then the pandemic started to bite down and everything shut.' Sally inhaled. 'So did dad. As soon as the government ordered everyone to stay at home, we organised ourselves into a little bubble.'

Fagan nodded silently. 'Thank you for speaking with us

today Sally. You've been brilliant.'

'Look, there's something else I have to tell you. But I'm scared I could get into trouble.'

'Ok.' Fagan said.

'Dad spent about two years planning the exhibition. Six months before it was due to start, he contacted an archaeologist at Cambridge.'

'And this archaeologist was called Robert Turner?' Fagan guessed.

Sally nodded. 'When the news revealed who was murdered at Skenfrith castle, I knew there had to be a connection.'

'It could have helped if you contacted us to tell us what you knew.' Fagan said calmly.

Sally nodded, looking mournful. 'You see, I'm a bit superstitious. When dad used to talk about Norman Cuthbert, he would always mention an unusual ring that Cuthbert wore. It was gold with a scarab emblem. Dad said he'd first asked about it when he studied under him at Cambridge. Cuthbert told dad that he was part of the team that unearthed Tutankhamun. They broke into the tomb before the official opening. Cuthbert said that he took one item from the tomb, the ring he always wore on his little finger. Dad told me Cuthbert was wearing the ring the day before he was murdered. When dad saw the body the next day, the ring was gone.'

Fagan nodded. 'Why did your dad contact Professor Turner?'

'Dad had read there was a dig coming out to Abergavenny to solve the riddle of where Alice's last resting place was. He knew the daggers were part of map that would reveal where Alice's treasure was buried. He contacted Professor Turner about the daggers. Turner visited Dad to view the daggers. But he instructed dad to hold on to them until the dig had actually started.'

Fagan snapped his notebook shut. 'You've been very helpful Sally, thank you.'

'Does this mean you will finally investigate the possibility that dad was murdered?'

Fagan looked at the plastic bags Sally handed over. 'It will be a long journey, but we'll look into it.'

Tears welled up in Sally's eyes. 'Thank you.'

C H A P T E R 3 8

2:30pm

Fagan clutched the steering wheel, staring at the road ahead.

'You've been quiet since we left Sally's.' Stacy mentioned.

Fagan inhaled before blowing out his cheeks. 'I'm just trying to take it all in. For the past few days, all I have had is one big history lesson. I've been told stories about ancient battles, knights of old and now the curse of Tutankhamun. It's just made my head spin a little.'

'Are we out here to arrest Barry for the murder of Norman Cuthbert in 1975?'

'We need evidence for that.' Fagan suddenly had an idea. 'Evidence, yes. Shit, why didn't I see that?' He tapped a button on the steering wheel. 'Call George.'

The phone rang several times before Walker answered. 'Hello young Fagan, is everything ok? Have you solved the big case yet? Heard they found another stiff at Grosmont castle.'

'Not yet George. Do you remember what you told me about the evidence that was gathered from Tintern abbey when you investigated that murder that took place in 1975?'

'It disappeared.'

'Straight away?'

'No, it was taken back to Abergavenny. I think some blood samples were taken from the sword. But a few days later, the evidence vanished.'

'Do you know Lord Barry, who lives out by Skenfrith castle?'

'Oh yeah, he's another character I could tell you a few stories about.'

'Another one who used to frequent the London hotel, I'm guessing.'

'A bit of a card shark back in the day. They used to play poker in one of the upstairs rooms at the London. A lot of money used to change hands. Lord Barry, Bob Benson, Ernie Brown, Bill Nelson.'

'Benny's dad.' Fagan said.

'That's the one.' George paused. 'I just remembered something.'

'What?'

'When the evidence was taken back to the police station, Lord Barry turned up. Back then, it was just Malcom Barry before he inherited the title. I remember Barry having a lengthy chat with Bob Benson.'

Fagan smiled. 'Now it's all starting to make sense. If Benson was bent, he would have handed over the evidence to Barry.'

'That was my guessing at the time. Benson listed the murder as unexplained. That was the last I heard of it.'

'Thanks George.' Fagan said before hanging up. 'What a tangled web we are weaving here. Ok, let's look at this from the beginning, starting with Norman Cuthbert. Renowned archaeologist. Helped uncover King Tut's tomb. Stole a trinket from the burial chamber. Goes on to travel the world and finds information regarding this Alice of Abergavenny while in Jerusalem. Builds an obsession with her. He goes to the dig in Tintern in 1975. Finds the daggers and gives them to Tony James. Cuthbert is then murdered and all the evidence vanishes, courtesy of Bob Benson.

James keeps the daggers for forty-five years before deciding to showcase them in an exhibition. He then contacts Turner and agrees to hand over the daggers so that Turner can locate this lost treasure of Alice. Tony James publicises the exhibition in the museum. That attracts Lord Barry, who has an argument with him. There's a break in at the museum, the daggers are stolen. A few months later, Tony James drops dead of a heart attack. His daughter believed he was murdered. Plus, James sent that cryptic text to Nigel Thomas saying he knew who stole the daggers. Thomas responds by asking who, but James doesn't answer. He must have been in the murderer's company when he sent that text.'

'There's a lot of ifs, buts and coconuts in there, guv.' Stacy remarked.

Fagan inhaled. 'I know. It's like what Watkins said the other day. This is turning out to be a right da *Vinci Code*.' An idea exploded in Fagan's mind, like fireworks on a bonfire night celebration. He slammed on the brakes and skidded into a layby.

Stacy barely hung onto the latte she had just bought.

'Of course.' Fagan declared.

Stacy steadied her cup. 'Guv?'

'What if this is more than just about buried treasure and religious artefacts? There could be another element at play.'

'Like what?'

'Family and legacy. When we found the body of Turner the other morning, DS Watkins mentioned Dan Brown. I downloaded his book last night, *The da Vinci Code*.'

'I've seen the Tom Hanks film. Never read the book.'

'I'm a bit of an insomniac so I started reading it last night. The curator at the Louvre museum in Paris is murdered and laid out in a pose similar to Leonardo da

Vinci's Vitruvian man.'

'I'm not really an art lover so I have no clue what you are talking about.' Stacy remarked, sipping from her latte cup.

'It doesn't matter. The main plotline of the book is that Jesus was supposed to have hooked up with Mary Magdelene and started a family. A bloodline that survived into modern day. In the story, the curator of the museum is part of that bloodline. When *the da Vinci Code* was published, the Vatican went apeshit. Accusing Dan Brown of heresy and writing blasphemy.' Fagan gathered his thoughts. 'What if we are dealing with something similar here? What if Lord Barry is a direct descendant of Alice of Abergavenny?'

'Which would give him claim on whatever the archaeologists find.'

'Exactly.'

Stacy thumbed the screen on her phone. 'Trouble is, Lord Barry is ninety-four years old. I don't think he could have murdered three people in as many days.'

'But Lord Barry could have murdered Cuthbert in 1975.' Fagan suggested.

'So who's been carrying out the recent murders?'

'That's what DS Watkins is helping me discover.' Fagan checked the rear-view mirror before pulling back out onto the country road. 'We'll interview Barry about Cuthbert's murder in 1975. But until Watkins gets back to me, that's all we can do.'

The car continued along the country road.

'You just mentioned being an insomniac. How come?'

'Something that happened nearly thirty years ago. Kept me awake since.'

'A case?'

Fagan nodded, recalling a distant and traumatic

memory. 'I was just a snotty nosed Detective Constable. Working for Merseyside CID. We were part of the homicide unit. One night, we got this call to Liverpool docks. A prostitute had been brutally murdered. The piece of shit who murdered her really went to work.' Fagan swallowed. 'She was heavily pregnant at the time of her death. Weeks from giving birth. The murderer cut the baby out of her womb and slit the poor little bugger's throat.'

Stacy almost choked on her latte. 'Jesus.'

'Two months later, we were called to Kirby to attend another killing. It was the same MO as the Liverpool docks murder. Heavily pregnant prostitute, the baby pulled from her womb and slaughtered. Then the notes started to arrive at the station. They were addressed to me.'

'The killer knew you?' Stacy questioned.

'That's what the assumption was. At one point my CO considered me as the killer. Over twelve months, the killer murdered six women. All heavily pregnant, all had their babies cut from the womb and murdered. And then he just stopped. I remember the last note he sent me. He taunted me, saying I would never sleep until he was caught. He also promised he'd return. But that was almost thirty years ago. I haven't had a decent night's sleep since.'

'Must have been hard for you.'

'It was. All those women brutally murdered. Serial killers are a law to themselves. They can operate in plain sight. Harold Shipman was a prime example of that.'

'I've only now got around to watching Dahmer on Netflix.'

'I watched that last year. The man who killed those prostitutes in the nineties called himself the foetus killer. The press had a field day over it, labelling him as Liverpool's answer to Jack the Ripper. But let's focus on the task at hand.' Fagan said, diverting the conversation. 'What does the internet say about Lord Barry?'

Stacy called up Google. 'It says here Lord Barry lives at Skenfrith. Owns fifteen hundred acres of land. His bloodline stretches back a thousand years.'

Fagan smiled. 'Like I just said, it's all about family.'

'Like the *Fast and the furious* films.' Stacy smiled.

Fagan recalled a visit to Evans' house a few days earlier. 'A friend of mine tried to convince me to watch those the other day.'

Stacy stared at the screen. 'This is interesting. Lord Barry led the Welsh Nationalists march in October last year. I remember that, because a load of us were sent to Cardiff to police the rally. There were over ten thousand people at the march. About a hundred arrests were made.' Stacy scrolled further down, reading more information. 'Oh wow, this is really interesting. Have you ever heard of a group called Meibion Glyndwr?'

Fagan processed the name. 'Yes, I believe they were an activist group in the seventies and eighties. I suppose in this day and age they'd be classed as a terrorist group.'

'It says here Meibion Glyndwr first appeared in 1979. They targeted eight English-owned holiday homes within a month. Over a ten-year period around 220 properties were damaged. There were several other groups who also claimed responsibility for the attacks. Mudiad Amddiffyn, which means the movement to defend Wales. Then you have Cadwyr Cymru, that means keepers of Wales. There was also a group called the Welsh Army for the workers' republic.' Stacy mused. 'Sounds almost communist.'

'I never understood those who want to break away from the UK.' Fagan said. 'I used to get fed up listening to Jimmy Krankie in Scotland. Always banging on about Scottish independence.'

Stacy laughed out loud. 'Do you mean Nicola Sturgeon?'

'That's the one.' Fagan smiled. 'Thank god she's no longer in power.'

Stacy looked back at the screen. 'Lord Barry came out to support Meibion Glyndwr. He claimed they were the only ones who had the guts to stand up against English imperialism. In 1980, the police launched Operation Tân, which means fire in Welsh.'

Fagan shook his head. 'It was a waste of time. They raided a couple of places, but no one was ever charged with anything.' An idea popped into Fagan's head. 'Do us a favour. Access the police central database to see if any properties were targeted in Monmouthshire.' He flicked the indicator lever. 'Let's see what secrets Lord Barry has to reveal.'

C H A P T E R 3 9

2:37pm

Fagan looked out across the landscape. In the distance, the cylindrical Keep of Skenfrith castle towered above the trees.

'Nice place if you have the money to run it. Must cost a fortune to heat.' Stacy commented, looking up at the ancient-looking manor house.

The door opened, revealing an elderly man who supported himself with a walking stick. Despite his age Lord Barry was quite agile. He marched across the driveway. His Barbour wellingtons crunched on the gravel.

Fagan looked at him, smiling.

'If you're lost, then you can ask directions at the pub. Otherwise you are trespassing on private property, so please leave.'

'Lord Barry I take it.' Fagan said cheerfully.

'Who's asking?'

Fagan held up his warrant card. 'Detective Inspector Marc Fagan. This is Constable Stacy Flynn.'

'If this is about what happened at Skenfrith castle, then I have nothing to say without my solicitor.'

'Why would you need a solicitor, Lord Barry?' Stacy asked.

Barry perched on his stick. 'What do you want?'

'We'd like to ask you a few questions about the incident the other night.' Fagan answered.

'I just said I had nothing to do with that. Now piss off

before I call the...' Barry stopped, realising how ridiculous his threat sounded.

'Can we have a quick chat inside please, Lord Barry?'

Barry stood firm for a few moments before nodding. 'If you must.' He turned and walked back towards the house.

'That's an impressive looking ruin.' Fagan remarked, pointing towards a spire hidden behind some oak trees.

'It's what remains of an old abbey. Destroyed by Henry the Eighth during the Reformation.' Barry answered. 'This way.' He instructed, leading them into the house.

Fagan and Stacy were led through to an impressive drawing room. The walls lined with paintings of Barry's ancient ancestors. Two suits of armour guarded the entrance to the drawing room.

Fagan looked towards a large fireplace. A sword was mounted, together with a shield. Hanging over the sword and shield was a large portrait of another ancestor. Dressed in chain-mail armour wearing a worn white vest decorated with the distinctive Knights Templar red cross.

'A very proud man back in his day.' Barry stated. 'Hugh De Barry was a twelfth century knight who swore allegiance under the banner of Alice of Abergavenny.'

'I was told that Alice only had one male knight. The rest were all female.'

Barry smiled. 'History rarely gives the answers we want Inspector Fagan. My ancestor and other Templar Knights true to the cause, joined Alice's crusaders while she was in Jerusalem. He felt that the Knights Templar were no longer faithful to god. Once they established themselves in the Holy Land, they became greedy. Most of them breaking their vows and raping the city's female inhabitants.'

'So he made it back home with Alice?'

'And built this magnificent manor house.'

'Do you think he knew where Alice buried the spoils of

war?'

'I'm certain of it. But so much history has been lost over the years. Or even stolen?'

'Stolen?'

'Yes, the English raided the lands of the Welsh nobility.' Barry glanced at the picture. 'My ancestors fought off many attacks from the English.'

'Why did they pick on Welsh nobility?' Stacy asked.

'Jealousy.' Barry replied smugly. 'When news spread that Alice had returned from the Holy Land, the English launched a series of attacks on the Welsh Marches. Obviously wanting to get their hands on Alice's treasure hoard. Hugh De Barry established this stronghold to make sure invading armies would not breach the Welsh Borders. In 1178, a battle ensued on the banks of the river Monnow. Alice's forces took one hundred English prisoners. It is said she cut off their heads and used catapults to launch them over the river where the opposing army was camped. This was enough to deter the English from launching more attacks on Alice's forces.'

'Why the fierce loyalty towards her?' Fagan asked.

Barry frowned. 'Did you know, Inspector Fagan, most people who live in Wales are not even true Welsh? But the descendants of immigrants. The result of invading armies or just relocation over the centuries. Stripping away our proud culture. Alice was special, because she was of special heritage.'

'Special heritage?' Stacy said.

'It is assumed Alice of Abergavenny was just a servant girl who...'

'I know the story.' Fagan cut Barry off in mid-stream before he had a chance to launch a historical lecture.

'Do you?' Barry shook his head. 'Most people can't remember what they had for breakfast, let alone any history, especially Welsh history.' Barry walked over to a glass display cabinet that contained an ancient looking book.

Fagan remembered he had seen a sketch of the book in Turner's journal the day before. The same book Cuthbert claimed to have seen the night before he was murdered.

Stacy walked over, closely followed by Fagan.

Barry looked at the book. 'The story of Alice of Abergavenny. This book is nine hundred years old.' Barry took a deep breath. 'Alice was the daughter of William FitzMiles. But he denounced her.'

'Why?' Stacy asked.

'To protect the bloodline. William FitzMiles was the decedent of Gruffydd Llywelyn, the last king of Wales. FitzMiles had no choice but to protect his daughter from English assassins who were hunting down descendants of Welsh royalty. At the time King John considered the Welsh as a credible threat. FitzMiles was slaughtered and his lands seized. Meanwhile, Alice plotted her revenge against her father's murderers and carried it out with ruthless efficiency. She then mingled amongst the locals until her journey out to Ireland with her lover.' Barry stared down at the book with a nostalgic look on his face.

'Proud family history, then.' Fagan said.

'Very proud.' Barry stated. 'Sworn to protect the legacy of Alice.'

'Are you part of the dynasty?'

'Good heavens no. But one day, Alice's descendants will reveal themselves and claim their rightful place. Ushering in a glorious future, producing the future princes of Wales who will rule over this green land.'

Stacy glanced at Fagan, trying hard not to smirk.

'I thought we already had a Prince of Wales.' Fagan remarked.

'I take it you're referring to that watered down family currently sitting on the throne of England.' Barry mocked. 'There hasn't been a true Prince of Wales in over a thousand years.'

Fagan switched subjects. 'Do you have any CCTV on your property, Lord Barry?'

'Just on the front of the house.'

'No clear view of the road?'

'No, I'm afraid not.'

'Can you verify your whereabouts the other night? The night of the murder over at Skenfrith castle?'

'I didn't murder that archaeologist, Inspector Fagan. I'm ninety-four for God's sake. The poor fellow was stretched out and crucified according to the news.' Barry gestured towards the drawing-room door. 'Now the tour of my family's history is over. You can both leave.'

Fagan couldn't help himself. He glanced at the broadsword. 'What about Norman Cuthbert?'

Barry glared back at Fagan. 'I'd watch your tone if I were you Inspector Fagan. Accusing people of things they've supposedly done is kind of your forte, wouldn't you say? Weren't you responsible for Ben Nelson's attempted suicide a while back?'

It was now Fagan's turn to return the glare. 'Thank you for your time, Lord Barry.'

Stacy stood her ground, scrutinising Barry. She noticed the ring on his little finger, remembering what Sally had said earlier. 'That's an interesting ring you have on your finger Lord Barry. Looks Egyptian, is that a scarab?'

Barry brought his hand up to his chest, covering the ring. 'Yes.'

Stacy glanced around the room. 'Such a strange item to see amongst all this medieval Welsh heritage.'

Barry summoned an answer. 'I have a taste for many

fine things, Constable Flynn.'

'Can I ask where you acquired an unusual piece of jewellery?'

Barry stared back at her. 'No, you may not. Now please leave.'

Stacy smiled back at Barry before following Fagan towards the door.

CHAPTER 40

2:59pm

'Well, that was interesting.' Stacy remarked.

'Nice job, asking him about the ring.' Fagan said.

'I remembered what Sally talked about earlier. It's too much of a coincidence Barry wearing a ring similar to what she described.'

Fagan gathered his thoughts 'So, it's 1975. Cuthbert finds the daggers and the map. Gives the daggers to Tony James. He sketches a detailed copy of the map. Then he burns the map in front of Romano. Cuthbert is then murdered and his ring taken by Lord Barry.'

'Which means Barry could have murdered Cuthbert.' Stacy added.

'We won't know that until forensics gets their hands on that broad sword above his mantlepiece. Besides, he could quite easily claim that ring could have come from anywhere. Unless we have evidence the ring belonged to Cuthbert we are dead in the water. Remember the story that Cuthbert told Sally's dad. He stole the ring from king Tut's tomb.'

'But we have reasonable suspicion. So why aren't we arresting him?'

'Because I want the person behind the three murders over the past few days. Then we'll move on Barry. Watkins is heading back from Cambridge with information that's going to blow this case wide open.' Fagan mulled over the situation. 'Thing is, the Vatican isn't exactly squeaky clean, is it? If this Splinter of Christ is that important to them, it's definitely worth murdering someone for.'

'Kind of putting yourself out on a limb guv. How do we know Barry won't do a runner?'

'Because the man is passionate about where he lives. Did you catch that nonsense about the true king of Wales?'

'Yeah, it was a bit weird.'

'Didn't you mention Barry led the Welsh Nationalists rally last year in Cardiff?'

'Yeah.'

'I'm wondering if Cardiff police are still running that facial recognition program.'

'They are.' Stacy revealed. 'It caused a shitstorm a few years ago with human rights campaigners. Saying it was a breach of everyone's privacy. I have a friend I trained with at the academy who works on the program.'

'I'm hoping they'll still have footage of the rally as it moved through central Cardiff.'

'They probably do. Stuff like that is always useful to have on file. Just in case something kicks off at future rallies.'

'I'm sending you a picture. Can you forward it on to your contact in Cardiff and run it through the facial recognition program?'

'Sure.'

Fagan's phone buzzed. He tapped a button on the steering wheel. 'DI Fagan.'

'Sir, it's Brooks. Where are you?'

'We've just spoken to Lord Barry regarding Turner, why?'

'Two things. First, they've found Turner's car several miles outside Hereford on the Ross Road. I've pinged the location. Secondly, I have just sent you some images captured in Abergavenny Morrisons a week ago. You're going to want to look at it straight away.'

'Ok, we'll head towards Turner's car. I'll look at the pictures you've sent me.' Fagan spotted a country café. 'Fancy a coffee at the Copper Kettle?'

'Yes.' Stacy smiled. 'I could do with one of their toasted teacakes.'

Fagan flicked through the images that Brooks had just sent him. He zoomed in just to check he wasn't seeing things. 'That lying sack of shit.' He handed his phone to Stacy, who scrutinised the image.

'It's Thackery.'

'Talking to Ross Smith a week ago in Morrisons. Look at the time frame on the video.'

'So he has visited Abergavenny.'

'Yeah, the twat has been lying to us all along. The question is, what was he doing speaking to Ross Smith? And what were they talking about?' Fagan felt sadness for Smith. 'Smith didn't deserve to die. He was just caught in the middle of something that was beyond his understanding.'

'Are we going to at least arrest Thackery?'

Fagan considered Stacy's request. 'I don't know.'

'You don't know.' Stacy looked surprised.

'Look, the situation is this. We have reason to suspect Lord Barry may have murdered Norman Cuthbert in 1975. But we can't rule out the Vatican being behind his murder, either.'

'But Father Romano was murdered this morning. Putting Barry back in the frame.' Stacy said.

Fagan sensed doubt gnawing away at him. 'All Barry has to say is that Cuthbert gave him the ring. At best, we could charge him for perverting the course of justice. According to George, a few days after Cuthbert's murder, the evidence just vanished. Courtesy of bent copper Sergeant Bob Benson. That evidence is hanging on the wall in Barry's medieval mansion.'

'Whoever murdered Turner, Smith and Romano wants their hands on the splinter of Christ.' Stacy said. 'Or as you have said. This could be more than just about some religious artefact.'

'The question is, how do we link this all up?' Fagan looked at the image of Thackery and Smith. He swiped the screen, revealing another image of Smith grabbing Thackery by the arm. 'Smith was collateral damage.'

'How do you mean?'

'He was never part of this. It was pure coincidence that he bumped into Thackery in Morrisons last week. That must have spooked Thackery.'

'When did the dig out at Bont start?' Stacy asked.

'About three weeks ago.'

'But Thackery only arrived yesterday.'

Fagan nodded. 'That's what we were led to believe. But this image shows he was in Abergavenny last week. Which means he knows someone from this town.'

'Who?'

'No clue.'

'No clue, or keeping your cards close to your chest?'

Fagan smiled at Stacy. 'You'll get used to it. It's how I always work a case.'

'But Smith was a druggie. It's a stretch that he recognised Thackery.'

'I don't know. I'm sure I'd recognise someone if they gave me five grand. No matter how off my face I was.' Fagan pointed to the picture. 'Smith is grabbing Thackery's arm as he walked by him. You can see the look on his face that he recognised him. There was a large amount of cash in his flat. According to Darren Stephens it wasn't drug money.'

'It was hush money.' Stacy took a guess.

Fagan glanced at her. 'Yeah, it was hush money.' He picked up his mug and drained the contents. 'We'll drive out to the location that Brooks pinged. See if there is anything useful to be learnt from Turner's abandoned vehicle.'

A49 – Aconbury - Herefordshire– 3:53

'Detective Inspector Tracy Berkeley, West Mercia Police.'

Fagan scrutinised Berkeley's warrant card.

Berkeley looked back at the abandoned vehicle. 'Our boys found it a few hours ago and ran a number plate check. Pretty nasty shit going on your side of the border.'

'It certainly is.'

'The keys are still in the vehicle.' Berkeley explained. 'We did a quick sweep of the area and found no one. Our boys thought the owner was desperate for a piss and jumped over a fence. We've just spoken to a lorry driver who comes through here every day. He said he noticed the vehicle yesterday.'

'It's a wonder the vehicle wasn't stolen.' Stacy remarked. 'Leaving the keys in the vehicle was pretty sloppy.'

'Or they were in a rush.' Fagan suggested.

Berkeley shook his head. 'This is a pretty remote location, despite being on a main road. We get the odd vehicle theft in Hereford. Tesla is all the range at the moment for thieves. The boy racers in Hereford tend to go out towards Leominster way.'

'The murderer could have been in a rush.' Fagan looked towards the main road. 'I don't suppose there are any traffic cameras along this stretch of road?'

'Not until you get a few miles outside Hereford.' Berkeley said.

Fagan glanced at Stacy. 'It's all country roads from here to Skenfrith and Grosmont. CCTV will be non-existent. Let's check out Turner's vehicle.'

Three CSI officers were searching the vehicle.

Fagan slipped on a pair of latex gloves and approached the car. 'Anything interesting?'

'We've had a dog in the car. There are a few spliffs in the ashtray. Less than two days old.'

Fagan examined the interior of the vehicle, noting that Turner kept his car spotless.

The forensic held up a bag. 'We did find one thing.'

'What is it?'

'It's known as gallium aparine. It grows everywhere. My wife dries the leaves out and makes tea with it.'

Fagan's mind suddenly exploded.

Stacy could see Fagan had suddenly worked something out. 'You've got more of a clue who our murderer is.'

Fagan gave her a sidewards glance. He grinned. 'By any chance, is it also known as goose grass?'

The forensic nodded.

'Thank you.' Fagan handed the bag back and made a hasty retreat towards his car.

Stacy gave chase. 'Who's our suspect?'

'Until Watkins gets back, I can't be sure.'

'Are we at least going to arrest Thackery and question him?'

'No.'

'But we have Thackery on CCTV speaking to Ross Smith.' Stacy sighed.

'I just need to piece all this together. I need you to do that electric vehicle check as soon as we get back to Newport.'

'Already done.'

Fagan looked at Stacy.

She handed over her phone. 'There are only seventy-five people in Abergavenny who own electric vehicles. Four of which are Tesla.'

Fagan swiped the screen until he stopped at a name. He smiled and exited the document. 'Perfect.'

Stacy stared blankly at her phone. 'Guv?'

'I know this is frustrating for you. As police we're supposed to share everything. But we are in the end game here of this case. We'll gather the team at the incident room in Newport and see what they have.' Fagan paused. 'Then we can arrest Thackery.'

'Thank Christ for that.'

CHAPTER 41

Newport Central police HQ – 4:49pm

Thackery watched as Fagan entered the interview room with Stacy. It had caused a lot of embarrassment when police arrived at White Castle to arrest him concerning the murder of Robert Turner. But he knew it would only be a matter of time before someone connected the dots. Fagan had briefed his solicitor before the interview.

Fagan tapped the record icon on the screen of his phone. 'Interview with Damien Thackery in connection with the murder of Robert Turner. Also in relation to the murder of Ross Smith. Present in the room is Mr Thackery's solicitor, myself Detective inspector Marc Fagan and Constable Stacy Flynn. Mr Thackery, do you understand your rights?'

Thackery tapped his finger on the desk.

'Mr Thackery, do you understand your rights?' Fagan repeated.

'Yes.' Thackery seemed to jump out of a trance.

Fagan pushed a CCTV image he had printed out across the table towards Thackery. 'I am showing Mr Thackery an image of him taken in Morrisons in Abergavenny just over a week ago. Mr Thackery, do you recognise the man in the picture who can be seen talking to you?'

Thackery gave the picture a quick glance. 'No comment.'

'His name is Ross Smith. He was found dead in his flat yesterday afternoon. Would you know anything about that?'

'No comment.'

Fagan leant back in his chair, inhaling. 'I have given you a lot of room regarding what has happened over the past few days. I have also held back on that dig in Bont and the other sites. I have let you carry on. I have to admit, even I've been caught up in all the excitement. Buried treasure, lost relics, legends of this Alice of Abergavenny and a journal that is packed full of clues to treasure hidden all over the world. But now my patience has run out.' Fagan paused. 'This isn't some thriller novel or a blockbuster film. This is reality Mr Thackery. Real life, in which five people have been murdered for the sake of buried bloody treasure. Let's reflect, shall we. First, you have the unsolved murder of Norman Cuthbert in 1975. Next, you have the suspicious death of the local museum curator in 2020. We have evidence that could prove the man may have been murdered in his own home. Then we have Robert Turner. Slain like some kind of sacrificial lamb. Ross Smith followed the day after. And now Father Romano, who was found dead at Grosmont castle first thing this morning. We have Turner's car, which was found on the outskirts of Hereford. Our forensics team is scouring the car. They have already found something, Mr Thackery.' Fagan gestured at the CCTV image. 'I'm going to ask you one more time. Did you know Ross Smith? Because it certainly looks as if you did in this picture.'

'We've also watched the footage.' Stacy took over. 'It shows Smith having what looked like a heated conversation with you.'

Thackery glanced at Stacy. 'No comment.'

'Damien, listen to me.' Fagan said. 'I'm quite confident that you didn't murder any of these men.'

'Good.' Thackery blurted out. 'Because I've had fuck all

to do with any murder. If you think you're going to pin anything on me, then you can forget it.'

'But you will be charged for perverting the course of justice. Which can carry a hefty jail sentence.' Fagan made eye contact with Thackery's solicitor. 'It doesn't matter if you have a fancy solicitor. You will do jail time for not being honest about what you know. Especially when we are dealing with five murders over a space of nearly fifty years.'

'I had nothing to do with Cuthbert's murder!' Thackery shouted. 'Jesus fucking Christ, I was born in 1970. I was only five when he was killed.'

'That maybe so Damien. But four of the murders have taken place within the last three years. Three in as many days.'

'No comment.' Thackery said in a defiant tone.

'Who are you protecting, Damien?' Stacy asked. 'Is it because of that journal you are all so desperate to get your hands on? It will be a long time before you are funding anything. Is that journal really worth spending time in jail for?'

'You lot do not know what you are dealing with. You have no idea how far these people will go to protect secrets.'

Fagan and Stacy glanced at each other.

'Five people have been murdered. I think it's very clear to us what lengths these people will go to keep secrets. Who exactly are the people you're referring to?'

'They're fanatical. I'll give them that. Wanting to preserve their heritage. They don't want anything to get between them and finding this so-called lost treasure of Alice. Thing is, I have had my own team looking into Alice. They have found nothing. Cuthbert and Turner were chasing rainbows, nothing but rainbows.'

'At the end of which will be a big score for anyone who

finds it.' Stacy added.

'What do you mean, they're fanatical?' Fagan asked. 'Fanatical about what?'

'Welsh independence, of course.'

'Welsh independence?' Fagan repeated.

'Like that fish woman from Scotland, there is a group that want's Welsh independence.'

'And the name of this group?'

'I don't know.'

'You don't know, or don't want to tell us.'

'The only contact I have had with them is through Lord Barry.'

'You know Lord Barry, how?' Fagan pressed.

'He first contacted me in 2019, when Robert announced there was going to be a new hunt for the lost treasure of Alice.'

'When exactly in 2019?' Stacy asked.

'Around November.' Thackery revealed. 'After Robert publicly announced that he was launching a new project to locate the treasure of Alice, it attracted a lot of attention.'

'This attention wouldn't have been in the form of threatening notes, would it?' Fagan recalled having an earlier conversation with Sarah York.

'How do you know about those?'

'A little birdie told me.' Fagan replied. 'What did the notes say?'

'It was usually the same bullshit. All sinners will perish. But there were one or two that went into details about how a crown belonged to Alice.'

Fagan took a long sigh. 'Crown?'

'Turner wasn't just looking for the Splinter of Christ. Apparently there was some sort of golden crown amongst other things.'

Fagan slumped forward, cupping his hands over his

face. *Here we go, another trip down medieval memory lane.* 'Ok, tell me about this crown.'

'That's the thing. I don't know much about it. Turner kept everything close to his chest. I gave a brief interview for his blog because I was the co funder of the dig.'

'Did Turner mention anything about the Vatican being involved with the dig?'

Thackery shook his head. 'They didn't want to be named publicly as the co funder. The Vatican wanted to remain anonymous.'

'Typical Vatican, hiding in the shadows.' Stacy mocked.

Fagan interlocked his fingers. 'So it's 2019. Turner announces he's going to have one more go at finding this treasure of Alice. When exactly in that year did he contact you?'

'September 2019, he first approached me about funding. Thing is, that bitch of an assistant of his didn't want me involved.'

'Why?'

'Why do you think? Because of what I did ten years ago.'

'The incident with the Templar coins.' Fagan guessed.

Thackery nodded. 'I didn't start out to do what I did. The original plan was to fund more digs.'

'When did Turner first show you the journal he had in his possession?' Stacy asked.

Thackery stalled on an answer.

'Damien, we know Robert showed you the journal.' Fagan revealed. 'We know he used it to lure you in. To fund the dig out at Bont.'

'I had already seen that journal ten years ago.'

Fagan stared back at him.

'How do you think we found that hoard of coins? Everything Turner did throughout his career was done with the help of that journal. Even before he got his hands on it,

Cuthbert had almost filled it. He was the man behind Robert's success, not Robert. All he did was ride on the coat tails of Cuthbert. He wanted his hands on that journal before Cuthbert had even died.'

'What makes you say that?'

'Because that's what Romano told me yesterday. Cuthbert worked with many noted archaeologists in his day. The most famous of all, Howard Carter. In the 1920s Cuthbert travelled around the middle east with several scholars who were there just to steal as much as they could.'

Stacy was intrigued by what Thackery was revealing.

'What, you think archaeology is an honest profession? Most of the top museums in London are filled with items that were stolen from countries across the world. The glorious British empire plundering the countries it ran. Carter, Cuthbert and Turner. They are all alike. Wanting to get their hands on as much treasure as possible.'

'But you're just the same, Damien.' Fagan pointed out. 'The woman I was with yesterday, Amanda Rhys, said you've profiteered from stolen artefacts from all over the middle east.'

'Don't make out I'm the only one doing that sort of thing. The various wars over the past several decades have given a load of treasure hunters opportunities to steal things that didn't belong to them.'

'Why don't we get back to the matter in hand, namely the murder of Professor Turner? You said Lord Barry contacted you in November 2019. What did he want?'

'He wanted me to stop funding Turner's project.'

'Did he threaten you?'

'No, he had a bit of a moan about what Turner was planning to do.'

'What about the daggers stolen from Abergavenny

Museum?'

'No comment.' Thackery answered.

'Seriously, after all you've just revealed, we're back to no comment.'

Thackery stroked the thick greying stubble that wrapped around his chin.

'What do you know about the daggers stolen in 2020 from Abergavenny museum?'

'I didn't have anything to do with the death of that museum curator.' Thackery insisted.

'We're not saying you did?' Stacy said. 'But now you've mentioned it, suggests that you know something.'

Thackery took a deep breath. 'Turner knew who had the daggers.'

'Tony James, the museum curator.' Fagan guessed.

'Yes. Just after Robert made it public that he was going to have one last go of finding the treasure of Alice, the museum curator contacted him. He told Turner that he had seen the article he published in a magazine.'

'Did Turner tell you how he knew Tony James?'

'They both worked on the dig at Tintern. Where the daggers were found. He said that at the time of Norman Cuthbert's murder, both men made an agreement. They would wait until the heat had died down surrounding the murder of Cuthbert. Turner kept the journal and James kept the daggers.' Thackery shrugged. 'I guess they just forgot about one another. Turner didn't think that Tony James was in Abergavenny until he published that article. James was due to hold an exhibition featuring the daggers. The dig was due to start in March 2020, around the same time.'

Fagan pointed at the CCTV picture of him and Smith. 'It still doesn't explain how Ross Smith fits into all this.'

'Lord Barry contacted me in January 2020. It was after

James had published an article. He said another dig team was being organised to find the treasure. But he needed the daggers. One of the daggers is a key to a vault. The other pointed the way.'

'But without a map, the daggers are useless.'

Thackery nodded. 'I ran a check on the company that handled the security at the museum and found a weakness.'

'Ross Smith.'

'By then, Smith had been sacked from his job. That's when I offered him five grand to break into the museum and steal the daggers.'

'After which you gave to Lord Barry.'

'Yes.'

'Did Smith ever meet Lord Barry?'

'Yeah, he was with me when I handed over the daggers. Before anyone could do anything, the country was in lockdown and the dig was abandoned for nearly three years. Then, towards the end of last year, the university gave the go ahead for the dig to resume. That's when Turner showed me the journal again. He thought because of the lockdown, I'd lost interest in funding the project.'

'Did he promise you could have the journal after the dig was over?'

Thackery let off a snort of derision. 'Turner was never going to keep the promise. He would have held onto that journal until he was on his deathbed. I decided to go back to Lord Barry and offer to pay for the daggers. But he turned me down.'

'When was this exactly?'

'Two weeks ago. I tried to speak to him on the phone, but he wouldn't talk about it. He said I'd have to meet him face to face.'

'And you just happened to pop into Morrisons when

Smith was in there.'

'Yes.'

'He recognised you in Morrisons that day.'

'I don't know how. The bloke seemed like he was smoking weed all the time.'

'Ross Smith remembered you from your meeting in 2020 when you paid him five grand to break into the museum. Did he demand more money from you in exchange for his silence?'

'Yes.' Thackery admitted.

'How much?' Stacy asked.

'Ten grand.'

'I'm suspending this interview until further notice.' Fagan tapped the stop icon on his phone.

'I didn't have anything to do with Turner's murder, or anyone else, for that matter. If I were you, I would arrest Lord Barry. He seems to know what's going on.'

'You will be released on bail, Mr Thackery. Until a time when we decide to charge you for perverting the course of justice regarding the murder of Robert Turner.'

Thackery stood up and left the interview room, followed closely by his solicitor.

'God, I need a drink.' Fagan announced.

'What exactly is going on here, guv?' Stacy asked. 'Why did you stop the interview?'

'I'll tell you exactly what's going on. A lot of people stabbing each other in the back to get rich, that's what.' Fagan stood. 'Come on, let's have another chat with Sarah York about Turner's role in all this. I have a feeling the sun didn't shine out of his arse.'

CHAPTER 42

White castle 5:59pm

York could tell by the way Fagan was marching towards her, she was about to face another barrage of questions.

'So.' Fagan sighed after ushering York away from the rest of the dig team. 'It would seem we are back to square one, doesn't it, Sarah?'

'In what way?' York sounded apprehensive as she spoke.

'In the way the lot of you have been bullshitting me over the last few days. I have a good mind to drag you down to Newport and charge you with perverting the course of justice.'

'Ok, what's been said now?'

Fagan shoved his hands into his pockets and looked towards the castle. 'You failed to mention something about a lost crown. Instead, you've been banging on about this splinter of Christ.'

'Who told you?'

'Who do you think? Damien Thackery, when I questioned him less than an hour ago regarding the murder of Turner and four other people. I'll say to you what I said to Thackery. I have given you a lot of room.' He gestured towards the castle. 'I could have brought this whole operation to a halt, which would have ended your little treasure hunt.'

'I never thought things were going to turn out the way they have. I warned Robert not to go ahead with the dig.

But he just ignored me.'

'What has this crown got to do everything?' Stacy asked.

'Robert first discovered information regarding a crown four years ago. It was one of the reasons he wanted to go after the lost treasure of Alice. As for the crown, it's supposed to have belonged to someone called Gruffydd Llywelyn. Allegedly, the last king of Wales. It is rumoured that Alice was a direct decedent of Llywelyn. For decades, the final resting place of the crown has been rumoured to be hidden with the splinter of Christ.'

'Why have you only now told me about this?'

'Because of the threats Robert had received when he publicised he was going to start a dig out in Bont.'

'Do you think any of these threats were made by Lord Barry?'

'I had a feeling he was connected with all this. Barry had an argument with both Cuthbert and Robert about the crown.'

'Robert told you this, did he? But you said previously they only had an argument about the splinter of Christ.'

'Yes.' York admitted. 'When Robert was just starting out, he said that Cuthbert took him under his wing. By then, Cuthbert was in his seventies. The man had been all over the world looking for lost treasure. He'd compiled that journal while on his travels. When they began the dig at Tintern, they didn't expect to find anything. But then Cuthbert's team unearthed the sword and the daggers, together with the map. The map held the key to finding both the splinter of Christ and the lost crown of Llywelyn. Cuthbert also had another favourite student.'

'Tony James.' Stacy guessed.

'Yeah. Both Robert and Tony were bitter rivals at Cambridge. Robert was the first to discover the sword with

Alice's seal. Then a day later, Tony discovered the daggers. Cuthbert took the credit for both finds.'

'That must have pissed both Turner and James off.'

'It did. Cuthbert wanted all the glory to himself. He saw the way Howard Carter died and was determined not to die in poverty. Norman was dedicated to the splinter of Christ and the lost crown of Llywelyn. Before his career came to an end.'

'He didn't count on his life coming to an end first.'

'No, he didn't.'

'Do you think Robert or James had a hand in Cuthbert's murder?'

'No, I am certain of that.'

'So who murdered Cuthbert?' Fagan asked.

'If I were to put a finger on it, I'd say Lord Barry.'

Fagan remembered what George had said to him a few days earlier. 'Did Robert ever go into detail about what happened at the time of Cuthbert's murder?'

'They'd been at Tintern for over two weeks. Robert was convinced there wasn't anything to find. He told Cuthbert the legend of Alice of Abergavenny was just that. Robert said he should concentrate on other artefacts that Cuthbert had outlined in his journal. But Norman was determined to find Alice's treasure. That's when Robert discovered the sword. He told me that once he had unearthed it Norman became aggressive towards him and took the sword away immediately. A few days after when the daggers were discovered by James, Cuthbert seized those as well.' York paused. 'Robert told me that Norman held a grudge.'

'A grudge against who?'

'Howard Carter.'

'What, the bloke who discovered Tut's tomb?'

'Yes.'

'Go on.' Fagan sighed. 'I'm listening.'

'When Norman arrived in Egypt at the end of October 1922, he was eager to make an impression on Howard Carter. So he set about undermining Carter's assistant, Arthur Callender. Cuthbert soon became Carter's main assistant. When Lord Carnarvon arrived in Cairo, Cuthbert and his young daughter, Evelyn, had a brief affair. Cuthbert thought his feet were under the table with Carnarvon's daughter. The night before the tomb was to be opened in the presence of the Egyptian department of antiquities, Howard Carter, together with Cuthbert, Evelyn and Carnarvon, broke into Tutankhamun's burial chamber. The story goes that Cuthbert and Evelyn were the first to enter the tomb. That's when they decided to take one small item from a chest they found packed with valuable objects. The tomb was sealed up for the official opening. A few months after the opening of the tomb, Evelyn and Cuthbert had an argument about who should take credit for the first one to enter the tomb. Carnarvon forbid Cuthbert from going anywhere near his daughter.'

'And Robert revealed this to you?'

'Yes, he told me because Cuthbert promised Robert that he would never freeze him out of anything. After falling out of favour with Lord Carnarvon, Cuthbert was kicked off the dig and found himself out of a job. For the next ten years he travelled all over the middle east, learning all he could about archaeological sites that had yet to be unearthed. Cuthbert logged everything in that journal. In 1932 he teamed up with another archaeologist, called Max Mallowan.'

'Here we go?' Fagan rolled his eyes. 'Another history channel montage.'

York looked right at him. 'Who happened to be married to Agatha Christie.'

'Ok, I suppose that's interesting.'

'In 1952, Cuthbert was in Jerusalem at a templar tomb. It was there, he found a pendant that bore the seal of Alice of Abergavenny. The trinket was also accompanied by several parchments which told the tale of Alice and her exploits in Ireland. That's when Norman became interested in Alice. Robert also told me that Mallowan encouraged Cuthbert to pursue the legend of Alice. To find his own Tutankhamun. For the next twenty years, Cuthbert catalogued the middle east and Europe, gathering evidence of Alice's exploits. Chronicling everything in that journal. He also travelled to South America and other parts of the world, filling the journal with as much information as possible. When you actually look through it, Robert contributed very little. Then, in the early seventies, he hit the jackpot at a dig just outside Monmouth at the Agincourt hotel. Scrolls were found relating to Alice coming into possession of the crown of Llywelyn. When she returned from the Holy Land, the people of Wales gave her a hero's welcome. She returned to Monmouthshire and was visited by a group of clerics who were in possession of the crown. They told Alice that she was a direct descendent of Llywelyn and that she was the rightful ruler of Wales.'

'I take it she accepted her role.'

'No, Alice had the clerics murdered.'

'Look, I know you archaeologists are all about history and love a good story. But can we skip to the part where Cuthbert was found with a broadsword sticking through him?'

'When Robert found the broadsword baring the seal of Alice, Cuthbert took possession and kept it with him. A few days later, when they found the daggers, he took them back to his room at a hotel in Abergavenny.'

'Would that be the Angel Hotel?' Fagan asked,

remembering what George had told him a few days earlier.'

York nodded. 'But he kept the map with him. Lord Barry and Father Romano arrived just after they found the daggers.'

'Do you know if the Vatican was funding the dig?'

'No.' York replied. 'The dig was being funded by Mallowan and Agatha Christie. Robert told me that when they started the dig, they both visited Tintern. There was a lot of publicity surrounding their visit. It's like I mentioned before. Robert was convinced other students on the dig team were feeding information back to Lord Barry.'

'What happened on the night Cuthbert was murdered?' Stacy asked.

'Father Romano and Lord Barry wanted to take possession of the daggers. Which at the time had the map with them. Barry knew about the lost crown of Llywelyn. Romano was interested in recovering the splinter of Christ. They both tried to negotiate with Cuthbert, but he didn't want to know. That's when he torched the map in front of Romano and Barry, after sketching a duplicate in his journal.' York paused. 'Robert wasn't superstitious or anything like that. But he once said, Cuthbert's greed and obsession with Alice stemmed from dig in the Valley of the Kings.'

Fagan couldn't stop himself from laughing. 'Are you telling me that Cuthbert was affected by the curse of Tutankhamun?'

York shrugged. 'There are those in the archaeological community who believe that some things are best left buried. Lord Carnarvon died less than a year after he discovered the boy king. Along with others who were at the dig site. Carter himself died penniless. Virtually no one showed up for his funeral.'

'Ok, so Romano and Barry tried to convince Cuthbert to hand over the daggers. He said no and burnt the map. Then what happened?'

'There was a massive argument.'

'Did Robert witness this argument?'

'Yes, so did Tony James. Robert said they were arguing well into late evening. He told me that Cuthbert had a go at him and James. So they decided to leave.'

'They left Cuthbert alone with Barry and Romano?' Stacy asked.

'Yes, it was just the three of them left.' York inhaled. 'That's when Robert and James decided to break into Cuthbert's hotel room and steal the daggers and the journal.'

Fagan smirked. 'Just like those two idiots who broke into Robert's room at the Agincourt hotel.'

York nodded. 'The next morning they returned to Tintern, Robert said that he was feeling guilty that he had stolen the journal the night before. So he took the journal to the abbey to hand it back to Cuthbert. Robert said he had a massive argument with Tony James, who was determined to hang on to the daggers. When they got to Tintern, the police were there. Robert said that he saw Cuthbert's body with the sword.'

'So Robert wasn't exactly the saint you have been making him out to be.'

'Robert had his issues. But since he was diagnosed with terminal cancer, he became more obsessed with finding Alice's treasure hoard. He knew time was running out.'

'In more ways than one.' Fagan added. 'Did you witness any confrontation between Lord Barry and Robert?'

'No.' York responded. 'When we first started the dig a few weeks back, Robert went to meet with Lord Barry on his own.'

'But he never told you what their meeting was about.'

'Robert just mentioned that Lord Barry was ranting and raving about the dig team disturbing the site at Bont.'

Fagan glanced at Stacy. 'What's the chances Turner knew who murdered Cuthbert?'

'I'd say pretty good.'

'But there's no way Barry or Romano could have murdered Robert.' York stated. 'They're elderly. There's no way they could have murdered Robert in that fashion.'

'Which means our suspect is still at large.' Stacy added.

Fagan looked towards the castle. 'How are things progressing?'

'They're not. I have deciphered all the texts on the shield. But nothing that suggests where the last resting place of Alice could be. The text which speaks of a place where the devil dined during the crucifixion could be anywhere.'

Fagan smirked.

'However, the shield itself could be worth a fortune if it belonged to Joseph of Arimathea. But just try proving it.' York looked at Fagan. 'How are you coming along with identifying who killed Robert?'

'We're getting there. The murderer can't stay hidden for long. I'll let you know when we have something.'

'So what's the plan guv?' Stacy asked as they climbed back into the car.

Fagan stared at his phone that had just pinged. 'Watkins has been held up.'

'We could arrest Lord Barry in connection with the murder of Norman Cuthbert in 1975.'

'No, I should imagine Barry has already called his lawyer. And it's all about proving it. We know that Turner and James were both witnesses to an argument that took place between Barry, Romano and Cuthbert. They left, returned to the Angel hotel to steal the journal and the daggers. The next morning, Turner had a change of heart and decided to return the stolen journal. But when he arrived back in Tintern, Cuthbert was already dead. Turner keeps the journal and James keeps the daggers.'

'I see our problem now. If Barry murdered Cuthbert, there is no way we'll be able to prove he did. Because the only witness to the argument is dead. Barry will just blame everything on Romano.'

Fagan nodded. 'He was obviously present when Cuthbert was murdered. Because he stole Cuthbert's Egyptian ring, you noticed earlier.'

'Do you think we should pay Sally another visit? It's clear that her father wasn't totally honest with her. He said that Cuthbert gave him the daggers, when in fact he stole them.'

'My guess is that he was protecting her from the truth. This has been all about lies from the very beginning.' Fagan's phoned pinged again. He smiled as he read the text.

'What is it?'

'Watkins has just e-mailed me the information I needed to piece this all together. Now I can make my move. We'll head back to Newport and organise a team. We have to be quick. Timing is everything now.' Fagan started the car. 'Then later on we'll make our move.'

CHAPTER 43

Angel Hotel – Abergavenny – 8:32pm

'Let me tell you about a young woman who went on a remarkable journey. It is also a story about greed, murder and the hunt for lost treasure.' Amanda smiled at the assembled audience. As with a few nights previous the room was packed with enthusiastic historians. Even the South Wales Argus had sent a journalist to cover the evening's talk. 'However, this is not a tale for the fainthearted. It is a tale full of death, murder and betrayal. It is a story that resonates to this very day. This is a tale about a woman scorned, and her rise to power. You could almost compare Alice of Abergavenny with Boudicca. Although, Alice's story has a more victorious ending than Boudicca's. Alice was supposedly just a humble serving girl who lived locally. However, we now know more about Alice because of interest shown by various academics over the years. If you have any questions, please put your hand up and ask away.'

Hands soon shot up into the air.

Amanda pointed at a man. 'Yes.'

'Do you think Alice is actually buried around here?'

Amanda sipped from a bottle of mineral water. 'I am certain of it. Why else would they have sent an archaeological team from Cambridge to look for her lost burial place? Although let's not forget the terrible events that have befallen the dig team. A prominent archaeologist was murdered in a brutal fashion a few nights ago. And just this morning, another gruesome murder took place just up the road at Grosmont castle. But let us not dwell on the macabre. Instead, let us embrace the legend of Alice of Abergavenny.'

A woman raised her hand. 'How much do we really know about her? I have looked online and there is virtually nothing known about her.'

'You're right, there's very little information. But the internet can't always tell us what we need to know. Many local people don't realise what a fascinating history this town has. When Boudicca led the revolt against the Romans in 60AD, A Roman garrison was dispatched from the island of Mona. Now known as Anglesey. The garrison travelled down through Wales and camped out at a fort where Abergavenny castle now stands. They stayed for a few days before marching on, bringing an end to Boudicca's campaign against the Roman empire.'

'But what about Alice herself? I know the information on the net isn't that accurate. So how much do you know about her?' The woman asked.

Amanda looked back at her. 'For over ten years I was a researcher at Cambridge university. I came across various texts regarding Alice's exploits. There aren't that many women in history that achieved what Alice accomplished during her lifetime. What I know is this. Alice wasn't just a humble servant girl that history would have you believe. The account of her exploits by Gerald of Wales isn't entirely accurate. Alice was the only child of William FitzMiles. He was a nobleman that lived in Abergavenny in the twelfth century. It was a time when sons were preferred over daughters. FitzMiles loved his daughter very much but was forced to disown her. Why did he do this? FitzMiles himself was a figure of myth and legend. It is said that he was descended from Gruffydd Llywelyn.'

Muffled whispers reverberated around the packed hall.

'I thought that would get your attention.' Amanda grinned.

'Who was this Gruffydd Llywelyn bloke?' A voice called out from the assembled audience.

'For those of you who don't know, Gruffydd Llywelyn, he was the last king of Wales.'

More whispers.

'Gruffydd Llywelyn was killed during the battle of Brecon in 1093AD. But that's only the beginning of his story. For Llywelyn's ancestors descended from an ancient Welsh lineage. Gruffydd Llywelyn was a member of the house of Dinefwr, which was a family that stretched back to the Roman period. There are text that record the House of Dinefwr were part of the uprising against the Roman empire. In 410AD the Romans were finally expelled from Britain. Just sixty years later, in 476AD, the Roman empire fell. Following the defeat of the Romans, Britain underwent a period of turmoil. Different rulers from all over, fighting amongst themselves. The house of Tewdwr was no different. Constantly having to fend off other would be conquerors from Merica, or England as it is known today.'

Another hand went up. 'Is all this written somewhere?'

'Yes it is?' Amanda answered, looking towards a man in the front row. 'Thanks to the hard work of my good friend, Lord Barry, we have pieced together the events of the day. Just after the Romans fled Britain, the Dinefwr king commissioned a golden crown. To be worn by himself and all his descendants. Over the years, the crown passed down the family. At one point, ending up in the hands of Arthur, as in King Arthur.' Amanda stopped speaking to gage the reaction of her captivated audience. 'And yes, I am talking about the actual King Arthur, who blessed the crown before handing it back to the Dinefwr king. The golden crown was kept well-guarded until it was handed down to William FitzMiles. However, by then the house of Dinefwr had grown so much. There was infighting and murder, not unlike your average episode of *Game of Thrones*.'

laughter spread throughout the room.

'The golden crown was a sought after relic. Whoever wore the crown could rule over Wales. But FitzMiles, despite being a rich land owner, had no interest in being king. Although the crown was passed to him, he refused to wear it. But he also refused to give it away. FitzMiles married the daughter of a nobleman, Seisyll ap Dyfnwal. Who owned lands in present day Monmouthshire, which, back then, was part of the old kingdom of Gwent. Dyfnwal offered his fourteen-year-old daughter to FitzMiles to secure an alliance between the two families. But tragically FitzMiles' young wife died two years after giving birth to Alice. Outraged by the death of his daughter, Dyfnwal launched an attack on Abergavenny. But was unable to capture the castle and the town. For nearly twelve years, Dyfnwal launched a campaign to take the castle and the crown. Finally, in 1165, there was a massacre in which William FitzMiles was captured and beheaded. However, before the attack took place, FitzMiles instructed a cleric to spirit the golden crown away.'

'What about Alice?' A member of the audience asked.

Amanda continued. 'By the time the final attack took place. Alice had already been disowned by her father. But FitzMiles did not disown her for being a girl. He did it to protect her. She was sent to live with a local family who had no particular standing, but wasn't allied with anyone at the time. After the castle had been taken and the murder of her father, Alice planned her bloody revenge. She was able to establish herself as a servant in the

Dyfnwal house. Then in 1167AD Alice made her move. In October of that year, she crept into Dyfnwal's bed chambers. As his wife lay sleeping, Alice plunged a dagger into her chest. Dyfnwal woke and tried to call for help. But Alice convinced him to stay silent. For Alice had discovered that Dyfnwal's wife was unable to bear children. So she offered herself to him. And when in the throes of passion, Alice slit Dyfnwal's throat. As he lay dying, Alice revealed her true identity and that her father had died at his hand. Alice fled into the night.'

'Are you saying that Alice seduced her own grandfather?' An audience member enquired.

Amanda nodded, taking another sip of mineral water. 'Incest wasn't exactly against the law back then. A year after these events, Alice travelled to Ireland with a knight who had betrothed himself to her. But tragically Alice's lover was killed in battle. For the second time in her life, Alice was left alone. Both heartbroken and enraged, Alice went to the commander of the army and said that any prisoners should be beheaded. So in one afternoon Alice murdered seventy prisoners by chopping off their heads and returning them back to the opposing side. A cleric called Arthur of Monmouth wrote an account of what transpired.' Amanda looked down at her notes. '*Up to seventy Irishmen were taken prisoner, and the brave knights had them beheaded. They gave an axe of tempered steel to a servant girl, who beheaded them all. And then threw their bodies over a cliff. While their heads were returned to the Irish masters who had sent them into battle. For the servant girl had lost her lover that day in battle. The girl who served the Irish thus, was called Alice of Abergavenny.*'

'What happened after the battle?' A man asked.

'After Alice had beheaded the seventy men, she retired

to her dwelling. A knight who had witnessed the slaughter visited her. It is thought his name has been lost to history.' Amanda broke out into a smile. 'But now this evening, I can reveal who that man was. His name was Robert de Payens.'

Blank expressions stared out from the audience.

'A name none of you are familiar with. But what if I told you that Robert de Payens was the grandson of a man called Hugues de Payens?'

A few of the audience recognised the name, nodded enthusiastically.

'For those of you who are still not familiar with the name. Hugues de Payens was the founder of the Knights Templar.'

A chorus of excited whispers broke out.

'Robert de Payens offered Alice the chance to go on a quest to the holy land. To walk in the footsteps of his grandfather. Together with de Payens and Aurthur of Monmouth, Alice travelled through Europe. They recruited thousands of followers, who were mostly female. By the time they reached Jerusalem Alice commanded an army of several thousand. And so her greed for wealth and power grew. In eighteen months, she sacked the towns and villages that surrounded Jerusalem. Arthur of Monmouth chronicled her quest.' Amanda looked towards a stand on which stood the chronicles. 'This manuscript is the actual text that Arthur of Monmouth wrote and has been in Lord Barry's family for generations. For he is a direct descendent of Arthur of Monmouth.'

Barry stood up and bowed to the excited audience.

'Arthur of Monmouth was the brother of Hugh De Barry, another descendent. When Alice returned to her native Monmouthshire, she built a manor house. That contained a vault where she stored the spoils of her quest. Supposedly, the treasure she amassed included the splinter of Christ. But this is not the greatest treasure in the vault. Shortly after she had returned, Alice was approached by a cleric who presented her with the golden crown of the Dinefwr king. The cleric told Alice that she was the heir and the rightful ruler of Wales. But Alice wasn't interested in ruling the land her ancestors ruled over. Her lust for wealth had consumed her. So she had the cleric murdered, and the crown was hidden away in the vault. Alice already had a price on her head because of her deeds in the holy land. She bore four daughters and entrusted them with the secret of the vault of treasure. After Alice died, her daughters had the manor house destroyed and the vault containing the treasure was sealed off. To this day, its location remains a mystery. Over the centuries, people have searched for Alice's lost treasure but so far have yet to find anything. History claims that Alice's descendants were eventually wiped out.' Amanda inhaled. 'But that is not the case. Alice's linage still exists to this very day.'

More excited whispers.

Amanda smiled at her captivated audience. 'Tonight I can reveal to you ladies and gentlemen, that I am a direct descendent of Alice of Abergavenny.'

The room plunged into silence.

'I had no idea until my grandmother passed away several years ago. Before she died, she told me everything. After doing genealogy research I discovered my ancestors were in fact from around here. Five years ago, I moved to Abergavenny to look for my ancestors. That's when I met Lord Barry, who has been helping me piece together this nine hundred-year-old puzzle.'

'Is that why you murdered Professor Turner?' A voiced shouted from the back of the room.

All eyes focused on Fagan, who was sitting in the back row.

CHAPTER 44

The Angel Hotel

Fagan removed his fedora hat and placed it on the empty chair next to him. He stepped out from the row of chairs and strolled slowly towards where Amanda was standing.

Everyone was staring at him.

'I couldn't put my finger on it at first. But right from the beginning, you have been at the centre of this mystery haven't you Amanda? Or should I say Sonya. Sonya Asker.'

Amanda maintained her smile. 'Inspector Fagan, I have no idea what you are talking about.'

Members of the audience were firing angry stares at Fagan.

Fagan shoved his hands into his beige trench coat pockets. 'It must have been the opportunity of a lifetime for you.' He glanced at the people sat in the room. 'She's telling the truth about more or less everything. You were a researcher at Cambridge until eight years ago when you were sacked from your job. What Amanda is failing to tell you good people tonight is that she was fired from her job for stealing from Professor Turner. The man who was murdered the other night.' He paused. 'You've already seen the journal that Turner owned when you originally stole it from his office. If it wasn't for CCTV, then it would have been lost forever. Or until you would have been able to get your hands on the daggers. Which you eventually did.'

'And you have evidence to prove all this, do you?' Amanda said calmly.

'As a matter-of-fact DS Watkins has been on a fact finding mission to Cambridge today. Funny, he couldn't find any reference to Amanda Rhys. So he talked to a few people at Cambridge who knew Professor Turner. That's when someone told him about the theft that took place. It was reported to the police, so it was just a matter of running a quick check. You were caught an hour after you stole the journal. But an hour is all you needed. To see where the lost treasure of Alice was hidden. But you needed the daggers, at least two of them, anyway. Turner pressed charges, and you were sacked from your post in the archaeology department. Something you failed to mention in an earlier conversation with me.'

Amanda stared back at Fagan. 'Really, DI Fagan, I think you're letting that trench coat go to your head.'

Fagan smiled back at her. 'You decided to move to Abergavenny to see if there was anything to this so-called lost treasure of Alice. It is then that you changed your name to Amanda Rhys. My colleague has already run your name through the DVLA. You assumed the new name in 2018 when you moved here. It was easy for you because there is no legal process involved changing your name, unless you have to update your driving licence or passport. You can simply move to a different town and assume a new identity. You bided your time, made friends, settled in and waited. In the meantime, Lord Barry had already contacted you. All you needed was the daggers.'

Barry stood. 'I hope Inspector Fagan, you have a damn good lawyer. Because you're going to need one by the time I am through with you.'

Fagan ignored Barry. 'Then, as luck would have it, the daggers surfaced. In the form of the exhibition at

Abergavenny museum. A place that you had already attempted to get a job. But it wasn't enough for you to contact the museum curator and simply ask to use the daggers to aid you in finding Alice's lost treasure. You already knew Turner was coming to Abergavenny to look for the treasure. You already told me you were familiar with him. Which would have made it easy for you to keep up with his online blogs. Plus, you had already tried to steal the journal he owned several years previous. When he announced he was going to have one last go at finding the treasure, you set a plan into action. What you didn't expect was covid bringing the country to a halt. You read that Damien Thackery was one of the dig's sponsors, so you contacted him. You already knew he had a reputation for double crossing people. So it was easy to convince him to pay someone to break into the museum and steal the daggers.'

People turned their heads towards Amanda.

'Again, DI Fagan, this is all just speculation.' She said calmly.

'What you didn't count on was Tony James doing detective work of his own. He somehow discovered that you had information regarding the missing daggers. He decided to confront you about the matter. So he invited you to his house. Because of your knowledge with plants you concocted a mint tea which you laced with a local poison. But you were sloppy, you disposed of your gloves in the waste bin. It would have been easy to murder someone during lockdown. What you didn't expect, was Tony's daughter having suspicions about her father's untimely death. She even approached you about it. But you convinced her that her father had suffered a heart attack. Just like what the police believed. Tony's daughter fished the gloves out of the bin. Even as we speak, they are on their way to a lab for forensic testing. As is the tea strainer found on the kitchen worktop, you left behind. You see, you were arrogant enough to believe that there would be no investigation into his death. You also knew that because of lockdown restrictions, the police wouldn't have been able to deal with a full on murder enquiry.'

'Can you even hear the dribble coming from your mouth, DI Fagan.' Barry mocked.

Fagan locked eyes with him. 'Then we have you, Lord Barry, a man of many traits.'

'You're an absurd fool to think that I had anything to do with Turner's death.'

'No, I don't. But what about the murder of Norman Cuthbert in 1975? When the daggers were found at Tintern. You knew they were the key to finding the lost treasure of Alice.' Fagan glanced at the manuscript. 'Because it's probably written down in that old manuscript you have brought with you tonight.' He looked at Amanda. 'You said it yourself when I spoke with you the other day. Alice's scribe documented everything. Which meant he had to have written something down about the daggers.' He looked back at Barry. 'You were arguing with Cuthbert when he found the sword and the daggers. Along with Father Romano. Both Turner and James were witness to this argument. But they left when you two were still arguing.'

Barry grimaced. 'I hope you're not accusing me of murdering Norman Cuthbert.'

'There were just three of you that night, Cuthbert, Romano and you.'

'And it was Romano who murdered Cuthbert.' Barry claimed.

'It's easy for you to say that. But if Romano had murdered Cuthbert, I doubt very much if the Vatican would have left you alive to tell the story. The last thing you were expecting was Romano to turn up nearly fifty years later. I mean, how could you have known he was still alive? So when he arrives at the site, it turns everything upside down for you.'

'Now you're just embarrassing yourself, Di Fagan.' Amanda said.

Fagan sensed his phone buzz in his pocket. He checked his messages, smiling at the screen. 'I don't think so. You see, while you have been giving a history lesson here at the Angel. My team acquired a warrant to search your home.' Fagan held his phone high in the air with a picture of two daggers. 'Our team has found the two remaining daggers.'

The colour drained from Amanda's face.

Fagan tapped out the word, now, on his phone and hit send.

Several seconds later, two double doors opened at the back of the room. Stacy marched into the room, leading a small army of uniformed officers. 'Ladies and gentlemen, we would like everyone to remain seated, please.' Her voice carried over a shocked looking audience.

Fagan stepped up to Amanda. 'I guess our date is off later on. Amanda Rhys, I'm arresting you for the murder of Robert Turner. You do not have to say anything. But, it may harm your defence if you do not mention when questioned something which you later rely on in court. Anything you do say may be given in evidence. I am also arresting you in connection with the murders of Tony James, Father Romano and Ross Smith. You do not have to say anything. But, it may harm your defence if you do not mention when questioned something which you later rely on in court. Anything you do say may be given in evidence.'

Stacy stood behind Amanda. 'Your hands please.'

'This is outrageous. You cannot do this.' Barry

protested. 'Do you have any idea who you are dealing with here?'

Fagan walked up to him. 'Lord Barry, I am arresting you in connection with the murder of Norman Cuthbert in 1975. You do not have to say anything. But, it may harm your defence if you do not mention when questioned something which you later rely on in court. Anything you do say may be given in evidence.'

'You have no idea the chain of events that have set in motion this evening, DI Fagan.' Barry sneered.

A uniform took him by the arm. 'This way please sir.'

'Get off me, you flat footed imbecile.' Barry pulled away.

Stacy led Amanda towards the exit.

As she passed Fagan, she glanced at the trench coat he was wearing. 'Well done, Lieutenant Colombo. But the game isn't over.'

CHAPTER 45

Newport Central HQ – Three days later

Fagan stared at Amanda.

Her stare was fixed in front of her. This was a woman who didn't look too bothered about the situation that faced her.

Fagan opened the file he had brought with him. He took time to read through some notes.

Amanda's solicitor sat next to her, scribbling quietly.

Fagan inhaled. 'Ok, so help me understand all this, Sonya.'

'It's Amanda.' She fired back quickly. 'And as for understanding anything, DI Fagan. I seriously doubt a backward flatfoot like you could tie his own shoelaces, let alone understand what has transpired here.'

Fagan nodded. 'Oh, ok, we're down to calling me names now are we? The other day you were all for inviting me to your place and making homemade lasagne. Incidentally, the police searched your home the other night. You know, the night you were supposed to have cooked me lasagne. You'd already prepared two dishes. I had them both taken to a lab for analysis. One dish was laced with hemlock. A very deadly poison. I've had some terrible dates with women over the years, but none of them have tried to kill me.'

Amanda briefly glanced at Fagan.

'And as for me being a backward flatfoot. I'm not the one facing multiple murder charges. And if I'm as backward as you believe, then why are you sat there? I mean, you've obviously put a lot of planning into whatever twisted game you're playing out here. Trouble is, like any criminal, you left clues for me to follow. On the outside you seem like a decent person. You're well educated. You've made a lot of friends since you moved to Abergavenny five years ago. Settling in nicely, getting a job at the local museum, after Tony James, the former curator, died during lockdown.' Fagan glanced at the file. 'It says here that you are the lead member of the Abergavenny historical society. You took over in August 2019. I have been looking at the Facebook page. Arthur Grant, the man who used to run it, died suddenly. According to his friends he had a massive heart attack.' Fagan swiped the tablet. 'You posted a comment on the page when Tony James announced his death. Can't believe he's gone. What a sweet man. I only visited him at his house yesterday.' Fagan looked at Amanda. 'Why did you pay this man a visit?'

'Don't tell me you think I murdered him.' Amanda sighed.

'No way to tell is there. He was cremated and his autopsy didn't really reveal anything significant. But let's not dwell on that, shall we. Let's talk about you.' Fagan looked down at his file. 'Let's see, you were born in April 1968. Daughter of David and Susan Asker. You lived at a place called Marshland St James in Norfolk. Tell me about your parents, Sonya.'

'I told you, it's Amanda.' She fired back.

Fagan rolled his eyes. 'Ok then Amanda, tell me about your parents.'

'They were murdered.'

'Do you have evidence to prove this?'

'They died in a car accident in 1995. The police report at the time said that the cables to the brakes had been cut.'

Fagan looked down at the report. 'That's what it says here. But that's about all. There's nothing to suggest who sabotaged the brake cables.'

'That's because Turner was a clever bastard who was able to get away with murder.'

Fagan sat back in his chair, glancing at Amanda's solicitor. 'You think Professor Turner murdered your parents in 1995?'

'I don't think DI Fagan, I know.'

'But how do you know?'

'Because that's what my grandmother believed.'

Fagan glanced at his notes. 'Your grandmother being Sylvia Asker.'

Amanda stared at Fagan before nodding.

'I've been doing a bit of historical research myself over the past three days. Your grandmother wasn't originally from Norfolk, was she?'

'No.'

'It says here she was born in Monmouth in 1927.'

Amanda glanced at Fagan. 'How do you know that?'

'The police have access to all kinds of data. We can access family trees if needs be. Because that's what this is all been about, lineage and family, isn't it? Tell you what, your family history is an interesting read. You never knew your grandfather, did you?'

'No.' Amanda sighed. 'I did not know my grandfather.'

'Until your grandmother told you who he was.'

Amanda nodded.

'Lord Barry?'

'How do you know all this?' Amanda demanded to know.

'We accessed your father's birth certificate. Malcolm Barry is the named father. What I want to know, Amanda, is how your journey began?'

'It began with the murder of my parents, that's how.'

'They obviously meant everything to you.'

'Of course they did, didn't yours?'

'So why do you think Turner was responsible for their deaths?'

Amanda didn't answer.

'Amanda, you are looking at spending the rest of your life in prison. You'll have plenty of time to spend in the prison library reading up on all the history you want. What is the point of keeping secrets? You've no family left to speak of. You never married, never had children.'

'My father was a student of archaeology.'

'Along with Robert Turner and Tony James.' Fagan guessed.

'Yes.'

'What happened?'

'My father knew about our family history from a young age. He was encouraged to go to university and study archaeology.'

'At Cambridge I take it.'

'Yes.' Amanda answered. 'At the time Norman Cuthbert was head of the archaeology department.'

'Was it your grandfather who told him to study archaeology?'

'Yes.'

'I have a friend who is a history buff. You've already mentioned him, Nigel Thomas.' Fagan pulled out a sheet of paper from his file. 'He's sent me a load of stuff here. This is an article from the Abergavenny tribune in 1968. The article in question covers a dig at the Agincourt hotel and how clues to a fabulous lost treasure belonging to Alice of Abergavenny had been unearthed.' Fagan pointed at a black-and-white photograph. 'This is Norman Cuthbert, meeting with the mayor of Monmouth at the time. Can you see who else is in the picture?' Fagan put his finger on the photograph. 'That's a young Lord Barry. And if you look closely at the photo of Norman Cuthbert, you can see something tucked under his arm.'

Amanda focused on the photograph.

'It's the journal that Cuthbert had compiled during his lifetime as an archaeologist. That's when Lord Barry first found out about the possibility this lost crown of Wales could be buried around Monmouthshire. Lord Barry is a fascinating figure, isn't he.' Fagan looked down, turning a page in his file. 'It says here that he was the founder of a group called Cadwyr Cymru, which means the movement to defend Wales. He was arrested in 1969, during a demonstration at Caernarfon castle on 1st July. It was during the investiture of Prince Charles. Ten years later, Lord Barry was questioned in relation to thirty four arson attacks on homes in the Monmouthshire region, all owned by people from England.'

Amanda smiled. 'And yet police were unable to prove a thing.'

'Yeah, you're right. He even sued for compensation.' Fagan looked at Amanda. 'So, I take it your father was at the dig in Tintern in 1975?'

Amanda hesitated before nodding.

'He obviously contacted Lord Barry and told him all about the dig. That's when Lord Barry turned up with the Vatican. Join forces, so to speak. Try to get their hands on the journal that Cuthbert owned. Which would lead them to this splinter of Christ and the lost crown of Wales. But Cuthbert was having none of it. He was just as hell bent on finding the treasure. Which is why he hid the daggers and the journal at the Angel hotel. But he didn't count on two things. Turner and James breaking into his hotel room and stealing the daggers, plus him being murdered. Your father must have been pissed off. He missed the opportunity to get his hands on the daggers, along with the journal. You want to fill me in on the rest, Amanda?'

Amanda inhaled. 'My father graduated from Cambridge university and went to work at a museum in Oxford. Twenty years after the events in Tintern, my father contacted Turner to talk to him about the events that summer.'

'Let me guess, Robert confessed to having stolen the journal from Cuthbert's hotel room.'

Amanda nodded. 'My father told Lord Barry, who offered Turner a lot of money for the journal.'

'But Turner, like Cuthbert, refused to sell it.'

'Yes.'

'What happened then?' Fagan asked.

Amanda hesitated.

'Amanda, what happened?'

'My father threatened to go to the police and tell them that Turner had withheld vital evidence regarding the murder of Norman Cuthbert.'

'You mean the journal? That's why you think Turner murdered your father, to silence him?'

'I just told you. I don't think he murdered them, I know.'

'But knowing isn't the same as having evidence. Is that why you got a job working at Cambridge? To get close to Professor Turner in the hope you could get your hands on the journal?'

Amanda nodded.

'But you were caught stealing it.' Fagan glanced at the file. 'What made you move to Abergavenny?'

Amanda shrugged. 'Just seemed the right thing to do. I sold my grandmother's house, and I had no family left in Cambridgeshire. My grandmother had already told me that Lord Barry was my maternal grandfather.'

'How did you come to know Tony James, the curator at the Abergavenny museum?'

'That was purely coincidence. I genuinely wanted a job at the museum. I walked in one day and asked if there were any positions.'

'That's when you started to form a friendship?' Fagan surmised.

'Yes.'

'But you didn't know he was connected to all this until he had an article published in the Abergavenny Chronicle, which showed the pictures of the daggers.'

'We thought the daggers had been lost.' Amanda explained. 'When Robert Turner announced he was going to start a dig at Bont, we knew that if we could get our hands on the journal, we'd be halfway to finding Alice's treasure.'

'And then Tony James announced the exhibition in which the daggers would be the centrepiece.'

She nodded.

'How did Damien Thackery factor in to your plan?'

'Dickhead.' Amanda snorted. 'An arrogant prick.'

'You obviously knew he had a reputation for being connected with stolen artefacts.'

'It was easy to find out. There are loads of articles about him.'

'When did you first contact him?'

Amanda puffed out her cheeks. 'October 2019. Just after Turner announced in an archaeology magazine that he was going to have one last go at finding the lost treasure of Alice. He named Thackery as his benefactor. It was a simple case of contacting him and luring him in.'

'And how did you do that?'

'Lord Barry showed Thackery the journal that Alice's scribe kept. It was just a case of feeding him a pack of lies about the manuscript being important in finding the treasure.'

Fagan took a deep breath. 'So, Turner had announced the dig to find Alice's treasure. James had published an article about the exhibition. That must have been the perfect storm of opportunity for you.'

'It was.'

'Until covid hit?'

'Actually, covid happening created more opportunity.'

'How so?'

'We set a plan into motion. The original plan was to steal the daggers and the journal together. Store them away until things died down. However, when lockdown happened, we decided to just go after the daggers. We persuaded Thackery to front the money to pay someone to break into the museum.'

'Ross Smith?'

Amanda nodded. 'Thackery ran a check on the security company that supplied equipment to the museum and found the weakest link, which was Ross Smith.' She paused. 'Ross Smith was never supposed to have been part of this. Stupid idiot, should have been content with the five grand Thackery gave him.'

'Why did you murder him?'

'Because when news broke to the media about Turner's death. He turned up at the dig site. He saw me with you. I can't understand how he recognised Thackery. They had only met once, and that was over three years ago.'

'And that was your first mistake, Amanda. Leaking information to the media regarding Turner's murder. When I interviewed you the other day, you mentioned Turner was staying at the Agincourt hotel. I had DS Watkins run a check to see if the media had mentioned where Turner was staying. The media didn't mention the

Agincourt, which means you had information that only the dig team and the police knew about. We have Thackery on CCTV in Morrisons Abergavenny.' Fagan explained. 'He's seen talking to Smith. What was Thackery doing in Abergavenny a just over a week ago?'

'We were going over final plans to get hold of Turner's journal. Thackery just popped into Morrisons for a bottle of wine we were going to share. That's when he bumped into Smith, who asked him for more money.'

'Did Thackery hand over any money?'

'He had no choice. Smith was going to blow the lid on everything.' Amanda paused. 'Thackery handed over ten grand. But Smith became greedy and asked for more as soon as he heard about Turner's death. It was stupid of me.'

'What was?'

'To leak so much information to the press. I gave them everything including information on the missing daggers. Smith obviously recognised them when he saw them on the news.'

'That's why he asked for more money. He knew how rich Thackery was.'

'Yes.' Amanda sighed.

'So you went up to his flat. You saw he was off his face so you murdered him with the dagger.'

'You think I wanted to do that?' Amanda snapped.

'You tell me. I mean, you told a good yarn the other day regarding Alice of Abergavenny. You obviously admire her for what she did all those years ago. Slaughtering her way through the holy land.' Fagan paused. 'Tell me about Tony James.'

Amanda shifted in her chair, clearly uncomfortable with the question.

'It's no good squirming, is it. You obviously murdered

Tony to stop him revealing who stole the daggers. He found out, didn't he?'

Amanda took a few seconds before nodding. 'He wasn't supposed to turn bloody detective.'

'But he did, and he discovered you were involved. So you went to his house and gave him the poison tea. I have to admit Amanda, it was the perfect murder, wasn't it? Proper Agatha Christie style. May 2020, the country was in full lockdown. No contact was allowed with anyone. Tony was a creature of habit, three glasses of orange juice a day. When he found out you were connected with the theft of the daggers, he invited you to his house.'

Amanda nodded. 'I promised him the daggers would be returned as soon as we found Alice's treasure.'

'But you weren't going to return the daggers, were you?'

'No.' Amanda admitted.

'You obviously thought you got away with the perfect murder. The lockdown, minimal autopsies carried out. No labs to run toxicology analysis. Unless there were obvious signs of foul play. Tony was in his eighties, so any pathologist would have concluded that his time was up, and he simply had a heart attack. Only five people could attend a funeral. They cremated all the bodies to reduce the risk of infection. But the one thing you didn't count on was Tony's daughter turning detective herself. She kept the tea strainer, mugs and the gloves you disposed of in the bin. They're now at a lab being analysed.'

Amanda glanced at Fagan.

'And then there are the clues you left behind. Namely seeds from the goosegrass you mentioned when you said you were a forager. They were all over the place, on Turner's body, on Smith's body, and on Romano's body. When we found the seeds on Romano's body, that's when

I twigged. You had to be connected to all this. That's when I sent DI Watkins to Cambridge to acquire the information I needed to connect you to all this. I mean, you already told me you were from that part of the world and you knew of Robert Turner, if only by reputation.' Fagan inhaled. 'So, what about Turner and Romano?'

'What about them?' Amanda responded.

'You obviously planned to murder both men, because you had two of the daggers sharpened to make them effective murder weapons. You had the other two daggers that would help locate the lost treasure of Alice.'

'Turner deserved what he got.' Amanda glared at Fagan. 'When I drove that dagger into his back, I felt a release.'

'I think you're confusing release with revenge. I'm just wondering, why all the theatrics?' You went to great lengths presenting the bodies. Making it look like a series of murders from a dan Brown novel.'

Amanda shrugged. 'Given what Turner and Romano were, I thought their deaths should be fitting.'

Fagan turned the page in his file. 'According to phone records acquired, you were in contact with Turner the day before he was murdered. These are some very heated texts you sent him. By the looks of things he had no intention of handing over the journal. That's when you sent him a picture of the daggers. Then you lured him out to Skenfrith castle before murdering him. I take it you did the same with Romano, luring him out to Grosmont castle before killing him. Everything has been taken away Amanda. Your house has been stripped. Your electric car is undergoing extensive examination.'

Amanda wiped a tear away.

Fagan studied her for a few moments. 'All this for the sake of lost treasure. Or is it more than just about getting rich? When I arrested you the other night, you said to me, the game isn't over. What did you mean by that?'

Amanda remained silent.

Fagan tapped a tablet he slid towards Amanda. 'I am showing the suspect a picture which was captured on CCTV last October in Cardiff last year.' Fagan pointed at the tablet. 'This is you last year at a Welsh independence rally. You can be seen standing next to Lord Barry, who is the founder of Cadwyr Cymru. Is that what this is all about, Sonya? Independence for Wales.'

She glared back at Fagan, her eyed filled with rage. 'I told you, my name is Amanda.' She seethed.

'And I don't give two flying fucks.' Fagan responded calmly.

'DI Fagan, my client has been very cooperative throughout this interview. I would like to take a break and discuss matters with her.' The solicitor requested.

Fagan stared at Amanda for a few moments before nodding. 'Interview suspended.' He tapped the stop icon on his phone.

'Inspector Fagan.' Amanda called out as Fagan headed for the door.

Fagan turned.

'You would have died a glorious death.'

Fagan stared back. 'Excuse me?'

'The meal I had prepared for you. The poison was concocted to kicked in when your heart rate accelerated.'

'What's that supposed to mean?'

'It means, if you would have kept our date, you would have died in the throes of passion.' Amanda smiled and winked at him.

An icy cold sensation raced up Fagan's back.

E P I L O G U E

The Cantreff Inn – Two days later

'Here he is. Look, Hercule Poirot.' Evans called out as Fagan walked through the entrance.

Jackie pointed at a newspaper. 'You've made the front page of the Chronicle Fagan.'

Fagan read the newspaper headline.

Local woman arrested for murder in dramatic Agatha Christie style raid

'Everyone is talking about this now. You've put Abergavenny on the map with this one.' Jackie placed a shot glass of brandy on the bar.

'That wasn't my intention Jacks.' Fagan remarked, reading the article.

'I take it you're throwing the book at her?' Edwards asked.

'Oh yeah, we have her on three counts of murder and one suspected murder.'

'That basically makes her a serial killer. A serial killer in Abergavenny. Make a good Netflix series.' Evans stated. 'What about Lord snooty arse? You arrested him as well.'

'Lord Barry is on bail. Probably sat in that manor house at Skenfrith laughing his head off.'

'But didn't he murder some bloke back in the seventies?' Edwards asked.

Fagan knocked back the brandy. 'That's the assumption,

but try proving it. The only witness to the murder of Norman Cuthbert is also dead. So Barry can blame everything on the Vatican priest, Romano. Plus, age is on his side. I suspect he will play the senile old git who can't remember anything card.'

'What about poor Ross Smith? He didn't deserve to die.' Jackie said.

'We found his fingerprints all over Turner's car when we examined it. He was at Skenfrith castle the night Turner was murdered. He drove the car and dumped it just outside Hereford. Our murder suspect said she promised Smith more money if he helped. The silly twat was just a pawn, an expendable pawn. Desperate for money.' Fagan stepped back from the bar. 'Anyway, I haven't got time to hang around you lot. I have a meeting at the Agincourt Hotel.'

'A meeting or a date?' Jackie winked at Fagan.

'Just a meeting, Jacks.' Fagan looked at Evans. 'Don't forget to drop George off at the Agincourt at the arranged time.'

Evans nodded.

The Agincourt Hotel

Fagan savoured the last of his rump steak. 'That was the best steak I have had in a while.' He reached into his pocket and pulled out his wallet.

'No, it's on me, DI Fagan.' Sarah York insisted.

'So, what's the latest with the dig?'

'It's being wound down. Cambridge has ordered everyone to abandon the site. I can't believe we were so close.' A tear trickled down Sarah's cheek. 'I can't believe Robert is gone.'

'It would have only been a matter of time before the cancer got to him.'

York nodded.

'What are your plans for the future?'

'I do not know. The only thing I know is that I don't want to be anywhere near the archaeology department at Cambridge at the moment.'

'I don't blame you.'

'I'm sorry I led you on a wild goose chase. I'm sorry I lied. I guess I got swept up in all the romanticism and hype surrounding Alice of Abergavenny.'

'I'm afraid you won't be seeing those daggers any time soon. This is going to be a lengthy trial.'

'What about Thackery?'

Fagan inhaled. 'He's got an expensive lawyer, along with Lord Barry. Amanda, or as she's actually called Sonya, will spend her remaining years in prison.'

'Then all has been lost.' York sighed.

Fagan smiled as George Walker entered the bar. A carrier bag was tucked under his arm. 'Not entirely.'

'Young Fagan.' George smiled, handing over the bag. He looked at York, tipping his flat cap. 'Young lady.'

'Can you give us a moment please, George.' Fagan asked.

'I'll go and grab a pint.' Walker turned and headed for the bar.

Fagan slid the journal out of the bag and placed it in front of York.

She stared back at him. 'I thought this would be used as evidence.'

'We have the murder weapons. That's the main thing. This is just immaterial.'

'Still, won't they be looking for it?'

'Let me worry about that.' Fagan assured her.

York wiped away tears. 'Thank you.'

'Now you can have your own adventures. You said it

yourself. There's a hundred years' worth of hidden treasures in that book.'

'I think for now, I'll have a quiet life.' York looked down at her ring Fagan had mentioned in an earlier conversation. She slid it off her finger and pointed at the figurehead etched onto the front. 'This is Fortuna, the Roman goddess of good fortune and luck.' York placed it on the table in front of Fagan. 'May she bring you good fortune, DI Fagan.' York stood and picked up the journal.

George returned with his pint. 'Good-looking girl.' He remarked as York walked out of the bar.

'Too young for me George.' Fagan said, examining the ring she had gifted him.

'That's a nice looking trinket you have there, young Fagan. What is it?'

Fagan smiled at George, recalling a line from an *Indiana Jones* film. 'Fortune and glory George. Fortune and, glory.'

The end.

Detective Inspector Marc Fagan will return in, 'Melody from the Dead.'

Help an independent author.

Many thanks for buying a copy of The Dead and the Buried.

Before you take to Amazon and hammer me about grammar please stop to pause.

Please e-mail and tell me if there are any problems with the book.

If you have enjoyed what you have read then please by all means spread the word to other avid readers.

If you would like to be added to my mailing list please e-mail me at the link below. You can also click the follow button on my Amazon page.

Many thanks
Jason Chapman

Jasonchapman-author@hotmail.com

Other books by Jason Chapman

The UFO Chronicles

The fallen

Codename Angel

The Angel Conspiracy

The Angel Prophecy

Detective Sergeant Samantha Drake

Dystopia

Avalon Rising

Signals

Project Genesis

Quality declaration

Please note, this book has been written in UK English. US English and UK English differ slightly.

I have taken every care to produce a quality item. As an independent author, it is hard to find people who will edit for a fair price. With the cost of living crisis biting down, it gets harder with every passing day. Most editors and proof-readers cost thousands of pounds. Way beyond the budget of most struggling indie authors. As a result, independent authors are often criticised for producing sloppy work. Packed with mistakes and a poor use of grammar. It can be an ulssacl struggle against reviewers who ignore the storylines and concentrate on missing full stops or speech marks. I am constantly updating my books, reading through them. Making sure you the reader enjoy the stories I write. I use AI software to help me with my writing and editing. It's not perfect, but it's better than just giving up.

Mainstream publishers label independent authors as desperate, inexperienced, self-published cry-babies. There are many indie authors who work hard to perfect their craft. Producing exciting stories for an ever-hungry reading public. Often writing better stories than many of the top bestselling authors. It comes down to two choices. Chase the dream, or give up because you simply can't afford it.

OFFWORLD
PUBLICATIONS

Printed in Great Britain
by Amazon